EARLY PF

This is my first book by Shari. And I can absolutely guarantee you it will not be my last. This book has it all, it has EVERYTHING!!

ASHLEY GAYHART, EARLY READER

OMG! I loved Man Flu. This book is sweet, sexy and hilarious. I haven't read a book that had me laughing so much and the hot sexy tension between Logan and Hannah. I loved reading the journey of Logan and Hannah story and meeting other characters along the way.

I love reading Shari Ryan books. Never disappointed and her books always take me to a happy place.

BELINDA VISSER, EARLY READER

Man Flu by Shari Ryan is one of the best books I've had the pleasure of reading this year. Cover to cover Ryan causes readers to relate, hope and laugh!

EMILY GOODWIN, SOUTHERN VIXENS BOOK OBSESSION

Do you want funny? Do you want sexy? Do you want sweet? Do you want it all? Look no further!! You've found it right here!!! Hannah and Logan, just *sigh*

First of all, I believe Ms. Ryan's take on the "man flu" is hilarious and one hundred percent accurate!!! You'll be laughing until you almost pee yourself!!

KATIE REISTER, EARLY READER

I was laughing so hard from beginning to end. I loved everything about this story. Poor Hannah's life as a single mother seems to be just one mishap after another.

NORA FRESSE, EARLY READER

MAN FLU

SHARI J. RYAN

ABOUT THE AUTHOR

Shari J. Ryan is an International Bestselling Author of heartbreakers and mind-benders. Shari was once told she tends to exaggerate often and sometimes talks too much, which would make a great foundation for fictional books. Four years later, Shari has written eleven novels that often leave readers in tears, either from laughing, or crying.

With her loud Boston girl attitude, Shari isn't shy about her love for writing or the publishing industry. Along with writing several International Bestsellers, Shari splits her time between writing and her longstanding passion for graphic design. In 2014, she started an indie-publishing resource company, MadHat Books, to help fellow authors with their book cover designs, as well as providing assistance with the self-publishing process.

While Shari may not find many hours to sleep, she still manages to make time for her family. She is a devoted wife to a great guy, and a mother to two little boys who remind her daily why she was put on this earth.

Make sure you join Shari's Twisted Drifters Reader Group at: http://bit.ly/2e17FsX

facebook.com/authorsharijryan
twitter.com/sharijryan
instagram.com/sharijryan_author
bookbub.com/authors/6090
amazon.com/author/shari-j.-ryan
goodreads.com/shari_j_ryan

ALSO BY SHARI J. RYAN

Last Words

Manservant

Raine's Haven

Spiked Lemonade

Queen of the Throne

A Heart of Time

A Missing Heart

A Change of Heart

No Way Out

Ravel

House of Tinder

TAG

The Schasm Series

Copyright © 2018 by Shari J. Ryan

All rights reserved. Except as permitted under US Copyright Act of 1976, no part of this publication may be reproduced, distributed, or transmitted in any form or by any means, or stored in a database or retrieval system, without the prior written permission of the publisher.

The characters and events portrayed in this book are fictitious. Any similarity to real persons, living or dead, is coincidental and not intended by the author.

ISBN-13: 978-1983774942
ISBN-10: 1983774944

*To Gia and Annelle.
Friends like you are hard to come by, and I'm not sure what I'd do without you. When I need a laugh, you're there with the perfect material. Thank you for inspiring me to be the goof I've always been. Love you, ladies!*

ACKNOWLEDGMENTS

I'm incredibly grateful for the support, love, and help I receive every day. It seems like I have an abundance of that in my life, and that makes me lucky.

Lisa, thank you for your constant honesty and realness. I know I can always, always, always depend on you, and that means the world to me, always. (See what I did there ...)

Linda, my rock, who I hate going a day without talking to. Not only do you provide the best platform for me to thrive on, you're an amazing friend to me too. I couldn't think of a better person to walk next to throughout the publishing process.

Julie, Julie, Julie, there aren't enough words in the dictionary to tell you how much I love and cherish you and our friendship. Thank you so much for everything you do every day, and for picking up my pieces when I break down.

My beta ladies, I'm so grateful for our private chat sessions and your honesty. Our jokes and laughs keep me going every day, and it means the world to me that you've all stuck by my side for so long. You haven't gotten sick of me yet, and I'm very grateful for each one of you! xoxox

Twisted Drifters, bloggers, readers, and co-authors, you make this industry—this "job" the best one out there. I love what I do because of you. Thank you for loving me enough to read what's inside of my crazy head.

To my family: You have been so supportive of my journey, and I'm forever grateful.

My boys—Bryce and Brayden—never let your future spouses know the truth about the man flu. You are strong little boys, and you can power through anything you put your mind to … even the sniffles.

BECAUSE OF YOU...

Josh, oh Josh. My man, who currently has the flu. Ironic, right? I love you so much for acting out some of the scenes in this book so I could write such an accurate portrayal. You make the man flu look as easy as childbirth, and I respect the hell out of that.
If only this book were about you... Just kidding.
Thank you for being my passenger on this crazy little trip. If I didn't have you as a partner to laugh with, I'd just look crazy laughing all alone. I love you more than anything, and I hope you feel better by time this book releases. xoxo

MAN
Flu

PROLOGUE

One Year Ago

"I now pronounce you officially divorced," I say while staring at the bathroom mirror. "You may kiss your reflection, since that's the only person you know you can trust, and live happily ever after with." That's all I have for a self-help pep talk on this lovely occasion today. No one else knows about the divorce, so I can't even go celebrate or anything. Time to buy a new vibrator, I guess.

In any case, I've kept this to myself because if anyone were to ask Rick about the split, he'd inform them I was 50 percent at fault because I wasn't as horny as the twenty-five-year-old he found on Tinder. When I start sharing the news with mutual friends or our extended families, Rick's story will come out, and I don't want anyone to know how often I avoided sex with my sleazeball husband. He thought his porn addiction should be a turn on, but it wasn't my thing. The different scents of perfumes he would come home smelling like didn't help either. I had no idea who else he was sleeping with, but I assumed it was a common occurrence.

Before Rick tried to explain his side of the story—how his infidelity and ensuing divorce were partially my fault, I wanted to put an announcement in the newspaper, so everyone knew not to address me as "Mrs." or wonder why I have a big white indent on my left ring finger. It would be like a wedding announcement, but the opposite.

I was about to get to it, but then I remembered that announcements are typically written in third person to make it sound like someone cares enough about them to make a formal statement in the name of love. *Come on, no one cares that much.* If I remember correctly, I wrote ours, and it was something like: "Congratulations to Rick and Hannah Pierce on their recent nuptials. May they be happy and in love for all their days together." So, because I was lame enough to write my own announcement back then, now I have to undo it and say (as if I'm someone else talking for me, of course): "Condolences and congratulations to Rick and Hannah Pierce on the event of their divorce. After ten long years of bliss, or hell together, depending on which one of the couple you're talking to, Rick was caught cheating on Hannah. Since there are always two sides to every story, we wish the newly divorced couple the best of luck being single, lonely, and washed up, and eventually wrinkled, forever. Unless you're Rick, of course, since he's already moved the hell on."

Since I decided against the divorce announcement in the newspaper, I feel like I've come a long way, maturity wise. Instead of a public mortification, I opted to drop a laxative in Rick's coffee this morning, hand him his last box of crap, and tell him to get out of my life, and *my* house too ... I won that part. Then again, we're talking about a habitable box filled with ten years of memories—memories that should all be burned inside of a flaming bag of shit and left on the doorstep of wherever he ends up.

I'm not bitter. I'm thrilled to start my life over at thirty-two with a toddler in tow. There are going to be men knocking my door down once the word gets out that I'm single. Although, it'll probably just be the police because hopefully, someone will realize I haven't been seen in months. Other than that, I've got this all figured out. I'll quit my job, learn how to homeschool when it's time, order all household items and groceries from Amazon, and request that their new drone thing drop off my deliveries so I don't have to see anyone. If I request that my goods are delivered to the back porch, I won't even have to open the front door. The best part is, I can eat like shit, wear yoga pants but never work out, and avoid all human contact with friends who want to gush about their amazing marriages and how hungry their sexual appetite is after so many happy years.

My therapist said that the first day of divorced life will be the worst. Well, I think I've already made some great strides toward my new future today.

Shoot, I forgot to add something to my list of things that need to be thrown out. My phone. It's a part of the cleansing portion of starting over. The damn phone is blaring N'sync's "Bye Bye Bye," and I wish whoever is calling could hear the ringtone instead of me.

I answer because I need to adult, even though I'm on my way to not adulting anymore. "This is Hannah," I answer.

"Hannah, it's Alan. I just wanted to make sure you're going to be rejoining us tomorrow? I realize you are finalizing your divorce today, but there are some pressing issues we need to go over if you can make yourself available."

Alan Mole is the *wonderful* CEO of the company that employs me. He's the one who cuts the checks for my salary, the one used to calculate my percentage of earned alimony and child support, so I'm screwed if I leave my job. At least it's me getting screwed this time and not some twenty-five-year-old chick, but this does put a kink in my great plan. "Yeah, Alan, I'll be there with bells on tomorrow." I hang up and switch to the *Words With Friends* app, waiting for the next victim to experience my nasty wrath of rude words. It's what I consider to be therapy, so I suppose throwing my phone out wouldn't be the best idea, after all.

Dickle15 would like to challenge you to a game. Do you accept?

Dickle? Sure, why not? How do people come up with these horrible usernames, or find me, for that matter? Maybe I should have been more creative than HannahP84.

Dickle starts the game with the word, **shatter**. Nothing like starting a game with a seven-letter word. It's on, Dickle. It's on. You picked the wrong player this time.

I continue the game with the only word I have to play at the moment. Ironically, it's the word **heart**, and so begins another funny episode of "Karma's Picking on Hannah."

This will all get easier.

It will get better.

Whatever goes down, must come back up.

Oh, and karma will eventually figure out its got the wrong person, Rick. Just wait.

CHAPTER ONE

MONDAY MORNING. NEED I SAY MORE?

365 Days Post Divorce

As a little girl, I was told to study hard, get good grades, go to college, get a decent job, find a nice man, and have a family. My dad told me it would make for the perfect life, and I would be set up for success.

Like a good daughter, I listened. I did everything he said to do, but there were some things he forgot to mention, like the moments that grow in between those life goals and then sprout into the form of ugly weeds—the ones that don't tear out of the ground without some plant killer. Except plant killer won't work on an ex-husband, or would it ...?

"Good morning, boss-lady," Brielle sings as she follows me down the row of cubicles and into my office.

My office. Alan, the old-fashioned kind of businessman, and my company's CEO, shockingly offered me a promotion to the Director of Marketing position earlier this year after I laboriously trudged through the Manager title, levels one through five, even though there are only supposed to be three levels. In any case, it made me feel like I could check off the box next to "successful career."

"Good morning, Brielle, how was your weekend?" I sometimes live vicariously through Brielle's weekends because she's in her mid-twenties and living it up. She has very different goals in life, which makes me wonder if my dad might have been wrong about the certain path that would lead me to success and happiness.

Ever since I got my first *Cosmo* magazine in the mail when I was fifteen, I've had a thing for the publishing industry and dreamt of snagging a job in New York City, working for one of the big, women's magazines. I imagined a tall, glass building and lots of high-class people walking around all day. I might have watched too many movies in the nineties and got my hopes up too high because some of the choices I made in my twenties got in the way of my dream. I couldn't give it up completely, though, so I settled for a smaller magazine here in the suburbs of Massachusetts. I mean, I've got my own office, so it's something.

It's also pink, like baby-girl pink. It was a joke—a high five by a couple of my male co-workers, for being upgraded to an office. I love jokes … *if* they're executed properly. However, I've been finding it difficult to work for a woman's magazine while being one of only two women in my department.

"My weekend was fab. First, on Friday night, Adam and I went to Via and met up with some friends. We totally closed down three different bars that night. I don't even know how it was possible, but clearly, it was." She sweeps her hair to the side, and I can't help but watch as each strand falls perfectly back into place. "I was wiped out on Saturday, so I slept until abouuuuut, I don't know … elevenish? I got manis and pedis with the girls, then had lunch with my old college roomie." She takes a breather because she's been talking for a minute straight, but I know she isn't done. "You know, it's seriously getting dark out way too early. I can't deal. Anyway, Adam and I hit up Boston for the night and spent the night at a mod hotel, which was super chic. You should totally check it out sometime. We went to bed wicked early for some reason," she said with a wink, "but I just couldn't make it past three that night. I must be starting to break down in age. Gosh, I don't know how you function in your thirties." I've learned to ignore Brielle's lack of a filter. It's great for honesty, no so much for modesty.

"Wow, that sounds like a busy weekend," I tell her. "Are things better with Adam, now?" Her six-month relationship has been on the rocks, and I guess this weekend was supposed to be a make-it-or-break-it situation.

"Eh, we didn't really have a chance to talk too much." I'd ask how that's possible, but I know how it's possible. I just really don't care to hear it. I preferred other activities besides talking at one time ... back when.

"Understandable," I tell her.

"Sunday was pretty much just a lot of 'non-talking,' if you know what I mean." She winks and jiggles her eyebrows.

I got it. You have more sex than a red-light district, and I'm dried up like a prune. I hope that state of being isn't a permanent feature, like the whole saying: *If you don't use it, you lose it.*

"I got what you're putting out there," I tell her with a mom-ish wink. "I'm glad you had a good weekend."

"No problemo," she chirps while scanning through her phone. "So, you have a ten o'clock appointment with the new temp, a three o'clock sales meeting, and a date with Dickle at seven." She covers her mouth and pulls in a sharp breath before continuing. "I can be at your house by six-thirty to take care of Cora if you want?"

Brielle is my spirit animal, and I think I might love her, but—

"Cancel my date. I'm not ready to meet Dickle anymore."

"Oh?" she questions in her high-pitched *I need to know more* tone. "What happened to your bet? I thought you kind of had a thing for him ... and his Dickle?" she snorts. It's been a year of talking to this guy, and she still can't say his name without laughing.

"I just can't. That last date I went on, you know, with Sergio—the one I met on that stupid Tinder thing? Maybe I forgot to tell you last week, but it was going okay until it was time to—" I make a nice hand gesture to my mouth. "You know? Anyway, he was super hairy, and he wasn't shaved or trimmed down there at all ..."

She places her hands up and closes her eyes. "Say no more. I did warn you about Tinder. It's either a hit or miss."

"I got a pube stuck in between my two front teeth, Brielle. This is life, at 'my age.'"

"I said, *say no more*," she enunciates more clearly. I know she doesn't enjoy hearing about my sometimes disappointing thirty-three-year-old life, but it's real, and she should know what might be in her future if she doesn't make the right decisions. I'm trying to be a good mentor. "On that note, I think I have some work to do." Brielle slides her phone into her back pocket and turns to leave.

"Hey, real quick ..." I pause to take a sip of the hot coffee as I watch my inbox pop open with a bunch of "Welcome to a big fat case of Monday" emails. "Sorry." I refocus my attention on her question-filled eyes. "How's the call list going for the event next week?"

"Ummm—good," she says, switching her focus to the window behind me. Yup, whatever she's about to say is a lie. She's been my assistant for two years, and I know the meaning of all of her body language. "I'm about halfway through." She takes a moment to look down at her manicure and proceeds to bite her bottom lip. *Lie, lie, lie.*

"You know, I gave you that list two weeks ago, right?" This is the part I hate about having an office. I don't want to boss her around, but she isn't always on her "A" game with the admin duties, which is kind of important, since she's an admin.

"I do, but some of our vendors like to chat. It's all a part of marketing. Hannah?"

"Right. Okay, let me know when the temp arrives." She quickly pivots away from my desk as her long, blonde hair flips over her shoulder like one of those Suave commercials, leaving me to watch her jog out of my office in her four-inch, leopard print Manolo Blahnik heels, kind of like a Barbie on her toes. I'd kill for her hair, clothes, body … I want to be her. I know I sound crazy, but her life just looks so easy.

I dig into my emails and get two cranky notes in when my phone dings with a notification from Dickle15.

The word: ***date*** is added to our two-day-long running *Words With Friends* game. How did he end up with those letters? That might explain all his skipped turns.

At least I have an *N* left, and there's a perfect spot next to an *O*.

A message appears in the sidebar. "Really? A bet was a bet, and I won the last five games in a row. You agreed to go out to dinner with me if that happened."

"I'm so sorry. I can't," I tell him.

"Why not?" he responds just as fast.

"I'm still not ready to be back in the dating scene." This is the third time I've broken a proposed date with him. Something is holding me back, and I don't know what it is.

"It's me, Hannah. There's nothing to be nervous about. We've been playing *Words With Friends* for an entire year. It's not like I'm rushing things."

"Dickle." I shake my head every time I type this man's name. I don't laugh like Brielle does, but he will not tell me if Dickle is his real name or just a fun username. "I love our conversations, and I don't want to ruin them." That's what this is. With Tinder or a blind date, I can run and hide. I don't feel like I can do that with Dickle anymore.

"Well, maybe you should find someone else to play with," he says.

No! Come on. Why can't anyone be patient? What's the rush? I don't understand how it can it be so easy to lose good things in my life. Not that Rick was good, but I thought he was at one point. *Whatever.* Now, I have no Dickle to play with. Men are so hard to understand. He even told me that he appreciated our conversations mostly because they excluded the most private information in our lives, and that wouldn't work if we knew each other in person. Doesn't he realize that?

"I'm sorry you feel that way," I tell him before closing the app. I suspected this would happen eventually. *Words With Friends* never should have added a messaging portion to the game. It was nice not having to chat when attacking someone with a ninety-point word. Sadly, I've gotten good at the game since it's my only real hobby outside of being a single mom.

I place my phone down, and the display doesn't even have time to go dark before the stupid thing starts ringing. I look down at the caller ID and curse life. Why? What could it possibly be this time?

I click to accept the call from the school and bring my phone up to my ear. "This is Hannah Pierce."

"Hi, Mrs. Pierce, this is Miss Ellen, the school nurse. I have Cora here with me."

I used to have a five-second heart attack every time the school nurse called, but I'm pretty sure I'm on their speed dial now. "Hi, Miss Ellen, is Cora all right?"

"Oh yes, but she has a bit of a hangnail, and it started to bleed." *Cora, a hangnail?* She has found more excuses to get out of school than I could have ever taken credit for at her age. She has the imagination and creativity of a mastermind.

"Can you put her on the phone, please?" I tell the nurse.

Brett, the vice president, my direct boss, picks this moment to walk into my office and takes a seat in front of my desk. Unfortunately, he's heard more than his fair share of my conversations with the school nurse.

"Hi, Mom," Cora says.

"Cora, sweetie, I need you to pull the hangnail off your finger, have Miss Ellen give you a Band-Aid, and go back to class. Please, Cora. I can't leave work this morning. You don't want Mommy to get in trouble, do you?"

"But, Mom, it hurts, and it's bleeding a little. You know I hate blood. It makes me sick, and I might throw up. If I throw up, I'll have to come home anyway. It's the school rules."

"Cora, okay, I understand. Can you put the nurse back on the phone?"

"Hello, Mrs. Pierce. How would you like me to handle this situation?"

"Could you please clip the hangnail and put a Band-Aid on her finger?"

"No problem, I just wanted to let you know we have her down here at the nurse's office," she responds.

I love how even though she calls me almost every day, it's as if I didn't speak to her just a day or so earlier. "These calls make me very nervous. Is there any chance we can save the hangnail calls for true concerns?" I'm probably out of line for asking, but it's seriously at least three days a week, and it's usually a mosquito bite, a splinter, a paper-cut, or a hangnail.

"I'm afraid I can't agree to that. It's the school policy that we notify you when Cora comes down to the nurse's office."

"Ok, great. Talk to you tomorrow, then." I hang up, frustrated as always.

Once I take a breath and unwind, I look up at Brett, whose eyebrows are hiked up an inch, and I'm wondering what he'll have to say about this.

"Seriously, that nurse is out to get you," Brett says with laughter.

"I've never heard of a school nurse who can't just put a Band-Aid on a paper cut or a hangnail!" I'm sure I came home from school with an ice pack after I broke my arm on the playground, and my parents had no clue what was going on until I told them. Now, this is the norm?

"When Caty was around that age, we got the same thing. Every single day. It's like once the kids figure out they can just leave class and take a little break for a bit, they'll find anything on their body that needs a Band-Aid and milk it for all its worth."

I close my eyes and shake the frustration away. "I should just switch the phone number on record to Rick's number, but then I'd be afraid something would actually be wrong with her and ... well, it's Rick, so ..."

"Yeah, you might feel better keeping that control. Plus, you'd start to miss those sweet little calls," he says. I'm not sure about that, but I suppose he's right. I cannot trust Rick with that crap.

"So, your new temp is starting today?" he says.

"Yes, he is."

"Good, good. Hopefully, this one will be better than the last few."

"I hope so too. I could use the extra hand to prepare for next week's event."

"Right, yes, for sure. It'll probably be good to take the temp with you onsite too if he works out this week." He smiles and takes a sip of coffee from his "World's Best Dad" mug.

"I'm not getting my hopes up yet, but we'll see." Brett's one of the only decent men in this office. He's been a work and life mentor to me since I started ten years ago, except I seem to have fallen off the path he led me on somewhere along the way. He's got this great marriage to an amazing woman, and three grown kids. I look up to him, hoping I'll be in his shoes someday, but it seems like I may have to travel to the moon and back before I figure my life out like he has.

I answer a few more emails, and somehow, it's already ten o'clock. "Hannah," Brielle pops her head in through the door. "The temp is here. I'm going to go escort him or her up."

"Thanks, Brielle."

I have enough work for three temps, but I'll take what I can get. Granted, this person will likely have no tech or marketing skills because the temp agency despises this company for a reason I'm still unsure of.

During the five minutes Brielle is gone, I manage to buzz through five more emails, all filled with rejections to proposed sales meetings. Why can't these people try the shit sandwich technique at least? (A shit sandwich is simply the process of layering the negative babble with a compliment at the beginning and the end. Then it's like nothing bad ever happened.) I swear, I'd respond quicker if they did it that way.

I hear the front door open and close, assuming Brielle is dragging along our newest employee for the week. We've gone through a half dozen temps and interns in the past month, so I don't have much hope for this one. The last woman our agency sent in didn't know how to "turn on" her email. I kind of just stared at her for a good five minutes before I walked out of her cubicle, but at least I kept myself from asking if she attempted any foreplay. I couldn't understand why the temp/intern agency would think to send an admin with no technical skills. I did have a little chat with the agency after that, and they promised to send only competent people to me from now on, so I guess we'll see.

Brielle knocks on my door before walking in, not that she typically does that, but I appreciate her setting a decent example for this person —err—man. I look up from my screen, finding Brielle in the shadow of the new temp. Like, he's a man's man. He's got to be at least six-foot-two, a lot of muscle going on there, salt and pepper scruff, but dark hair that isn't receding. He has crow's feet, but he's working them. He's not a recent grad. No way. He's dressed professionally, without fold creases on the sleeves that scream, "I just took this out of a plastic wrapper an hour ago," and his pants are hemmed to fit perfectly. I've been sizing him up for like thirty awkward seconds now, and Brielle is clearing her throat. "Hannah, this is Logan, our new intern," she says.

Intern? I stand up from my desk, and as I do, a button from my blouse catches on my keyboard drawer and pops off. Shit! I grab my shirt to hide the gaping hole as I reach out to shake Logan's hand. "It's nice to meet you, Logan."

"You, as well," he says, politely. Okay then, that is one deep voice. It's illegal to ask him how old he is, but interns are usually a little younger.

"You're an intern?" I question.

"Well, if you ask the temp agency, I'm an intern because that's what they were looking to place with you. In truth, though, I did go back to school for a bit a little over a year ago after I was relieved from my MLB contract because of an injury—and yeah, I don't want to bore you with my history, but I am technically an intern. However, we can go with temp if it makes you more comfortable, though."

Baseball player, tight pants, picturing him in them. *I'm the boss, stop it.* "Awesome, well it's great to have you. Do you have a resume I can keep on file? The agency didn't send me one." Shocking, with how organized they are.

"Sure thing." He opens his leather folder and pulls out a resume on actual resume paper, which I haven't seen in about ten years. "I take it you're proficient with email?" I ask for my personal, snarky reasons, but come on, who can't open a freaking email in 2017?

He laughs because he thinks I'm funny. I am funny. "Of course. As you'll see on my resume, I'm proficient with the Microsoft Suite, Adobe Creative Suite, and web development." Can I just make him a full-time employee now? I've never had an intern or temp with these credentials before. For that little fact, I'll let the agency off the hook for not sending his resume ahead of time. However, they could have sent me a headshot. That would have at least prepared me a little more for this interaction.

"Perfect! Brielle, will you get him set up in the cube outside of my office and have a tech team member come down and set up his email?"

"Of course," she peeps. Brielle stands back, allowing Logan to pass by her, and she looks over at me with a look of shock.

"What the hell?" I mouth.

"I know, right?" she mouths back. That's totally inappropriate of me, but he's inappropriate for looking so good.

As he sits down at his desk, I realize I can see right into his cubicle from my open door. So, it looks like I'll have to stare at him until the temp agency either steals him back or sells him to me.

I sit back down in my chair, glancing at my shirt bowed open in front of the roll on my stomach—the one I've tried so hard to get rid of with the four million crunches I've done this past year. I haven't been able to get rid of the last of the roll, and now it's taunting me.

Slouching into my chair, I grab the newbie's resume and hold it in front of me. Major League Baseball player. No way, I'm not buying it.

Five years at Northeastern University, two years playing in the minors, and ten years in the major leagues for two different teams. Plus, his degree is in technology, which makes him a very smart baseball player with no marketing experience.

I stand up from my desk and paper clip the inside of my shirt together, so I'm not on the verging of being inappropriate. I love Mondays. I really, really do.

I make my way into Logan's cube, finding him setting up his email without IT's help. I guess it's not a surprise since he's tech-savvy, but it's a good kind of reinforcement I need at the moment.

I rap my knuckles against the plastic lining of his cubicle, and he swings his desk chair around to face me. "How's it going, boss?" he asks. That's a lot of confidence right there for being in the office less than ten minutes.

I like it.

"Good, good. I have a few tests we require all interns and temps to take before starting any work. It's to help us gauge what level of tasks you'll be comfortable performing. Performing ... dear God. Stop. It's a combination of Word, Excel, PowerPoint, and some basic HTML. You mentioned you're proficient with those programs, so I'm sure it will be a piece of cake for you."

"Definitely. Is the test online? Do you have a link you want to send me?"

My head falls to the side. "Why are you starting out as a temp/intern, whatever?" He seems quite advanced to be claiming this junior title.

He smirks and leans back in his chair, crossing one leg over the other. He's way too hot to be working in this office with all these schmucks. Little pricks of pins and needles pinch my cheeks, and I can only hope I'm not blushing in his presence. He should stop smiling at me like that. "Well, the hiring agency had no permanent jobs available within a thirty-mile radius, but they had this intern position open, and it's five minutes from where I live, so here we are."

"But this isn't a temp-to-perm position. Isn't that what you're looking for?" I ask.

"Sure am, and I might just shock the pants off you and make you change your mind," he says confidently, with a wink.

Holy, no. This man cannot say that stuff to me. That's arrogant, and I don't need to be thinking about him taking my pants off ...

"We'll see about that," I regain my composure and say in my motherly tone that doesn't belong in the office. I sometimes wonder who I've become. Then, I realize it's obviously my mother showing through.

"I'm just kidding, but, hey, you never know. Someone might pick up and leave, and it could put you in the position to say, 'Well, Logan does know his stuff, so why not?' I'm a risk taker."

That's hot. No, it's admirable in a professional way.

"I suppose you never know what might happen," I tell him, trying my hardest not to stutter. I'm the boss. I need to act like it.

I tap the top of his cube and turn back to my office, forgetting what I even came to say.

"Oh, and yeah, send me that link when you have a second. The IT guy from upstairs already walked me through the setup, and my email is up and working. It's Logan@HouseMomsToday.com."

Yes, I work with all men for a magazine named House Moms Today—just like Cosmo, and just as I always dreamed.

"Great, I'll send that right over."

CHAPTER TWO

MONDAY AFTERNOON—IT SHOULD BE FRIDAY BY NOW

...

"Hannah, hold up, I need your signature on something," Nick, our head sales manager shouts over to me as I have one foot outside of the office door.

"Nick, can't this wait until tomorrow?" I need to leave now, or I won't make it to the bus stop on time.

"It'll really just take two-seconds. Come on." He's shoving the papers at me without a pen. "I need to get this in to the vendor by five."

"Well, why did you wait until just now then?" I push his hand back and move toward the elevator.

"It's two forty-five! The day isn't exactly over." For me it is. I work from home from three-thirty to five, and I've been doing so since the beginning of the school year.

"Thank you for that reminder, but I'm going to be late to pick up my daughter, and by the looks of it, you don't even have a pen on you right now. Oh—look, the elevator door just opened."

"You don't have a pen anywhere in that massive purse of yours?" Nick asks, looking down at my "mom-bag."

"I've got a pen," a voice chimes from around the corner.

Logan jogs over to the elevator and hands me his pen. While I should be thankful for his considerate gesture, I was happier not signing the paper. Nick knows when I leave. He just likes to make it known that it's disruptive to *his* schedule.

Nick hands the paper back to me and puts his foot against the elevator door to hold it open.

I press the paper against the wall and sign the damn thing before shoving it back into Nick's chest. "Now, please move," I tell him. As he's grinning at me with a shit-eating smile, I hand Logan's pen back to him. "Thanks, Logan. I appreciate it."

"You're a doll," Nick says with what he thinks is a charming smile. Little does he know, his smile only makes me want to punch him more. He's one of the pink wall painters, a real guy's guy who believes women don't have a place in the corporate world. Also, I was promoted ahead of him, which makes sense since I have five years on him here, but it annoys him. He and his counterpart, Taylor, are thorns in my side, oh, and golf buddies with Rick, of course—just a side effect of one of our company holiday parties a couple of years back when our spouses were invited. I should have known better than to bring Rick.

Logan slips into the elevator just as it's closing, and I'm suddenly barricaded in a life-size box with the scent of cologne I can nearly taste. It's like spicy rum and a sweet mango, mixed with a hint of sage. God, he smells good.

"Are you making a run for it already?" I ask him. I would be if I had the chance.

He gives me a quick chuckle and focuses on the blinking numbers above the door. "Nah, Human Resources wants to see me. I guess there's some transitional paperwork from the temp agency I need to fill out."

"Those agencies really like to make things challenging for us," I tell him, watching the same numbers slowly tick down toward the lobby.

"Where are you off to?" he asks. I suppose I should have told him I leave early three days a week. I obviously have this boss thing down, like a boss.

"I completely forgot to tell you, but I leave early and work from home in the later part of the afternoon."

"Ah, are you moonlighting?" That's not very professional to ask a boss. I wonder if moonlighting has a different meaning than the one I'm thinking. I think he's asking if I'm working a second job. Not that it matters.

"No, I have to pick up my daughter at the bus stop," I respond with a grim smile, knowing I just made myself look about fifty years older to this attractive man-temp.

"Oh, sweet!" He's more enthusiastic than I would have imagined, although I still know this attraction is only one-sided; therefore, it wouldn't matter if I had one kid or four. He probably has his choice of arm candy. "What's her name?"

How long is this damn elevator ride? I hit the lobby button again, but the door opens on the third floor, welcoming no one onto the elevator. I swear there is some asshole running floor to floor, chasing elevators all day, ghosting buttons just so we have to stop at every other floor to find no one waiting to get on. "Cora. She's five." Maybe that makes me sound a little younger than fifty.

"That sounds like fun," he says, glancing over at me, though I only notice through my peripheral vision because I'm too busy staring at blinking numbers to avoid his good looks that will surely be burned into my head for the rest of the day.

"She's definitely a barrel of monkeys and keeps me on my toes, but I love her." More mom talk, how cute. "Do you have any kids?" Of course, he doesn't have kids. He's the picture of single-manhood, plus he doesn't have a ring on his finger. Not that I noticed, but—well, he went to press the button just as I did and—okay, I noticed. However, I'm not wearing a ring either, yet I have a daughter. I should stop assuming.

"Unfortunately, no." Unfortunately? What single guy says that? Wait, no, what single guy who looks like him says that? He can't be real.

"Well, kids are worth the wait." Saying that makes me consider the thought of what my life would be like without Cora. If I had waited, I would have been left with nothing and alone after Rick's dick move, so I'm glad I got something out of that marriage, even if she is a bit of a challenge for one person.

The door finally opens after the world's longest elevator ride, and Logan presses his palm into the door, waving his other hand for me to walk out first. "Have a good night, Hannah," he says.

"You too," I reply breathlessly, as I jog toward the doors in my click-clacking heels.

I run outside through the pouring rain and hold my briefcase above my head to salvage what's left of the curl I tried to put into my hair this morning. I double click the key fob in my purse, and the doors to my minivan unlock. I jump across a puddle and duck inside, falling heavily into my seat.

Thankfully, the lack of traffic makes up for the extra two minutes I spent in the elevator. However, with the rain downpour, there's a line of five minivans parked against the sidewalk, and I'm the very last one, which means it will take a full minute to reach the bus stop. I won't be able to see the bus until it arrives—mothertrucker.

I dig around under the passenger seat for my umbrella, finding nothing but a bunch of crumpled drawings Cora smashed under there last week.

Mom, I need to borrow your umbrella for a minute. The memory of her saying that hits me as I jam my fingernail into whatever is metal and hard under the seat. Dammit to hell.

I look like death anyway; might as well just get this over with. I hop out of the van and trudge through the puddles, soaking my feet and legs. There is nothing better than wet feet inside of peep-toe pumps. As soon as I make it up the hill and over to the bus stop, I realize my paper clip has gone missing. How long has it been gone? I don't want to know how long my stomach has been visibly showing between the perky buttonhole and hanging thread of my blouse.

I clutch my shirt together, squeezing water out at the same time. Now seems like a good time to up the rain-factor too. Instead of just pouring, it's now flying in horizontally with the wind, as well.

With a quick glance down at my watch that shouldn't be getting as wet as it is, I see it's already a minute past the time the bus normally arrives. Thankfully, I'm here, but not so thankfully, I'm standing here like this.

Ten minutes goes by before the bus rounds the corner. Each of the other moms step out of their cars with their umbrella and a second one for their child. Not me, nope. No umbrella here. *Fabulous mother alert.*

As the bus empties out, Cora is the last one to jump off the bottom step right into a puddle, splashing me, as if I weren't already soaked to the bone. The joke isn't on me this time.

"Hi, baby-cakes, how was school?"

She tilts her head from side to side, her bouncy curls swaying with her movement. "It sucked."

"Cora!" I snap. As if she were using a megaphone, the other moms turn around and glare at me like I was the one who said the word "suck."

"Just saying it how it is," she chirps.

"Well, we don't use that—"

Like I needed icing on this freaking cake, a sports car flies by, hitting the unnecessary, massive drainage hole in the middle of the street, and drenches me from head to toe. I shield Cora, of course, but that mothertrucking bitch has got to go.

"Oh, it's Tiana!" Cora shouts.

Tiana, like the Disney princess, except she is no freaking Disney princess. She's Rick's peach-cake.

I click the button on my key to make the sliding door of the van open for Cora, and she hops in and closes the door behind her before I reach my door. I can take a guess that while Tiana was flying by, soaking me with rain and sewer water, she was taking a selfie that will somehow show me in the background, taking her wrath like a beaten, wet rat. That shit will appear all over Instagram tonight because that's what this twinklette does. She's a fitness guru with a side gig of promotion yoga on social media. They have those sorts of jobs now. To add insult to injury, she probably gets paid more than I do.

I drive around the block until I pull into our driveway, watching Tiana as she slowly pulls into her garage next door.

"Mom, why can't we pull into our garage? I don't want to get wet," says my princess who stood outside in the rain for less than thirty-seconds.

"Because, sweetie, all your dad's junk is taking up the space in there, so there is no room for our car to fit inside," I tell her.

"Minivan, mom, not a car," Cora corrects me. *Thank you for the reminder.*

Cora hops out of the vehicle and runs through the rain she was just complaining about, crosses over the small patch of grass between the houses and disappears inside of their garage. "Cora! No!" You have got to be freaking kidding me. "Cora Taryn Pierce!"

Now, running through the rain as I glance down at my watch, I confirm that I have five minutes before I'm expected to be on that call, and Cora is not in this garage. I've told her not to do this, yet it's like I've never said it at all, as with most things that come out of my mouth. I open the door that leads into Rick's kitchen and storm inside, searching for Cora.

I find her seated at their kitchen island, eating a cookie. "Do you want a cookie?" she asks me.

"Get over here right now," I seethe through my clenched jaw.

She hops off the stool and brings herself to where I'm standing. "Hannah, you look like you've been standing in a hurricane," Rick says with a snarky chuckle.

"Well, I kind of was, Rick. Actually, you kind of look like you've been through a hurricane too." I point to my ears, signaling at what I mean. "The hairs in your ears are sticking out ... too much thinking today? A little brainstorming? You must have too much wind going on in that head of yours," I say, sounding like the bitter ex-wife that I am.

He takes a cookie from the plate on the counter and chomps half of it down. With his mouth full, he redirects his attention to our daughter. "Cora, you know you're only supposed to be here on the weekends, sweetie. I know it's fun here, but we have to follow the rules, okay?"

Cora rolls her eyes and crosses her arms over her chest. "This is stupid. You two and your stupid rules. Why can't I go where I want to go, when I want to go there?"

Rick and I look at each other. It's the only time we have any mutual understanding for one another. Not that the divorce was my idea, but he *was* kind enough to make the decision for the both of us. Oh, and then he was kind enough to move in next door with his mistress.

"It's just the way things have to be, sweetie," Rick says to her with a loving smile.

"Can't you just come home now?" Cora asks again, just like she does every time she sees him. She doesn't understand what divorce means, or the whole "forever," thing for that matter. Rick is never moving back in with me, and we will never be together as a couple again. It's easy enough for me to understand, but still painful for Cora to comprehend.

"I'm afraid that isn't possible," Rick continues.

"It's because you fucked Tiana, isn't it?" Cora asks calmly and so surely, it steals every ounce of air out of my lungs. *Oh, awesome.* Unfortunately, Cora's last babysitter was a tremendously horrible influence over her, and now I'm trying to bring her newfound sixteen-year-old attitude back down to one of a typical five-year-old.

I grab Cora by the arm and drag her and her cookie out the door we came in. "Thanks a lot, Hannah," Rick says as I close the door behind us.

"Oh, you're so welcome. You're lucky that's all she said." I don't say another word until we're next door in our house, and I sit Cora down on the couch.

"First, we don't say the word fu—that word. Second, thank you."

"What does that word even mean?" Cora asks.

I inhale a slow breath of air and swallow the explanation I would like to give her instead of, "It means Tiana is a better friend to him than I am."

"Hmm, weird," Cora says. "Can I get up now?"

Before I answer her, she bounces off the couch and runs upstairs to her bedroom.

And ... my meeting with Brett started five minutes ago.

I run upstairs to my office-loft and dial in as I start up my laptop. *Of course, you need to do fifteen goddamn updates.* This machine is as done as my marriage, and I need a new one. I need a lot of new things.

"Thanks for joining, Hannah," Taylor says. "You're only five minutes late today—it's like a mom miracle, right?"

Something inside of me snaps when the smugness of his voice lingers in my head for a second longer than it should. "You know what, Taylor?" I spew his name as if it were the worst cuss word I've ever used. "Not only am I soaking wet from head to toe from the downpour I stood in for ten minutes waiting for my daughter, but then I needed to go drag her out of my ex-husband's house. As I'm sure you know, he lives right next door to me. So, yes, I'm five minutes late today. Any other comments you'd like to start this fabulous sales meeting with?"

There's silence on the other end of the call for a long pause. "This is our staff meeting, Hannah, so why don't we hold our private conversations until later, okay?" Alan speaks up.

Mothertrucker. I scroll through my phone, opening my calendar to see what the hell was on the schedule for today, and yeah, of course, it's a staff meeting. I swore it was a sales meeting.

More silence follows Alan's lovely statement until I hear Brielle's voice peep up. "I'll start by introducing Logan, our new temp. He'll be working with Hannah and me for the next few months while we hash out the new Anti-Hover-Mother segment."

"Nice to meet you all," Logan says.

Well, now my temp doesn't need to wonder about my personal life because I just vomited it out to everyone on the team, including him. This is my life.

CHAPTER THREE

TUESDAY: DON'T BE FOOLED, IT'S JUST AN EXTENSION OF MONDAY

My alarm—that I haven't heard in months— blares "Hit Me Baby One More Time" by Britney Spears. I sit up in bed, frantic that I haven't already woken up. Where's Cora? Oh no, not today. I can't today. I have a meeting with a new advertising rep, and Cora cannot be sick.

I pull myself out of bed and push my hair away from my face. Why can't it be Saturday? For once, I'd love for someone to wait on me hand and foot, have breakfast waiting for me, and maybe even do my hair before I leave the house. That will most definitely never happen, though. I suppose I should try to appreciate that I now have one less person to get ready in the morning because Rick can be Tiana's problem for as long as she'll take him.

As I drag my heavy feet across the hall, I hear a cough echo from behind Cora's closed door. Silently, I cry. Screw you, gummy vitamins. You're just candy with a label tricking me into believing you're boosting my kid's immune system for eight bucks a bottle.

I open the door and find her hiding under the covers. "Cora, sweetie, are you okay?"

She moans and pulls the covers from her head. "I think I'm sick." I reach over and press the back of my hand on her forehead, but I don't feel much heat. There's an ounce of hope, followed by another cough.

She runs her arm under her nose and pulls in a loud, wet snorting sniffle. "Can I have a tissue?"

I jog into the bathroom, grab the box of tissues and bring it back to her. "I'm sorry you're sick, sweetie."

She rips the covers off and hops out of bed. "It's okay, but I can't miss school today. A farmer is coming in to teach us about cows."

Holy crap, someone in heaven is watching over me. "Are you sure?"

"Yeah, I'm sure," she says. "There's no way I can stay home today."

Ditto, kid.

"Well, let me take your temperature, and if it's normal, you can go. Deal?"

"Deal," she says, following me downstairs into the kitchen.

I run the thermometer over her forehead and get a green smiley face on the display, telling me this girl is going to school today. "Yay!"

"Okay, go get dressed quickly, and I'll make your lunch."

Cora runs upstairs, coughing along the way, and I put her lunch together while firing up the coffeemaker. I'm going to need so much coffee to get through today.

By the time Cora comes downstairs, she has green boogers dripping from her nose, and her face is flushed. "You look miserable, sweetie."

"Can you just do my hair, so we can get out of here?" she asks. Cora never wants me to touch her hair. She'd rather leave the house looking like whatever the Lion King would give birth to.

I pull her hair up and tie it into a ponytail, sparing myself the horror movie screams I'd endure if I braided it.

"Cora, I need you to listen to me," I say while kneeling in front of her. "If you think you're well enough to go to school, I need you to try and stick it out for the day."

"I'll be okay, mom," she says with a sniffle.

I do the whole dog and pony show, dragging her to the bus stop and shuttling her onto the bus before finally hopping into my super-hot, gray minivan. Why do I have a minivan for one daughter? I was supposed to have three kids, but kid two and three will probably end up in Tiana's uterus now. It sounds way more depressing than it is, but really, it's a blessing. What would truly be a blessing, though, is if I could lose six seats in this God-forsaken spaceship.

I speed into the parking lot of Coffee Me and burn a little rubber while pulling into a front spot.

I jog inside, stopping behind the woman who's next in line. She turns around to see who's standing behind her, and of course, we recognize each other. "Hannah, how are you?"

Gill Sanford. Gill, as in Jill but with the twenty-first-century type of spelling, is a twenty-first-century type of mom. We met at a playgroup when Cora was six months old, and her daughter was about eleven months old. We tried to become friends, but it didn't work out. We live two very different lives, and our parenting techniques are slightly contrasting, to put it mildly. Every time we were together, it felt like the battle between the working mom versus the stay at home mom. We moms should be on a united front, but it isn't always like that, and it never has been with Gill.

She stopped talking to me when she found out I was going back to work after taking an eight-month maternity leave. I tried to keep our friendship intact, but she had no interest in talking to me at that point.

I'm not even jealous that she wears yoga pants every day, or that she somehow has time to spend at least an hour or more on her hair and makeup. She purposely looks sexy and cute, but like she just came from the gym where she could not have broken a sweat. Oh, and we can't forget about the tan with no lines and a smile with no flaws—the face of a mother without a hint of worry. I want to ask her how, but I don't want to hear the answer.

"I'm good, Gill, how are you?" I ask, sounding as exhausted as I feel and look.

"Are you sure you're good, honey?"

I wave her off with a snort that bellows deep within my throat. "Oh, I am finer than fine."

"I heard about the divorce." She just dives right in. It's been a year, but I was so good at hiding the secret that word didn't spread about Rick and me until a few months ago when Cora started school.

"So, anyway, how is Celli enjoying first grade?" I abruptly change the subject.

"She's just great. All straight A's, captain of her soccer team, and student president. I couldn't be prouder."

Yeah, they don't have captains in soccer at this age, nor do they have student presidents. Oh, and I'm almost positive a check mark on paper does not equal an A, but what do I know? "Wow, you must be so proud," I coo, placing my hand on her shoulder.

Her smile widens, but just enough that I can tell it's fake. "Can I help the next person in line?" *Thank you, barista chick.*

"Oh, and by the way, my daughter, you know, Cora, she can now wipe her own butt after she goes number two. I'm really proud of my little girl, so I totally get the pride thing." She looks at me like I'm speaking a different language and turns to face the barista. As if I can't see her, she twirls her finger beside her ear, calling me crazy without saying the word out loud.

Dumbass.

Breathe in, two, three, four. Breathe out, two, three, four. I hate people. All people.

"Good morning, Hannah," the barista says. I still can't seem to remember her name. I see her name tag each time I'm in here, but it just doesn't stick with me for some reason. "A large coffee with a shot of espresso, hold the froth?" I can't remember her name, but she remembers my order.

"You're an angel. Yes, to the coffee," I tell the woman.

"Ohh, you two know each other?" Gill pipes in as she waits for her green smoothie with the calories and carbs on the side.

"Hannah is a frequent customer," the barista says.

"I don't know how you do it," Gill says. "A single mom with a career. And you still manage to …," she looks me up and down, "match your clothes every day." That wasn't just a ditz comment. She's a bitch.

"Yup and I brush my own teeth and put my shoes on the right feet too. I'm moving up in the world," I laugh and squint one eye at her. What nerve.

The barista places my coffee up on the counter first, and I want to hug her for doing so, but I need to get the hell out of here before I run into someone else I don't want to see.

"Um, I actually placed my order before her, so …," Gill says as I open the door to leave. "Is your manager around?"

Holy crap, get a freaking life.

Back in the van I go, but at least I have my coffee. Oh, and I mindfully put a shirt on this morning that won't tear. I'm calling today a win.

I arrive at the office ten minutes early and take the stairs instead of the elevator because you know, it's that kind of day.

The office is fairly empty, and it's music to my ears. Maybe I can get through my pile of emails before anyone asks me for something this morning. Wouldn't that be something?

I make the long journey through the row of cubes and head right for my office, finding the Pepto-colored walls calling my name.

"Hannah?" I hear. I take another sip of my coffee and spin around to see where the voice came from, finding Logan at his desk. Dammit. Why? He's wearing dark jeans today, a white fitted, button-down shirt, suede penny-loafer boots, and that cologne that was burnt into my nose for hours yesterday. For someone his age, he still has thick hair, which is slightly coifed. His square jaw shows some of his age, as well as the very fine lines angling outward from his deep-set, topaz blue eyes. "You're ... uh, dripping over there." His voice snaps me out of my awkward, analyzing stare, and I find that I am, in fact, dribbling coffee onto the cheap Berber carpeting.

I right the cup. "Oh, crap. Sorry, I feel like a zombie this morning."

"I bet. Were you up partying all night with your daughter?" he asks through laughter.

All I hear is: *Your life must consist of cooking, cleaning, and homework. You're so cool, the best reason I can come up with for you to be tired is that you were probably partying with your five-year-old, instead of having any sort of real life.*

"That pretty much sums it up," I say, tapping my coffee cup into the air. "I hope your night was a little more exciting."

Logan leans back into his chair and rests his hands behind his neck, which happens to highlight rippled muscles along his biceps. "Not even a little bit. My sister is staying with me until tomorrow, and she's a slob. She's loud, annoying, and needs to go back home."

"Sounds like my daughter," I confess.

"She's twenty-eight going on five, so I can see how it might sound that way."

I head into my office, still chuckling at his words. "By the way, your appointment with Veggie Squeeze is at noon. I reserved conference room two for you since the walls seem to be soundproof in there, and I've managed to set up another meeting for you during the upcoming expo with GoGo Toys."

I place my coffee down on my desk and walk back out into the corridor between my door and his cube. "You booked GoGo Toys?"

"Yeah, the sales rep seemed eager."

"Holy shit." I press my fingers into the sides of my face. "I've been trying to book an appointment with them for a year—. You know, I didn't see any sales experience on your resume—"

"I like to talk," he says with a grin. *Don't smile at me. You're making me lose my train of thought.*

"You're amazing." I shouldn't have said that. Crap. Wow. Really? "I mean, keep it up, and uh, keep your calendar clear because you're joining me in today's sales meeting."

"Hannah," Brielle's voice sings from down the hall. "I saw your car. I know you're here."

"I wasn't hiding," I announce.

"You're not going to believe what happened after you left yesterday," she continues.

I have a feeling she's going to mention GoGo Toys and might not expect Logan to be here a half hour before work starts, but I'll let it play out.

"I'm sure I won't," I continue as I hear her bag drop in her cubicle.

"Logan, holy hottie, first. Second, he freaking snagged you a meeting with GoGo Toys."

There we go. Now I get to see Brielle become mortified as she realizes that Logan is here, listening to her. As a matter of fact, I can see into his cube, and he's smirking, but professionally, still maintains his focus on whatever he's looking at.

Brielle's heels scuffle against the carpet as she makes her way over to my office, where she notices Logan. She stops short between his cubicle and my office, then slaps her hand over her mouth. "Oh my Blahniks, you heard that?"

"Heard what?" Logan plays along.

"Oh, uh, nothing," Brielle says, trying to pull it off, but she's not hitting that mark as she spins around in a circle like a dog and twirls her hair around her finger. Smooth, real smooth.

Brielle makes her way into my office, beet red, and closes the door. "Holy shit. I can't believe I just did that," she says.

"Happens to the best of us," I remind her.

Brielle plops down in my guest chair and presses her elbows into her thighs as she leans forward. "Why do you think he's here, of all places, after playing for a Major League Baseball team? Wouldn't you think he'd be loaded?"

I guess that thought didn't cross my mind, but it's an interesting question. It makes me wonder what his story is, but I shouldn't care about his story. I'm his boss, and if he performs, I'll be happy. "Who knows? I don't know how all that stuff works. Maybe he broke a contract or something."

"I just can't believe he got GoGo Toys. It was his first call to them too. We've been trying to get them for like a year. Way to go, Mr. Batman, right?"

I lean back in my chair and cross one leg over the other. "Yes, it's pretty incredible." Brielle likes to talk, which voids my extra work time when I make it in early.

"You aren't going to fire me now that you have the dream temp, are you?" she asks.

Ah, that's why she's early. "You are my administrative assistant, and *Batman* is a temp for the marketing portion of the new magazine segment. You're safe, Brielle," I ease her concern with a smile. I need to try and stop sounding like such an old hag. I used to have spunk, joy, and a chipper demeanor when I talked to others. I actually saw myself as "cool," but even the word "cool" really goes to show how much I've aged this year. I even saw a gray hair the other day, and while I pulled it out, I sort of had a moment where I felt like my life was beginning to show the other side of that hill everyone talks about.

"So," Brielle says, starting the next segment of *Brielle Tells All.* "Adam and I had *the talk* last night."

The talk. The talk as in … he's finally going to pop the question, or did she finally ask him if he was cheating? I shouldn't find it mildly confusing that the two conversations go together.

I keep my focus on my emails, scanning for important information as she continues to fill my head with her Adam drama. I love Brielle and her stories, but they're endless sometimes, so I try to multitask. That, and the topic of cheating still causes a pain in my stomach.

When I found out Rick cheated on me, I didn't sit on the idea of staying with him for weeks and months on end. I made a split decision that moment I walked in on Tiana's perfectly toned and tanned ass in the air and told him I wanted a divorce, which was kind of like stabbing a knife through the fake topping of our wedding cake. Our marriage revolved around his career, and I sat in his shadow, celebrating every raise and bonus, praising his every great review, while constantly being understanding of his early hours and late nights. I never actually said, "What about me?" But it's all I felt for most of our relationship. Everything about us seemed fake.

Divorce was the key to my freedom. Who would have thought?

I've considered getting back on the saddle, and I've tried it with a few Tinder dates, but nothing feels right, so I stick with single-hood. "What do you think?" Brielle asks.

Shit. I didn't hear a word of what she said. "Well, what did you say to him?"

"What would you say to him?" she snaps back. I probably need the context before offering a realistic answer.

"I'd say ..." Uhh.

"I know, right? I was totally speechless. I don't know. I didn't exactly respond to him. I think I need some time to ponder the idea."

An email pops up as I'm thinking of my next response, and it's from Logan, so I casually click on it.

The email is short and says:

To: Hannah@housemomstoday.com
From: logan@housemomstoday.com

Subject: Just a little FYI

Brielle just told you her boyfriend asked her about a threesome, and she's considering it but wants your input. Not eavesdropping—the walls are very thin, and I can see your confused expression through the window.

— :) ~~Logan~~ Batman

Oh no. I knew the walls were thin, but I didn't think we were that loud. *Just lovely.*

A threesome? Is that like a normal thing to ask your girlfriend nowadays? There I go sounding old again. "Um, I'd have a hard time agreeing to that," I tell her. "Is the third party a man or a woman?" The thought popped into my head, and I wonder if that part of the question would have persuaded my premarital mind in a particular direction.

"It's his best friend, Fray," she says with a bit of a blush tinting her cheeks.

"Is Fray hot?"

She mouths the words, "Oh my Blahniks, yes. All of his friends are hot, Boston, city guys."

"Eh, so why not? Maybe it'll spice things up." As the words that are so not mine—could never be mine—but definitely came out of my mouth, offer her advice, I feel a little saucy suggesting such a dirty activity. Maybe it's the part of me that wants to live vicariously through Brielle and her pretty little self.

"You're so right," she says. "You should be a therapist, you know that?" Yeah, that'd be good. I'd be out of a job within a week. I'm going to go ahead and disagree with that opinion.

Brielle hops up from her seat and trots out of my office and back toward her cube.

I open my presentation that I've been working on for days but haven't managed to make a dent in, even though it needs to be ready by noon today. I work my best when I'm being rushed, so it's all good.

PowerPoint stalls as it populates the three slides I've already created. The file can't be that big. What the hell?

That could be the problem ... the three slides I created turned into thirty. I'm confused. These aren't my slides. I scan through them, and while there is no content on the slides, they are all set up and ready for the content.

Logan appears in my doorway as I'm wondering how this file ended up in my folder. "I hope you don't mind, but I did a little work on your presentation today. I noticed it wasn't too far along, so I created a few template pages for you to use."

I close my eyes, trying to understand everything he just said. "Wait, how did you know I had to do this presentation and didn't have it done?"

Logan takes the opportunity to sit down in the open chair and crosses one of his legs over the other. His pants pull snugly in the wrong—no, the right spots, and once again, it makes me wonder what he looked like in a baseball uniform. I shouldn't be wondering that. I'm his boss.

"Brielle told me you had been working on it, and she was kind of making fun of the fact that you hadn't quite figured out how to work the new version of PowerPoint yet. As I was finding my way around the Intranet, I happened to see the file, and since you were tied up with meetings yesterday afternoon, I thought you might not mind if I helped a little. I apologize if I overstepped any boundaries."

I could kiss him. Is he kidding? He basically did all my work, leaving me with just entering in numbers and words. That, I can manage. "You're quite the go-getter, huh?"

"Yeah, I'm not sure that's always a good remark," he says.

"I don't mean it rudely. You've been sort of killing it since you got here twenty-four hours ago, and you're probably going to end up taking my job." While I laugh at my joke, I realize I don't really find it funny.

"Your phone is lighting up," he tells me while glancing at the red light flashing.

With a pit already in my stomach, I peek at the caller ID. "Motherfu—." My reaction sort of slips out, but come on. "This is Hannah," I answer.

"Hi Mrs. Pierce, this is—"

"I know who you are," I mutter.

"Miss Cora has a fever of one hundred two, and she vomited in class. Unfortunately, we can't keep her in school with these symptoms. I'll need you to come and pick her up as soon as possible."

"I'll be there as soon as I can," I concede and hang up, then with my elbows on the desk, I take a deep breath, close my eyes, and let out a long sigh as I press my forehead into my hands.

Logan presses his hands into the armrests of the chair he's still seated in and looks at me with question, probably wondering if he should stay, go, or ask if I'm okay. Am I ever okay? Nope. Definitely, never okay. It's been a long time since I've been okay.

"Can I help you with anything?" he asks.

"Shit, shit, shit." Logan releases his hands from the armrests and settles back into the seat. "My daughter woke up sick. She insisted on going to school, but now she has a fever, accompanied by vomit."

"Oh man, and we have that meeting at noon," Logan reminds me, but he doesn't have to.

It's another defining moment in my life where I silently tell Rick to Screw off again while I think of a solution on my own, even though he could take some responsibility for his daughter on an inconvenient occasion.

I can't miss this meeting.

I hold up my pointer finger to Logan, telling him to wait a minute. I grab my phone and dial Rick's office number.

"Yo, this is Rick," he answers after the first ring.

Real professional. "Rick, it's Hannah, I need your help today. Cora is really sick, and I have a meeting I can't miss at noon."

"Hannahbananna," he draws out my name. Did he hear a word I said, or is he just ramping up to be his usual douchebag self? "Hannah, Hannah, Hannah. Babe, I can't. I'm meeting with a client at one, and it's in Newport, which is at least an hour drive."

"Mmhhm. I see. Well, as always, use protection, Rick."

"Hannah, you can't just throw that around whenever you feel like it."

"You're right. I'm so thoughtless sometimes. Go to hell, Rick." I can't think of anything appropriate to respond with since he's already way too familiar with every name I could call him. It's all moot to him anyway, so I hang up. This is how it has always been. I've always had to take the back seat to his career, even after the divorce, which is totally unfair, since I only ask him for help when it involves Cora, and she is his daughter too. I need to depend on his child support, yet I can't manage to better my life by not screwing up my job at least once a week. "Sorry, my ex is a dick," I explain to Logan. Way too personal, but it is what it is.

"How about, you go get her, bring her here, and I'll keep her entertained during the meeting?" he says.

Did I imagine everything he just said, or did he truly just offer to help me? I can't remember the last time someone offered to give me a hand, considering I don't have mom friends, and I don't exactly belong to the cooperative system of all those moms who are united and have some pact to help each other out in times of need. My single friends don't understand, and my parents are too busy cruising along the Mediterranean somewhere for the fifth time this year.

"She's really sick. I don't know if I should bring her into the office," I tell him.

"I take my Flintstones," he says. "I'll be fine."

"Logan, I don't know if you're trying to get a raise on your second day of work, but you're doing a damn good job, and I'm already considering it."

"Then my plan is working," he says with a snicker. "I love kids. I'll keep her entertained. Don't worry about it."

He must be gay. Straight men like him don't exist. It's an accurate assumption based solely on the diversity of douchery I'm surrounded with right here in this very office building.

CHAPTER FOUR

STILL TUESDAY. CAN I CALL TUESDAY A "SEE YOU NEXT TUESDAY?"

Like I do every time I'm going to or leaving from somewhere, I run, in heels because a lady wears freaking heels.

I should start wearing running shoes with my skirts and dresses, oh, and maybe lose the stockings and forget to shave. I wonder how long it would take for one of the clowns I work with to say something. It's tempting, but I'm not sure Logan needs to see how far I'd take something with those asshats. Not yet, anyway.

I'm buzzed into the school and jog into the office, then the nurse's office. Cora is asleep on one of the cots, and she's more than a little pale. "Hi, Mrs. Pierce," the nurse greets me. "The poor little thing came in here looking awful. I'm surprised she didn't have a fever before she left home this morning."

Is she accusing me of sending my daughter to school with a fever? She better not be.

"Cora insisted on coming to school today," I reply, "and she did not have a fever this morning."

"And you took her temperature?" the nurse asks.

Those are fighting words. "How dare you accuse me of lying!" I say, keeping my voice low.

"I'm not accusing you, Mrs. Pierce, I'm simply asking."

"Well, let me ask you something. Do you have children?"

"No, I do not."

"Then, do not judge my parenting. Are we clear?"

"I was not judging, but clearly, Cora is quite sick. I suggest making a visit to her pediatrician." I'm going to lose my shit in about two-seconds if I don't get us out of this place.

I lift Cora up, cradling her in my arms as I grab her backpack that's leaning against the cot.

"You'll need to sign her out," the nurse says, obviously waiting until after I've lifted my child up to remind me.

I sling her Shopkins backpack over my shoulder, grab the pen tied down to the clipboard and fill out the necessary information.

"Thanks a lot," I tell the nurse.

"Hopefully, Cora feels better soon," she says with a fake grin. What is her issue with me?

I carry Cora out to the car, shocked she hasn't woken up yet considering she has never been the type to stay asleep while I'm transitioning her from one place to another. Once she's strapped into her car seat, I dump her backpack below her feet and quietly close the door before falling into it and exhaling the exhaustion and pain in my chest. This seems like it's never going to get easier. I swear, some days I feel like I'm not strong enough to make it to the end of the day.

As I lug Cora into the office, I begin to question if she does need to be seen by a doctor. She hasn't woken up yet, but I can't miss this meeting. I check my watch for the thirtieth time in the past hour, knowing I now have less than fifteen minutes until the meeting starts.

"Just hang in there, kiddo," I tell her as we enter the elevator. While heaving against the wall and holding my forty-pound child like a baby, I can't help wondering what Rick is doing at this moment. I can imagine him sitting in his office chair with his feet up on his desk, shooting the shit with someone about golf.

For every minute longer this stupid elevator takes, my arms threaten to give out entirely.

The door opens, and I hobble into my department and down the corridor to my office. However, I have no idea what I'm going to do with her now that we're here. Spinning around, I kick one of the two chairs out from the wall and pin it against the other to make a bed, but I can't seem to make them straight.

Logan turns the corner and doesn't say a word before straightening out the chairs and peeling Cora out of my arms.

The release on my shoulders is pretty much the most incredible thing I've felt in forever, but I must look like a sweaty rat right now after running all over while carrying her.

"You have five minutes to freshen up and another five to prepare," Logan says. "I've got her."

I touch the back of my hand to her forehead, feeling the heat that wasn't there this morning. The fever is radiating from her now. "I need to get her some Tylenol."

Logan stares through me for a minute. "Okay, you'll only have like three minutes to freshen up, but hold on."

He jogs out of the department, disappearing without a mention of where he's going or what he's doing. I probably should have told him she can't take adult Tylenol. It's something only parents probably think about.

I kneel by Cora's side, allowing the fear factor in me to take over all other thoughts and concerns. I want to wake her up, tell her I'm here and make sure she's just sleeping off whatever this is, but maybe it would be better if she slept until after my meeting.

As promised, Logan returns within a solid ninety seconds, handing me a bottle of Children's Tylenol. "Um—dare I ask?"

"The receptionist downstairs has two small kids at home. That's why she only works half days. I figured if anyone had Children's Tylenol on them, it would be her."

I should have kids Children's Tylenol with me too. I'm failing so badly at this game, it's just sad.

"There's a better mom than me?" I ask with nervous laughter and a hint of sarcasm. I'm such a moron.

"Is Cora shy?" Logan asks, ignoring my question.

That requires a true laugh. "Definitely not," I tell him.

"Okay, I got this. Go do whatever you ladies do in the restroom, and I'll take care of this cutie-pie." I think my ovaries just skipped a beat.

I remove my hand from Cora's back and gaze up at Logan. "I don't know where you came from or how you ended up here in my office, but thank you. Honestly, from the bottom of my heart, thank you," I say, feeling a bit emotional, as tears threaten to appear in my eyes. Receiving help is something I've long forgotten about.

Logan places his hand on my shoulder and looks down at me with his hooded eyes. "You got this."

He isn't real. The warmth of his hand isn't real. The sensation running through my body like warm water after a coming in from the cold isn't real either.

The opening and closing of the department door *is* real, though, and my vendor is here.

"Shit," I mutter to myself. I guess there's no time to freshen up. I just have to hope I don't have raccoon eyes.

I head out of my office, but before I have one foot out the door, Logan grabs my arm and pulls me back in, closing the door behind me. My heart is beating in my throat, and for the life of me, I can't figure out what is going through his head or what is happening right now.

"I'm not trying to be inappropriate," he says.

Um, at this moment in time, he's free to be inappropriate, but I'm almost positive no one would want to be inappropriate with me in the current state I'm in. Words can't find their way out of my mouth as he presses the pad of his finger under my lower lashes and gently sweeps to the side. "Happens to me all the time when I'm running around. Damn eyeliner," he says with a wink.

"You wear eyeliner, huh?" It's the only sensible response I can conjure at the moment. My face has gone untouched for the last year and a half of my life, and having him fix my makeup like this feels almost like foreplay.

"No," he snickers. "My ex-wife did, and I've pretty much heard the pros and cons about the varieties of makeup more times than I care to share. She was a Clinique girl. My house smelled like new perfumes every day, and she never looked like the same person two days in a row. It was weird."

He's divorced. "That sounds terrible," I tell him. Terrible? We're talking about perfume and makeup. He didn't just say he had walked in on his wife cheating with someone hotter than he is, if that's even possible.

I glance over at Cora once more, watching as she turns over in the makeshift bed. "Go," Logan says. "They're waiting." He shoos me off.

I walk at a fast pace down to the conference room, then calmly make my way inside to find a group of casually dressed younger women—younger meaning, I must be at least ten years their senior. "Good afternoon, ladies. It's a pleasure to meet with you. I'm Hannah Pierce." I reach my hand out to the first woman who appears to be in charge, judging by the look on her face. I can take a guess that she's an all work, no play kind of gal.

"Caroline," she says, affirmatively.

"Nice to meet you, Caroline."

I take a moment to shake the other three women's hands, and we all take seats around the table.

I had the overhead projector set up so they could present their pitch, even though I've been the one eager to bring in their company as an advertiser.

The video takes just over ten minutes, and I made the mistake of shutting the lights off before hitting play. Now, I'm fighting my heavy eyelids, hoping I don't begin to snore, as well.

After the long drawn out explanation of why organic and BPA free are the two best combinations that earth has to offer right now, the video ends, and I lean back in my seat to hit the light switch.

With the research I've done, I know this relationship will be profitable on both ends.

"Ladies, I'm thoroughly impressed with what I've seen here today. I'll need to run some numbers by the rest of the executive team, but I think we can reach an agreement that will be favorable to both of our companies."

"I'd actually like to ask you some questions if you don't mind," Caroline says.

Facing the conference room window with the blinds only partially closed, I happen to see Logan running by with Cora cradled in his arms. What the hell is going on? "I uh—"

"Is everything okay, Ms. Pierce?" Caroline asks.

"No," I say, cupping my hand over my forehead. "My daughter is very sick."

Not one of them says a word. If they were moms, they'd say something. But they're all like twenty-three.

"So, can I still ask you some questions, or—"

My baby is sick, and I'm stuck in here with these tweenybots. I look down at my watch, which is such a no-no for sales, and in general, it's just a rude habit when talking to someone, but it is what it is. I pull in a deep breath, placing my trust in the hands of a hot stranger, who oddly enough likes to be around kids but doesn't have any of his own. People like him don't exist. I'm sure of it. At thirty-three, I think I would know. "Of course," I say, hearing the high-pitched bite of my voice.

"So, say we purchase the space of a web banner for the duration of three months—" I'm not sure I completely hear what comes after the first few words because my mind is spinning with worry.

"Yes, you're correct," I tell her. "A web banner for three months will offer you the highest exposure."

"That's not what I asked," Caroline deadpans.

"I'm sorry, could you repeat your question." My head is not at this meeting and not on veggies or ad space, or—*shit, is she talking again?*

"Would you be willing to negotiate in with a link on your sidebar as well?"

"Typically, that isn't something we do, but I like you, so yes, we'll offer that incentive for the first month of your plan."

"Great, so what about—"

"Caroline, normally, I wouldn't do this, but as I mentioned, my daughter is very sick, and I'm going to need to end this meeting a bit early today. Please don't take this as any form of disrespect, but my daughter must come first, before I can give you my full attention. I'm sorry."

"Okay, we'll—" Caroline looks around to the other three. "We'll be in touch, I suppose."

I ignore the frustration in her voice and jet out of the meeting room to go find Cora and Logan.

The moment I exit the department doors, I find them in the corner, hovering over a large plant.

"We didn't make it too far," Logan says.

Cora is leaning over the plant, vomiting.

"Oh, baby." I run over to her and take her hair from Logan's hand. "I am so sorry." I'm apologizing to both of them, but I'm looking at Logan.

"You think I haven't seen puke before?" he asks with laughter.

"I suppose." I've never been a fan of watching anyone else vomit their guts up, but it comes with the mom territory. I don't have a choice in the matter, but I want to spare Logan from the experience as much as possible, especially after all he's already done for me today. "Thank you for taking care of her."

"She woke up, interrogated me for a full two minutes, finished by asking who the 'hell' I was, then told me she was going to be sick." *Oh, Cora. Why? Why? Why?*

I place my hand on my forehead. "That's my daughter."

"Feisty little thing," he says.

Cora stands up and wipes her arm across her mouth, with a sickened look tugging at her sad eyes. "I think I feel better now," she rasps.

"Oh good, sweetie. Let's get you some water, and I'll take you home."

"Who is this beefcake? Is this the Batman man, Mom?" My eyes nearly fall out of my head, hearing her mention the words beefcake and Batman, which was only said by me late last night when I was talking to Brielle on the phone for a whole two minutes. Cora had been asleep for at least three hours when I made the call.

"Cora!"

Logan looks up toward the fluorescent lights and bites down on his bottom lip. I'm absolutely mortified and have nothing to say in response to this. I'll scold her later when we aren't standing in front of the *beefcake*.

"I'm just kidding," Cora says, dryly. "I already know his name is Logan, and he's your term."

"Temp," I correct her.

She shrugs her shoulders. "Same thing." Cora sighs and looks back over at Logan. "Do you know he was a baseball player?"

How did I produce this kind of spawn? "I may have noticed it on his resume," I say, realizing Cora has no clue what a resume is.

"Yeah, Logan and I are going to play when I'm better. I told him I'd kick his butt."

"Cora, we don't talk like that," I remind her. Why am I constantly reminding her how to not be like me? I feel like I read something when I was pregnant about every child being born as a cave-person, and it's our job as parents to teach them how to act like civilized human beings in the twenty-first century. Considering I still haven't figured it out for myself, how the hell am I expected to raise another human to act civilized?

"Sorry, I'll just beat him good," she corrects herself.

Oh, please stop, child of mine.

"Well, that sounds like fun, but Logan has a job to do," I say, trying to place some separation into this playing house situation we seem to be in at the moment. I don't know a thing about Logan, other than the simple fact that he's gorgeous and good with kids. I can take a simple guess that he's every woman's dream man, and I'm not part of a crowd he'd enjoy choosing from. Plus, I'm his boss, and I shouldn't even be having this internal dialogue thing going on. *Shut up, Hannah.*

"Does he work all day and night?" Cora asks.

"So, I'm going to head back into the office now," Logan says, pointing toward the doors. "How did the meeting go?"

"Oh, I'm pretty sure I blew it," I tell him.

His lip quirks downward, seemingly bummed. "Sorry about that," he says.

I kneel at Cora's side and pull her into me. "It happens." To me—the mother of one, the wife to no one, and a woman with the kind of luck she should have a black cat named Lucky.

CHAPTER FIVE

I MADE IT TO HUMP DAY ... MINUS THE HUMPING

The alarm goes off again. Crap. I knew I shouldn't have considered the slight possibility that Cora could be better this morning. That's not how these colds or viruses go. No, she'll be down and out for at least three to four days before she's well enough to play right before bed, then wake up like a zombie with green boogers draining from her nose the next morning.

I tiptoe down the hall and press on the white wooden frame of Cora's door, allowing in just enough light to see she's still sound asleep. She's usually a light sleeper, but when she's sick, alarms can be blazing, and she will not budge. As I kneel next to her bed, I touch the back of my hand to her forehead. Warm, but not as hot as yesterday. Her face is covered with dried boogers, and she's snoring louder than a grown man. Today isn't going to be pretty.

Whatever the case, she's not going to school. I leave her room and climb back into my bed like the child I wish I could act like. Maybe I can't act like a child, but I *can* hide under my covers and play Words With Friends for a bit. I open the app, wishing there was a new game request from Dickle, but I'm almost positive the fun from that game has passed. But hey, Aunt May wants to play another round.

This is what my life has come to. That, and Rick's living his happy little fantasy next door, blissfully unencumbered by his parental responsibilities. Mom thinks Rick cheated on me because I didn't try hard enough to please him, and Dad won't admit it, but I'm nearly positive he still likes Rick because he's an "old-fashioned kind of …" douchebag "who wears a suit and tie every day." Plus, divorce wasn't part of Dad's grand plan for me. As far as they're both concerned, I probably should have been more understanding of Rick's desires, apparently including his desire to sleep with more than one woman.

When has it ever been acceptable for a man to cheat on a woman and carry on like it was nothing? It makes me wonder about Mom and Dad's marriage. If that crap is cool with them, great, but I don't want to know. I'm a monogamous type of person, and I don't think it's too much to expect the same out of a partner.

I need to figure something out … something I don't want to figure out. I rip my pillow out from beneath my head and smother it over my face, pressing firmly into my eyeballs, which causes little black circles to swim in front of my darkened vision.

Just get it over with.

With a toss of my pillow, I blindly reach for my phone and search for the name Douche Nugget Rick. The phone rings once. *You're a douche.* Twice. *You're a douche.* Three times. *You're such a damn douche.*

"Hannahbananna, how are you, ex-darling?"

"Really?" My voice couldn't sound flatter or less affected by his insults if I tried.

"What's going on?" I hear a blender or something in the background, which strikes me as funny since Rick would never eat anything green or something that had a natural source of vitamins in it when we were together. He was a "meat and potato" kind of guy because that's still a thing and all, and it made him feel more like a manly man. As a result, I ended up making three dinners every night. Cora inherited his limited tasted buds but hates meat and potatoes. She prefers only pasta, and I can't eat like that every night, not at my thirty-three-year-old, post-child state of life. So, three meals it was, and not one, thanks. Ever. Now … now Rick drinks green smoothies for breakfasts and enjoys "cleansing his palate" with a nice hearty salad before lunch and dinner. Why? I almost laugh out loud while thinking my atrocious thoughts. Because Tiana is a size negative zero, she only has one chin, and she has make-up tattooed onto her face, so she never wakes up looking like a freak like the rest of the goddamn population. Oh, oh, and the best part, yeah, the best part of it is she has this Cuban, silky dark hair that makes a hair model look like they stuck their finger into a socket. There isn't a flaw to this chick, so Rick watches every calorie now. He needs to make sure he can remain suitable to be her arm candy or else—

"Hannah?"

"Uh, yeah, um, are you busy today?" I sound caught off guard even though I'm the one who called him. This happens often. My anger is still present a year later, but thankfully, that's the only emotion I have left for this man.

He chortles at my question, which enrages me more. However, Rick could pleasantly say, "Good morning, how are you?" and I'd still hate him enough to want to kick him repeatedly in the nuts.

"Yes, I typically work during the week."

He doesn't even ask why. Why else would I be calling him unless it had something to do with Cora? He's not asking "why" because he knows what this is about. He knows I call in sick way more often than he does, and he's the boss of his own penis—I mean company. Same thing, really.

"Cora is very sick, and I basically lost a sale yesterday because I had to bring our daughter to work for a few hours. Is there any chance you can have someone fill in for you today? I'm sure it has to be hard finding someone to lean all the way back in your desk chair and casually rest their feet on your desk for eight hours while you smile at every double D secretary that walks by, but I could use a hand."

"A hand?" Yes, that is all he took from that long-winded attempt of a slam. "You have a drawer full of vibrators the last time I checked, so I'm sure you'll be just fine."

"I swear to God, Rick, I will come over there and dump your green shit-drink all over your five-hundred-dollar shirt if you don't stop dicking around."

"Easy, easy, settle down now." *I'm not a dog, Rick. It's not worth it. It's not worth it.* "I think I have a solution that will help us both."

"No. No, that's not a solution. No."

"Hey, Titi!" That's t-e-e t-e-e, not titty like I prefer to call her.

"Rick," I grunt. "No, she is not watching Cora today."

"Hannah, she's home all day other than her online spinning class." I hate the way he says my name as if I'm a child who's begging for ice cream.

"No. Plus, what would she do with Cora during her spinning class?"

"I'm sure she'd skip it for a day."

"No," I keep saying, while also realizing I probably have no other choice.

"What's up, babe?" Tiana shouts from wherever, sounding obviously out of breath. Does she ever stop working out? Screw her and her nice body.

"Will you stay with Cora today while Hannah works? Cora's pretty sick, and Hannah can't afford to take any more sick time at her office." He just air-quoted the word office with his fingers. I know he did. I can tell by the way he said the word, and I can picture it in my head, just like he always did when I made mention of my job being as important as his. I was bringing in at least thirty-five percent of the household income, but it wasn't fifty-one percent, so I wasn't as important as mister C-E-freaking-O.

"Umm," I hear Tiana thinking out loud in the background.

"Hannah would really appreciate it, babe," Rick adds in. Not that he could make mention of Cora being his daughter too, and that it would essentially help him out. What Rick seems to forget is that our child support agreement was nearly in his favor since I bring in a decent salary. If I were to lose my job, Rick would be forking out a lot more dough, but he doesn't look at it that way.

The thought has crossed my mind. Just quit, live off my ex's alimony and child support, and bam, have it made, but my ego is too big for that. However, that doesn't mean I can't drop a hint and play the game.

"You know what, I'm just going to call in today. Cora needs me," I tell him.

"Didn't you just call me up all damsel-in-distress like because you're afraid of getting in trouble at work?" he retorts, just as I hoped he would.

"I did, but you know what, it's just a job right? What's the worst that can happen?" I continue.

"Well, you could get fired," he says with a guttural belly laugh. Though, the laugh does end abruptly, almost as if my brilliant ex-husband realizes what would happen if I got fired.

"I see what you're doing," he says.

"Oh," I play along with a high-pitched sigh. "You do, buddy?"

"Jesus, I'll stay home with her today."

"My hero," I lament. "Come get her." The second we divorced, Rick appeared to take on the role of a babysitter. Even when Cora stays at his house on the weekends, Cora plays on her Kindle for hours, or in between the time it takes Tiana to paint her nails whatever bold color she's chosen for the week.

"Yes, your hiney," Rick says before the phone disconnects. There's something unsettling about a child watching a child. I think Cora is more mature than Rick, and I'm not thinking that out of hate or distaste. She might be more responsible too.

I clamber out of my bed again and greet my full-length mirror with a snarl. No wonder he chose Tiana. I run my fingers through a bird's nest of hair standing at attention like a creature from Whoville.

I kind of stopped caring about the way I look a long time ago. I was comfortable in my marriage, and I guess I was stupid enough to think Rick loved me for what was inside rather than the way I looked when I woke up or came home after a long day at work. After all, I birthed a child and distorted my body into a dome house for nine months, leaving behind white zebra stripes on both sides of my torso. I thought a man was supposed to find it sexy after his woman went through the most brutal pain in the world. Instead, I ended up with the man who looked at me as damaged goods after childbirth. After Cora was born, he never wanted to sleep with me. If I took my clothes off in front of him, he'd turn around. I got the hint but had no desire to try much harder. He made me feel hideous, and now that's what I see in the mirror—small age lines, dark circles, dull hair, and a matching complexion. I'm hot stuff.

I look over at my alarm and figure I have at least ten minutes before Rick meanders over here with his stainless-steel juicing cup in hand.

I've gotten good at taking five-minute showers. There's no time for closing my eyes and glancing up into the shower head as I run my fingers through my hair. Nope. I step in before the water is completely heated, pump a handful of shampoo into my hand, lather for thirty-seconds, rinse, repeat with conditioner, and scrub a bar of soap over my body while the conditioner does its job for two minutes. Then it's rinse and rinse, run the razor over the important spots with very few strokes, and grab a towel. Done.

I drag a brush through snarls, feeling individual hairs plucked from my scalp since I don't take the time to spray in any product. A swipe of mascara and four lines of black liner, lipstick, perfume, and deodorant make my bathroom time complete in nine minutes.

The only good thing I do for myself is set out my clothes for work the night before and hang them on the back of the bathroom door. I can literally walk out of the bathroom fully clothed and ready to go.

I'm aware I could wake up earlier. It would solve my issues, but I'm so freaking tired that the thought makes me feel sick.

Just as I pluck the last button through the hole on my blouse, the doorbell rings. Maybe he could have considered that his daughter might still be asleep because she's sick. Though, he's never been around when she's sick. Leaving for the office before she wakes up and coming home a half hour before she goes to bed left Rick little time to get to know the day-to-day details of his daughter's life.

I take one quick look in the mirror, approving the improvement of my just-awoken look, and trample down the stairs to the front door.

I'm sure it's completely normal for a person to feel a need to punch their ex right in the teeth when they see him or her first thing in the morning, but why does he have to smile like he owns the whole goddamn world? "Cora is sick. Maybe you could take your perkiness down a notch."

"A smile always cheers people up, Hannah. Even the most miserable people can feel a little brighter when someone smiles at them. It doesn't seem to be working for you, though."

"Is that what this is?" I ask him. "You're trying to brighten my day with a smile?"

"Well, you do look a little miserable," he adds in.

"Our daughter is sick. Unlike you, I would rather stay by her side all day and feed her soup and keep her wrapped up in her favorite blanket."

Rick holds his hands up as if I offended him. "Whoa, whoa, who said I didn't want to do all that?"

I cross my arms over my chest and shake my head for a moment. "Rick, when have you ever done that?"

His smile fades into a straight line as he walks in and past me like he still lives here. "Come on in," I mumble sarcastically as I close the door. He pokes his head into the family room and then the kitchen, finding that Cora's not downstairs. "She's still asleep."

"Eh, kids like to sleep," he says while heading up the stairs.

"No, Rick. No, they don't." I follow him upstairs and pass by him to give Cora a quick kiss on the head before I leave. "Let her sleep," I whisper as I pass by him.

"I know, Hannah." Yeah, I'm sure you were just going to stand here and stare at her sleeping.

I shouldn't feel nervous about leaving Cora with Rick all day. He's her father, but he's so incompetent and self-centered that I feel I might be better off leaving her with Tiana. I don't know who's worse.

I have a little extra time this morning since I don't have to get Cora to the bus, so I'm skipping the bagged coffee and going for the real stuff. Two mornings in a row ... another miracle.

Like yesterday, there's a short line of people waiting to place their order, and I could stand here all day inhaling the roasted scent of fresh coffee, and whatever pastry smells like heaven. The chalk-written menu blurs into a colorful swirl as I daydream of a life where I could have just twenty minutes to myself every morning, but my daze is interrupted when a hand lands on my shoulder. "I think you're next," a man says. I shake my head around, clearing up my vision. Oh my God, how long was I daydreaming? "Hannah?"

I turn around as I take the few steps forward, finding Batman, the temp—Logan—behind me. "Logan?"

He turns and glances over his shoulder as if I were talking to someone else. "I think I'm the only Logan here," he responds with a chuckle. "Are you okay?"

"Yeah, yeah, of course I'm okay. Are you okay?" Why am I asking him if he's okay? He's obviously okay. I'm the one standing in the middle of a coffee shop looking like a lost child.

"You're still next," he says.

"Right," I hop up to the counter, facing the annoyed teenage girl with piercings lining her lips and eyebrows. Where is my normal girl whose name I can't remember? She knows what I want more often than I do. "Can I have a—" I look back up at the chalk writing, deciding between the hazelnut coffee and chai tea. I'm in the mood for something different today.

"We literally only have coffee and tea," she says, sounding bored, monotone, and stiff. When did I become so uncool? *I used to work in a Starbucks, you little twerp.*

"Thank you for clarifying," I tell her. "I'll have a medium hazelnut coffee."

"Sweetened?" she asks, looking around as if I've been thinking about this decision for an additional twenty minutes.

"Please," I tell her.

"That'll be four dollars," she says. I give her a ten, and she drops six bills down on the counter and pushes it toward me. *Kill with kindness.* It almost never works, but I still try. I put the six dollars in her tip jar, hoping she'll lighten up a bit. Why a girl her age could be so miserable is beyond me. I'd like to tell her what being a single mother is like while my ex lives next door with Barbie, but no one wants to hear my sob story. In fact, *I'm* sick of hearing my sob story.

She doesn't thank me for the tip or give me another second of her time. I toss the straps of my purse back up to my shoulder and slide down the counter to the pick-up area where a few teenage boys are hustling around to prepare the orders.

"That was rude," I hear Logan say.

"Rude?" the cashier giggles. She giggles at him but snarls at me. Do I come off as a bitch? Is that my problem and no one is telling me? Maybe my misery is rubbing off on other people. That's kind of sad, I suppose.

"Yeah, that was rude. She just gave you a nice tip for no good reason. Why not at least say 'thank you'? Has no one ever taught you any manners?"

"Guess not," she says with a shrug of her shoulders and a stupid smirk. "Hey, aren't you that baseball player? You look familiar. Logan Grier, right?"

"I get that a lot," he says. "I'll have a large black coffee."

"You are him, aren't you?" she says, ignoring his order.

Logan looks over at me, probably wondering what I'm thinking. He'll be happy to know I'm wondering the same thing. I had no clue how big of a deal he was because I pay absolutely no attention to baseball, or any sports for that matter. I'm sort of a moron when it comes to anything with balls … clearly.

"Did you get down the large black coffee?" he asks.

"Can I have your autograph?" the cashier replies.

Logan seems to be getting slightly agitated. He leans forward and says something to the girl I can't hear, though I'm quick to figure it out as she slides down the counter across from me and says, "Thank you for the tip, and I'm sorry for acting rude."

"Apology accepted," I say. "Thank you."

She spends little time in front of me before running back down to where Logan is standing. She presses a button on the register, and a stream of white paper unravels from the top. With a quick tear, she whips a pen out from below the counter and hands it to Logan, who signs his name. "Please, the black coffee before I'm late for work. My boss might kill me if I'm not there at nine." He peers over at me and winks. Smooth. Real smooth, Logan Grier.

"Your boss?" the girl laughs while punching in his order. "Aren't you your own boss?"

"Nope," he says without further explanation.

He hands her the money she didn't ask for, but she pushes his hand away. "It's on the house." He drops the money anyway and moves down the counter to where I'm waiting.

"These kids act like they're so privileged nowadays," he says to me.

"How old are you?" I ask him. I'm sure that's against another corporate policy, but I'm not at work, and I'm curious.

"Ms. Pierce," he addresses me. "I'm pretty sure that's a human resource violation." He's grinning, so I don't think he's serious.

"You're right. I don't know what I was thinking. I need to get going," I say, pointing to the door.

I take a couple of steps away when I hear soft laughter mixed with a breathy sigh. I'm the joke of everything. Everything. All the time. I press my palms into the door and force myself out into the brisk winds of winter in New England. I make it to my car when I realize I don't have my goddamn coffee. I'm not going back in there. No way. It's bad enough I have to see Logan all day and play the role of his boss.

I hit the button on my key fob and open my door just as a decorative Styrofoam cup is dangled in front of my face. "Forget something?" Logan asks. His voice is deeper than the passing wind, and the sound thuds against my chest, causing everything inside of me to reverberate.

"Kind of," I tell him.

"You were going to leave without your coffee?"

"Kind of," I say again.

"You know I was just messing with you, right?"

"Kind of." A smirk presses against my lips even though I try to fight it off. I was out of line by asking him his age. It shouldn't be something to smile about.

"You know my age can be Googled, right?"

Why didn't I think of that? Why? Because I shouldn't be thinking about him after work or before work, period. So, at least, he knows I wasn't crazy enough to start Googling him. *I should Google him.* "Of course, I know that. I know what Google is, in case you were wondering."

"I wasn't wondering," he replies. "And I'm thirty-five." He's older than me by two years. I'm not technically an old hag to him. Though, he might think I am since he doesn't know my age.

"You're thirty-three, right?"

"Did you Google me?" I ask playfully, with shock ripping through my words.

"Kind of," he plays back.

"My age is on Google?" Why would my age be on Google?

"Facebook, actually," he says.

Crap. I thought I disabled that. I shouldn't be allowed online.

"Do you get that a lot?" I ask, pointing at the front door of the coffee shop? "Recognized, I mean?"

"Sometimes," he says. "It hurts more than it flatters me. I miss baseball."

"I can imagine." Stop getting lost in his bluish, greenish, grayish eyes. He has very pretty eyes for a man.

"Oh, how's the little princess doing?" The way he says princess in his gruff voice makes me want to giggle like a young girl, but I control myself and clear my throat.

"She's pretty sick. I left her with her father for the day."

Logan presses his lips together as they curl at one side. "Poor thing. You probably just want to be home with her, huh?"

I'm struck with awe that he understands this. Not that it's hard to understand, but I kind of assumed that because he doesn't have kids, and since my ex-husband can't grasp the understanding, that no man would get it.

"Home with her is the only place I want to be today," I tell him.

"I'm sorry," he offers. "I'm sure she's in good hands, though."

The laughter flows freely. It was funny. I can't help it. In good hands. "Let me put it this way. I would have been better off leaving her with the cashier in the coffee shop."

"Ouch," he says with a snicker.

"Thanks for asking, though, really." I slide into my seat and place my almost forgotten coffee down into the cup holder. "I'll see you in a few minutes."

He waves silently before heading off in the opposite direction, which gives me the opportunity to stare at his butt that fills in his blue dress pants very precisely. I am officially a pig. That's a funny realization, considering my opinion of Rick.

The office is in the next parking lot over, but I feel the need to compose myself for a few minutes before making the fifteen-second drive. I cannot be looking at Logan's ass anymore. I cannot ask him any more inappropriate questions. I need to forget about his looks and charm, oh, and the way he was with Cora yesterday. It should all be forgotten. I'm his boss. Boss lady. That's me; I stick to the rules.

CHAPTER SIX

STILL HUMPING ALONG AND IT'S NOT EVEN NINE O'CLOCK

I waited a good five minutes and played three high-scoring words on Words With Friends with Aunt May while trying to forget about the fact that there's still no Dickle to play with. I'm sure Logan made his way upstairs by now. I didn't want to walk in together because the last thing I need is for anyone to speculate and start rumors. It would take very little for some of the lovely gentlemen I work with to come up with a juicy story.

I do my best to keep my head down as I head toward my office, acting like it isn't the least bit awkward when I walk by Logan's cube. I try not to look, but he's staring right at me as if he were waiting for me. Of course, he eases the discomfort by adding in a quick wink as he takes a sip of his coffee.

Is he trying to make me squirm?

I drop down into my office chair, feeling a bit breathless. Either age is catching up with me, or Logan has managed to take my breath away.

Forget about him. It's distracting. It's not going to happen. I already have enough to deal with in my life right now. Move forward. Work.

With a long blink, I go through the list of items I need to accomplish today. I need to take complete advantage since I'm getting an extra full day in the office this week. At the least, I can make up for the time I lost yesterday.

"Chickadee," Brielle sings as she dances into my office. "Look at you with a fancy coffee again? Two days in a row?" She looks surprised because she knows I don't usually have time to stop for coffee.

"Rick has Cora, so I splurged on my 'me' time," I tell her.

"Totes," she says with a high-pitched giggle as she plops down in my guest chair. "So, as you know, we have the expo next week, and our promotional materials should be in today, so we'll need to organize that when it arrives."

Crap. Why did I think we had another two weeks before the expo? I lose track of time so easily. Maybe I'm losing my mind, which would explain why I couldn't remember my phone number the other day. "You booked our flights and stuff, right?"

"Of course, like three months ago. However, I didn't book anything for Logan. Is he joining?"

One minute while I put fantasy together in my head before I give you a decision. All I can envision is a super-hot, thin version of me climbing into bed with Logan. It would be a pretty big letdown if he came because I know that wouldn't be happening. Plus, if I were to imagine he has a thing for thirty-something-year-old hot messes, it would require grooming that I've ignored for almost a year, which is terrible. That's why I don't use the bathroom fan when I take a shower. It needs to be all steamy in there before I go near a mirror.

"I don't know if it's a good idea," I tell her. "He just started. I think he should be focused on other projects."

"I think he should come," she argues.

"For what reason?" I question, curious to hear what she has to offer this argument.

"He's hot," she whispers.

"Okay, Brielle, sweetie, if you want to move up in your career, you'll need to figure out a way to focus your energy on career aspirations a bit more."

"So I can fly up the chain like you did so quickly?" she counters.

"Touché." She has a valid point, but still. "What real reason do you have?"

"He seems to keep saving your ass, so that should be reason enough."

Logan must have gotten wind of our conversation and has no

problem rolling back a few feet in his chair, bringing himself into view. "Did you mention me?"

The look of guilt frames Brielle's perky face as I stare dumbfounded at Logan. "We were just discussing an expo we have to attend next week."

"Oh, do you need an extra hand?" Can I just laugh out loud? He's so innocent the way he asks, and my mind goes to the dirtiest place possible. What the hell is wrong with me?

"You know, a lot of that equipment is heavy, and neither Brett or Alan are coming to this one."

I lean forward, placing my elbows down on my desk, and rest my chin in my interlaced hands. "Yeah, I suppose it would be good to have an extra hand." *No. No extra hands, Hannah.*

"No problem. Where is the event?" he asks.

"It's in Orlando at The Contemporary," Brielle says, clapping her hands together.

"The expo is at Disney?"

"We have a big market down there," I tell him.

"Well, I'll go book your flight and room," Brielle tells Logan. "This will be a great way for all of us to get to know each other." Because she hasn't made things awkward enough, she feels the need to throw me a not-so-casual wink.

"Wait, Brielle?" I call out as she's strutting out the door in her heels.

With a twist of her toes, she turns back to face me. "Yes?"

"You said you had the promotional material being delivered today. Wasn't that supposed to be done in-house?"

"I meant the swag items," she says. "Yes, you were supposed to design the promotional material for me to print."

Shit. "Right, I'll get that to you today."

"What can I do?" Logan asks.

"Once I have the graphics ready, you can bring them up to the print room and collate."

"I love being a temp," he says with a cute smile. I kind of wish I was the temp right now. I'd rather mindlessly collate than focus on creating a promotion while imagining my temp naked.

It takes me way too long to create these damn things, and it's just about lunchtime. Knowing I didn't bring anything to eat at my desk today, I stand up and grab my coat. "I'll have those graphics for you after lunch," I tell Logan as I pass by his cube.

"Hey, wait up," he says. "Where is there a good place to grab a bite around here?"

I stop and button up my coat. "There are a lot of cafes and fast food options in the center of town, about five minutes down the road."

He stands up and grabs his peacoat, which looks like it was tailor-made for him. "Which one are you going to?"

Wow. That's forward, but I'm not complaining. "I actually haven't decided yet."

"You don't like making decisions, do you?" he criticizes.

"I hate making decisions, because I feel like that's all I do," I tell him, honestly. It *is* all I do. I mother. I finance. I taxi. I chef. I'm sick of making decisions.

"I'm in the mood for a sandwich," he says. "Which is the best place to grab one?"

"Anthony's or Perka's," I reply, noting that we're now walking side by side out the door. I notice Brielle has already taken off for lunch, which isn't a surprise. She runs out at noon each day to talk to her beau of the month and sits in her car, drinking her lunch smoothie.

"Will you show me where I can find Anthony's?" he asks.

"On a map?" I ask, trying to be funny, which isn't working for me.

"No, like in person," he jests, elbowing me gently.

His friendly gestures hint at a lack of hierarchical attention. His demeanor is more on the lines of friendship, but maybe more. Except, I don't understand why. What's so exciting about me and my baggage full of drama that would cause someone to be so determined to have lunch with me? This is what a divorce does to a woman in her thirties. It kills every ounce of confidence a person could possibly have left, being so close to mid-life.

"I can do that," I tell him, while wondering if it's inappropriate to be having lunch with the temp. The men all have lunch together several days a week, and they're at varying levels of stature in the company, so I suppose this is no different.

"I'll drive," he says, as we step into the elevator.

"I can drive too. You don't have to do that," I tell him.

Logan turns to me and tilts his head to the side as if I'm crazy.

"Hannah, we're both grown adults. We don't have to play this game. I'm offering to drive because I want to, not because of any other reason. I know you're my boss and I'm a temp, but we're still people. Relax a bit."

I never wonder why so many people tell me to breathe and relax. I wear stress on my face as if it were makeup. It's hard not to.

I have no rebuttal to his perfectly stated explanation, so I wait the elevator ride out and follow him to the main doors. "Damn, snow. I was hoping we'd go all winter without a flake this year," he says. "Once the seal is broken, it's like there's an endless sky-size bag of flour pouring out all over this state."

I'm not sure we'd ever make it a whole winter without snow, but you're right about breaking the seal. Though, I do love the first snowfall, but only the first snowfall. Cora gets so excited. I forgot what it felt like to be in the snow as a child until she reminded me. I wish Cora were feeling better so she could enjoy the snow. "Or, at least at the beginning when it's white. I'm not a big fan of the brown and gray hues it takes on after a day or so."

"Fair point." We make it over to Logan's truck. Now, seeing it up close, it looks new and expensive, which reminds me that he doesn't financially need the temp position for our magazine. He's filling his time.

I open the passenger side door and look up about three feet to where I'm supposed to climb in. You gotta be kidding me. "I'm right behind you," Logan says. "I know. I'm an asshole."

I'm speechless and the unexpected touch of his hands on my hips makes me screech as he lifts me up effortlessly like I weigh no more than a feather. I'm now ducking into the cab of his truck and taking a seat on a polished leather seat that smells like a combination of shampoo and cologne. I shouldn't be in here. He shouldn't have just lifted me into his truck. I'm his boss. Why doesn't he care about this? Why do I have to care about this?

I can answer my question.

He doesn't need this job.

I'd have to be the one to fire him.

Without giving Logan more than a second to settle into his seat, I twist toward him and sweep my hair behind my ear. "What's your deal?" I ask him.

He doesn't seem surprised by my question. In fact, he presses his key into the ignition and turns the truck on without so much as flinching. I'm wondering if he even heard me. "What do you think my deal is?"

I absolutely love when people turn questions around on me. If I wanted to offer up that information, I would have done so. Obviously, I don't know the answer or I wouldn't have asked. Thoughts keep surfacing, but I shove them back down to where they belong because everything I want to know is still considered inappropriate. "I think you're just bored." It doesn't come out as nice as I meant it to sound.

"Bored, huh? Left or right?"

"Left."

"Yeah, I think you're bored," I unashamedly repeat.

"Could be," he responds.

"How could you not be?" I can play this game, although, I'm pretty sure I'll still lose.

"I think you're bored too," he says. I hope we're talking about the feeling of boredom and not my personality.

"Bored isn't an adjective I can describe myself as," I tell him. "More like overworked and exhausted."

"Same here, I guess," he says. His response boggles me. How could he possibly be overworked and tired?

"Right," I quip with a short chuckle.

"I should turn right?" he asks, jerking the truck into the right lane.

"No, no, I was agreeing, or actually not agreeing with you. I was being sarcastic."

"Ah, is that what that was?" He glances over at me and flashes a quick, half smile. At the same moment, I come to realize my slow beating heart has the capability of different speeds. Who would have thought?

"I don't understand your decisions," I tell him. If I had all the money in the world, I'd stay at home all day in my pajamas and watch trash TV. It would be amazing.

"There are times when those who appear to have it all, feel as though they have nothing. I loved playing ball, don't get me wrong, but there were many days when I told myself I'd kill to have a mindless desk job and know I wouldn't wake up needing to down painkillers before sinking into a tub of ice cubes."

I find myself enamored by his words and the way in which they casually slip off his tongue. I like that his past life and career aren't this big secret. I've never considered the life of a person who uses their body to make a living, wearing it down to the point of pain every day. I can hardly handle an hour-long fitness class, never mind practicing baseball daily at this age. "I think I understand."

"You think your life is challenging because you're raising a daughter on your own while dealing with a broken heart." He states this little fact, rather than asking or confirming. I can guess it's thanks to my little outburst yesterday on the conference call.

"It's challenging compared to other times of my life, yes."

"Right or left?"

"Left, then take a U-turn, drive a mile, and pull off to the right. We missed the cafe." I missed the cafe.

He shakes his head with another soft laugh. "Got it."

"I wanted a child," he says.

"Why didn't you have one?"

"I did."

That's all it takes to make my heart stop thundering in my chest, followed by a heavy silence that drowns us within the truck. My gaze drops to my lap, focusing on my intertwined fingers and the redness blushing at my fingertips from squeezing so hard.

"I'm sorry," is all that comes out of my mouth. I'm complaining about something he lost. I couldn't make this worse if I tried. "I'm one of those people who have chronic foot-in-mouth disease."

"Where did that saying even come from? Have you thought about it? It never fails. Whenever someone says that to me, I imagine them with their foot in their mouth." The image of myself or Logan doing such a thing forces the rollercoaster of a conversation into a fit of laughter.

"Turn here," I shout as I almost forget to tell him to turn again.

The truck jerks to the right and I skid halfway across the bench, bringing the seatbelt with me. Shouldn't that thing lock or something? *I guess not when fate wants me grabbing this guy's junk.* Of course, it takes a solid ten-seconds to realize where my hand ended up. "I think this might be grounds for a sexual harassment complaint." I whip my arm around, grabbing my hand as if I accidentally touched something scorching hot. Then again, the analogy works here.

He doesn't laugh after his statement, and a moment of fear pours through me. "It was an accident," I assure him.

"It's a good thing. If it wasn't, it would definitely be sexual harassment."

By the time Logan parks the truck in a spot outside the cafe, I feel like I have sweat dripping down the back of my neck, yet I feel like I'm standing inside of a freezer at the same moment. This has been the craziest ride I've ever experienced.

"Logan, is this a joke to you?" It's rude, but I'm honestly concerned about my job. Sexual harassment isn't something to joke about. It could ruin my career.

"A joke? No, I think I might be missing the whole job security fear tactic thing though, and I apologize if I'm making you nervous."

At least he's honest. "Is this what you do?"

"Take sharp turns into parking lots, so a chick grabs my dick? Not usually, though I can't say I'm upset at the way it turned out." Holy crap. How did we get here? He was as sweet as pie yesterday when helping with Cora, and now he's this … this … devil in a baseball player's hot body.

"No, I mean job hop and hit on women until you get fired."

"I can't say that's the case. Before this job, I was surrounded by a lot of dudes every day."

"So, it's just me? And you just pretended like you don't know where to get a sandwich when you live five minutes away from the office, didn't you?" I remembered that little tidbit of information as we were flying into the lot. He was pulling a fast one on me.

He holds his hands up in defense. "Okay, okay, I wanted to have lunch with you. Sue me. I'll quit being nice, okay?"

"That isn't what I asked," I tell him.

"Do I find you attractive and think it's kind of sexy that you're my boss? Yeah, Am I a little worried you're going right to Human Resources when we get back so you can report me? Only a little. It would get out into the news, and I'd have reporters at my door. Then it would get messy, but I'm a player. I play to win, and I know how to deal with striking out. What can I say?" He's cracking himself up, and I'm stifling the same feeling.

"A player?" I question.

"A game player," he corrects me.

"A game player where women are your bases?"

He raises a brow and quirks his lip a touch. "No, where bases are safe, and the only balls getting hit are the ones flying out of a park."

"Jesus, what kind of women have you dated?"

"I'm hungry. I say stupid things when I'm hungry." He hops out of the truck and rushes around to my side. I hadn't opened the door yet because I've been caught up in my thoughts, trying to figure out what the hell he's all about. I catch my reflection in the side mirror briefly before the door opens, and I honestly don't get it.

He offers me his hand this time, and I not-so-gracefully jump down. If he weren't there, I probably would have gone head first, but he saved that play too. "Thank you," I tell him.

"Sure, so, while we're eating lunch, can I ask you a favor?"

I glance over and up at him, along with the serious expression masking his face. "Okay?"

"Forget about work." If I do that, my thoughts go directly to Cora, wondering if she's feeling any better. Rather than calling her like a good mother would be doing, I'm having lunch with a man I'd be drooling over if I wouldn't be fired for it. I suppose I can drool with my imagination. I can do other things with my imagination too. Oh yeah, my imagination is good. It has always been good to me.

I look over at Logan as we're walking into the café, and he's naked. His ass has those side muscles that you could fit a fist into (not that I've tried). I've never felt an ass like that before. I wonder if it's all firm or if any part of it is soft. Also, it's hairless so is that because he waxes, shaves, or maybe he's just lucky? Because Rick's ass is hairier than his head, and it was nothing I fondly touched or looked at. When I did accidentally touch it, it felt like running my fingers through an old man's balding head with stringy hair.

"You look like you're not feeling so hot. Are you okay?" Logan asks as he opens the door

"Oh, I—I was just thinking about my ex-husband's hairy a—wow, okay, um, yeah, I'm fine."

The look on Logan's face is one of sheer discomfort. "I'm sorry, were you just about to say you were thinking about your husband's hairy ass?"

He releases the door to the cafe, closing us outside of the warmth. "Um."

"It's either a yes or no?"

"Why does it matter to you?" I come back with. Smooth, Hannah. Real smooth.

"Well, we were walking into the restaurant, I asked you if you felt okay and you shouted something about your ex-husband's hairy ass. Obviously, you can't blame me for wondering what the correlation is?"

There are many days, and moments within those days, where I just say screw it and release what my big trap was holding in. "Well, since I'm already at risk for sexual harassment, I might as well be honest with you and just say I was wondering what your ass looked like, and it made me realize I've never actually seen a nice-looking, naked ass because I was with my ex-husband since high school."

"I'm flattered that you think I have a nice ass, even though you've never seen it, hopefully, but if you knew your ex since high school, there had to be a point in time where he had a nice ass?" Logan crosses his arms over his chest as if he were honestly intrigued by my statements.

"Never," I tell him honestly. "It was his worst feature … before he cheated on me."

"Inferiority complex," he says.

"What?" I wrap my arms around my body because I'm beginning to shiver from the cold. Logan notices and reopens the door to the cafe. "I meant he was probably feeling down about himself since you probably have a pretty nice ass, so he needed to see if someone else would take him with his funky ass, or if it was just you."

"Wow," I say, walking into the warmth. I'm flattered he thinks I have a nice ass. That's sweet. Let's hope he never finds out that it's a little saggy, with a touch of cellulite mixed in.

"What do you eat here?"

"The roast beef sandwich is pretty good," I tell him.

"Good, go sit down. I'll grab us a couple of sandwiches. I'm sure you want to call to see how Cora's feeling."

I love you. That almost just came out of my mouth. It's a good thing I still have some sort of a filter left.

I take the booth in the back corner and call the house phone first to see if they're still there. No answer, though. I love calling Rick's phone. It's like the highlight of my life.

Yo? Rick speaking. Asshole.

"Yo, Rick speaking."

"Why do you need to announce yourself when you have caller ID?"

"Habit," he says.

"Kind of like infidelity?" Why can't I help acting like a five-year-old every time I talk to him? "How is Cora?"

"The fever broke. I had her in the tub for a bit this morning since she was freezing, but after some Motrin, she seemed to get a little energy. She's napping now, though."

"I feel awful that I'm not there," I tell him. It was an inside thought that should have stayed inside.

"She's in good hands, Hannah. I *am* her father. I can take care of her." He can't see me squinting my eyes at his words. How come he never took care of her while we were married? He was always too busy doing something else, to stop and give me a hand with her. Now he's father of the year because he's working from home like he does plenty of days a year, and she's napping.

"Okay."

"I'll give you a call if anything changes."

"Okay."

"Hannahbannana, cheer up. It's just the flu." His singsong voice drives through me like nails on a chalkboard, forcing me to hang up on him.

Logan is placing a tray down on our table as the conversation abruptly ends. "He's one of *those* guys huh?"

"What type is that you're referring to?" I'm curious as to what he took from whatever he heard.

"The schmoozer, smooth operator, who thinks he can win anyone over with a smile and a few nice words."

"Impressive," I tell him. "You hit the nail right on the head."

"How is Miss Cora?" he asks.

"Still pretty sick."

He juts out his bottom lip, releasing a soft sigh. "Poor kid." I want to ask about the child he mentioned in the truck, but it doesn't feel right bringing it up without him initiating it.

I dig into my sandwich, starved from the stress I've caused myself today, but for some reason, I'm unable to get through even half of the sandwich before my stomach churns in a way that tells me to get up and run to the bathroom as quickly as I can. "I'll be—"

Yup, I'm not making it to the bathroom.

Oh no.

I gag and expel the rest of my sentence out in chunks of roast beef.

CHAPTER SEVEN

AND THIS JUST BECAME THE WORST, MONDAYIST WEDNESDAY EVER ...

Please tell me I made it to the restroom. I'm not on the laminate wooden floor with dozens of people staring at me, including Logan, a man I've probably made up in my head, which would just add to my insanity.

With another round of impending bile rising through my esophagus, I grapple the leg of a nearby chair as the sounds of a dog with a hairball buck through my throat. My hair is pulled away from my face, which is pointless since it already has chunks dangling from the ends. Then, a hand touches my back—a warm hand. "Let me help you up."

"I don't think I can move," I try to say, though it comes out sounding as if I swallowed a porcupine.

Logan squats down beside me and hands me a wad of napkins. My hands are soaked in a puddle of coffee-laced puke, but I reach up to take the napkins, unsure where to clean first. Everything feels like it's in slow motion as I clean my face.

"Ma'am, we're going to need to ask you to move so we can mop. It's a health code violation."

"Hey man, give her a minute. She's clearly having a rough time getting up," Logan says.

"I'm losing customers," the man continues.

As the wave of nausea passes, anger fills the empty pit in my stomach. Who the hell says stuff like that while someone is obviously sick to her stomach?

A man.

I push myself up off the ground, saturating my hands in my vomit as I come to my knees, and Logan loops a hand around my elbow to help me up the rest of the way. I try to carry myself respectably to the restroom, attempting to maintain a sense of acting like a lady after that display.

After retreating from the restroom, Logan guides me outside. The fresh air feels good on my skin, but I can still smell the horrid scent of bile, and I'm afraid to look down at my clothes.

"I think you caught whatever Cora has," Logan says.

"Yeah, I think that's a good assumption." The words feel like rusty nails in my throat, and my head just became a twenty-pound weight I don't want to hold up for much longer.

"I'll get you home," he says.

"No, I have to get back to work. I have to plan for the event."

Logan snickers and runs his fingers through his short, dark hair. "No offense, but you're covered in vomit."

"I'll shower and change, but I have to be at work today."

"Okay, then." He looks at me like I have two heads but doesn't argue, which is nice. Most of the men I associate with are insistent and on the controlling side of the spectrum. "Let me take you to your house, at least, so you don't have to drive."

"It's just down the road a few miles." I try to offer a faint smile, but the tingling in my throat pauses all facial expressions and bodily movements. Please, no. *Just pass.* I don't know who told me this old wives' tale, but I'm staring up into the clouds, pulling in deep breaths as if it will wash the nausea away. Whoever came up with this shit is probably the same person who said to chew ginger gum for morning sickness. Gum causes saliva and saliva goes down and then comes back up. Bastards.

By some luck, the wave of sickness passes by like a putrid breeze, and I continue walking toward Logan's truck with his escorting assistance. I'm waiting for the lecture on trying not to puke on the luxurious interior of his truck, but it never comes.

"I'll tell you to pull over if I feel sick."

"We'll be okay," he says, placing his hand softly on my back. With a flick of his wrist, the passenger door opens, and he gently helps me up and inside. I lean my head back and close my eyes, wishing for the unsettling sensation in my gut to go away. The ride will not make it better. That much, I know.

My memories of feeling like death while pregnant with Cora play through my mind like an old movie. I would tell Rick I didn't feel well, and he'd tell me not to yak in his car because he didn't want it to smell like vomit for the next month. He had it pretty rough during my pregnancy, working from six in the morning until eight at night. I was asleep when he left and asleep by time he got home, and worked in between all that too.

"Are you hanging in there?" Logan asks.

"Mmm," I groan, scared to open my mouth. Then it dawns on me, though. He has no clue where I live, so we're driving aimlessly but in the right direction at least. Rather than popping the cork, I point in the directions he needs to turn, which works out fine up until we hit my street. The deep breaths, the tight jaw, the clenched eyes—none of it's working. Just a few more seconds until we make it to the driveway. I point a second too late, and he pulls into the wrong driveway. He pulls into Rick's driveway, but I don't care now as I push open the door, falling on the way. The moment my knees touch the pavement, an explosion of bile pours from my throat in old-fashioned, exorcist style. What the hell? I'm starting to wonder if I have food poisoning, but one would have to eat something for that to happen, and coffee doesn't count. I don't think.

The retching sound I make is basically a call for the neighbors to poke their heads out of their doors, looking for the source of the horrendous noises. Tiana is one of those neighbors, except I'm on her driveway, so she has more of an excuse to look.

"Rick!" she yells. "There's a truck in our driveway, and some woman is puking her guts out. Can you please get rid of them?"

It truly amazes me—even as I sit here with vomit dripping from my lips—what Rick saw in this woman beside her double D's, perky ass, and Botox-infused lips. Oh, she probably gives him head more than once a week. That must be where I went wrong all those years. Silly, Hannah.

"What the hell?" Rick says, stepping outside of his house, all manly and stuff. I also find this funny because Rick couldn't figure out how to fix a leaky faucet or plunge shit out of a toilet. He couldn't jump a car because he might get shocked, and changing the batteries in our smoke alarms was traumatizing to his ears, so I did all of that. Real manly, he was. Now he's coming out here like a tough guy, ready to kick some puking chick off his driveway.

A little rain, and it will be like this never happened. Relax, macho man.

"Sorry, man, I thought this was her house," Logan says to Rick. *What a nice introduction.*

"Hannah?" Rick questions while leaning down to confirm it's me, his ex-wife, the woman he was unfortunately married to for ten years.

"I take it you're neighbors," Logan says. "If you just point me to her house, I'll help her over there."

Rick laughs. Of course, he laughs. Why wouldn't he laugh right now? All the while, I'm wondering where Cora is if Rick is out here. If Cora ever hears one of us outside, she's through the door in a matter of seconds, which tells me she's no better than she was this morning.

"Yeah, we're neighbors all right," Rick continues. "Her house, my old house, whichever you want to call it, is right over there."

I'm using every bit of strength I have to look up at Logan and Rick, assuming the confusion Logan must be experiencing at the moment, though he did hear my outburst on the conference call yesterday, and I believe I blurted out something about living next door to my ex.

"Whatever the case, I just want to get her home," Logan continues, without missing a beat. Either he doesn't care to figure out the drama, he's already figured it out, or he wants to dump me at my house and get the hell away from me as fast as he can. I'd go with option three if I were him.

Rick steps in front of Logan to help me up. "Hannah, babe, come on. Let's get you home."

Babe? Home? No. No. No. No. He's helping me up, and I pull my arms out of his grip. "Don't call me babe, and don't refer to that house as home," I manage to grumble. "Logan, this is my dumbass ex-husband who had an affair and then moved in next door to continue destroying my life for as long as humanly possible." Now that I got that out, I would like to collapse back down to the ground and be left here on this soothingly cool driveway to die. It's all that's nice about this property.

Rick steps away, but Logan takes his turn trying to peel me up. Preferring his arms over Rick's, I comply like a limp rag, then cross the small patch of lawn in between our driveways.

"Hannah, are the keys in your purse?" Logan asks.

I nod once, hoping it's noticeable enough that he saw. In any case, he's back across the lawns, fishing my purse out of his truck. I hope there's nothing mortifying in there. He digs around for a minute before retrieving the keys. Since I have at least ten on my keychain, eight of which belong to doors I wouldn't be able to decipher, I point to the house key.

Logan opens the door and turns back around to help me up and inside the house. "Where is your shower?" he asks.

"No, no, you can't see me naked, Logan. That's against company policy," I say. My words sort of sound like I've had about five cocktails, and my stomach feels about the same.

"I won't look," he says. "You need to get cleaned up though."

"Yeah, I suppose. Then, I have to get back to the office before anyone notices I'm gone."

"There's no way," he argues. "You're seriously sick. You need to take it easy."

"I can't," I say.

"You have to."

"You're not my boss. I'm yours," I argue.

He gives up the battle and helps me up the stairs, where I point off to the right toward my bedroom. Normally, I would have spit-shined my house if I knew a man was coming over, never mind lightly straightening up the place. It looks like a tornado whipped through here at some point in the last week.

I always laugh when I watch the TV shows where a woman unexpectedly finds herself in a sexy predicament and spontaneously brings some hot guy home to her super clean, spotless house, as if she always lives that way. There needs to be some real reality TV shows, like this is what a house of a single, working mom looks like. Yes, it needs to be cleaned. Yes, the dishes are still in the sink from two days ago. No, the laundry has not been done in a week and a half, and no, my sheets have not been changed in at least five weeks. I'm gross, but surviving and keeping a child alive, so I'm thinking that's all that matters.

Just as I remember leaving it, my sheets are hanging off the bed, my comforter is crumbled in a ball on the floor, I have two bras hanging from the top of my hamper, oh, and a pair of panties just sitting there in the middle of the floor for no reason. My room might actually smell, but maybe that's just me.

"Sorry about the mess."

"Eh, we all have our days," he says.

I have mine every day. I like to be clean and organized, but I suck at it. I even Pinterest that shit just so I can be inspired to clean and organize, but still, no luck.

He sits me down on the edge of my bed, and another wave of thuds rolls through my head like thunder. Holy crap. What the hell is this?

Over the pounding of my head, I hear water squeal through the pipes before splashing onto the tiled floor of my shower.

"Okay, the water temperature is good, and you're all set. Are you going to be okay in there?" Logan asks. I lift my head, looking up at him and the concerned gaze in his caring eyes. The sunlight pouring into the room reflects off his face, making the blue in his eyes almost transparent. There isn't a flaw on his face, not even a chicken pox scar. How is that possible if he's older than I am? Shouldn't he have more than just two little crow's feet on either side of his eyes? And those only end up making him look sexier. God knows I have enough lines and age spots for the both of us, but still.

"I think so," I tell him. I push myself up and sluggishly drag my feet into the bathroom, closing the door behind me.

"I'll wait here for you," he says.

I should probably tell him to go back to the office or something, but I do want to get back to work, assuming this shower is like the magic healing solution I hope it is.

The hot water does seem to settle my stomach a bit, so I soap up and move through my routine quickly.

Crap.

There's a man waiting in my bedroom, and I have no clean clothes in here. Could this day get any worse? Why, yes, yes it can.

I step out onto my plush bath mat and reach for the linen closet to grab a towel—a towel that isn't where it should be. *Shit!*

I know I had at least one clean towel left. I don't even have a hand towel to dab myself up with, or clothes.

My hamper—I don't care if it's dirty. I need a towel.

I open the door a crack, peeking into my bedroom for Logan, but I don't see him.

"Logan?" I call out. After a second without hearing a response, I open the door a little wider. "Logan, are you still there?" If he's anywhere in the house, he would have heard that shout. Maybe he left. The house is so quiet, I'd be hard-pressed to think he's still here. For all I can imagine, Rick came in to find him.

I open the door and tiptoe out and over to where my hamper should be, but either I'm losing my mind, or there's a laundry fairy, which I'm certain there isn't. I circle around my room, looking for where the hell my laundry could be. You must be kidding me. I'm freezing, soaking wet, and there is no towel in this room.

I scurry over to my bed, ready to grab the comforter for warmth, but because this is the worst day of all worst days in the history of worst days, Logan has appeared at my doorway in what looks to be a state of shock—he's staring at my dripping, wet body with his mouth ajar.

CHAPTER EIGHT

WEDNESDAY JUST KEEPS F***ING HUMPING ME LIKE A HORNY DOG

He's as caught off guard as I am. Both of us gasp and turn around, but me turning around means I'm just showing off my backside. At least he's not looking—I don't think.

"What are you doing?" he asks.

"Looking for a towel. What are *you* doing?" I return the question.

"I threw your laundry in the washing machine. I was—" My room is clean. My panties are no longer on the ground. My bras are not on top of the hamper because the hamper is gone. My sheets and comforter are in place nicely, but I grab the heather gray feathery clump and wrap it around myself.

"I am mortified," I tell him, facing his back.

"I was trying to help," he says.

"This is not what it looks like," I tell him. I'm not sure why I said it, but it seems like the only thing to say in explanation of this sight.

"What?" he questions.

"Me, my body, my bedroom, and my cleanliness." It's right at this exact moment that I realize I've let myself go. I have stopped caring about myself. I look down, assessing how bad the view was, something I desperately try to avoid.

My stomach is flat thanks to the stages of grief from being cheated on, but I'm whiter than the ceiling, and then there's the whole jungle issue going on that I haven't tended to in quite a while. It's like a scene from the Kama Sutra book, circa nineteen-seventy-something. It's not pretty, nor is the dark hair lining my legs. What the hell have I done to myself?

"I don't think I can ever let you look at me again," I add in.

"Are you decent yet?" he asks.

"I've made a comforter burrito around myself, if that's what you're asking?"

Logan slowly turns around, peeking out of one eye first, as if he's scared to see what he just saw again. We've crossed so many lines in the last hour, I don't even know where the original line was.

He places his hands out before him as if I were a scared dog. "It's okay, just relax."

"Don't tell me to relax! I know what you just saw!"

"It all happened so fast, I didn't see much, if that helps," he says. He's lying. He's lying. He got a good look at everything.

"It doesn't help that you touched my panties."

"So what? I've touched jock straps that don't belong to me. It's just clothing."

"First, why would you be touching someone else's jock strap? Second, it's not just clothing."

"Look, I wanted to help you out. Clearly, you're having a rough time, and I didn't think I would be making things worse."

My head pounds a little harder, reminding me of its ever-so-apparent presence. "I'm sorry, I'm overreacting," I tell him. Am I, though? I don't know him all that well, and I'm his boss. I suppose anyone trying to suck up to their boss would do what he did today, maybe, but then again, probably not.

"How can I make this better?" he asks.

As if there's a way to erase the last couple of hours, my thoughts are instantly swayed into a different direction. *I'm going to vomit again.* With a tight hold on my blanket burrito, I jump from the bed, making it halfway across my room before I trip, landing so hard on my boobs that the pain itself purges the vomit from my stomach. I look like an avocado that's been stepped on. All I see is my vomit decorating my white comforter beneath me.

"My heart is literally breaking right now, Hannah," Logan says as he jogs into my bathroom, quickly returning with a wad of toilet paper. He gently cleans my face up. "What am I going to do with you?" He laughs quietly, not at me, but with me, if I had the energy to laugh.

I don't have the energy to even speak, so I just watch. How is it fair that I spent so much time with a man who couldn't care less about me and then meet someone who is willing to clean up my vomit within a couple of days of knowing me? I didn't think there was this type of kindness in the world. It doesn't matter, though. I was destined for dicks like Rick. Yeah, I know; calling him Dick got old a long time ago.

Logan cleans up as much as he can, covering up what's remaining with the extra blanket. His hand drapes over my forehead, and the scent of soap soothes me. "You're really pale. We might need to get you to a doctor."

"No," I croak out. "I'll be fine. I just have to get up and start moving around—get my mind off vomiting."

"You're burning up, though."

"I'm just embarrassed," I tell him, honestly. "I don't feel like I have a fever. I don't remember the last time I even had a fever."

"Do you just want to lie here for a bit, maybe?" he asks.

I know I said I want to get up and start moving, but his idea sounds better. "I think so. "He lowers himself down, bringing his knees to his chest. That doesn't look comfortable. He's in dress slacks and a fitted shirt. "You don't have to stay here," I tell him.

"I know," he says.

"You don't have to feel bad for me, either."

"I know that, too."

He stands back up and looks around the room before heading to my nightstand and grabbing the remote to my TV. Unsure of what he's doing, he powers it on, so I slowly twist my head to the other side, watching as he flicks through the channels until he finds a soap opera. "Yes, or no?" he asks.

"No," I tell him, trying not to laugh. "Not my thing."

He passes by a few more channels and finds HGTV. "This?"

"Yeah, I like that."

Three hours of HGTV and no more vomit. It's a win. Logan is still next to me, sitting quietly, watching the shows as intently as I have been. The silence and calm cause a storm of thunder in my chest when the doorbell rings. I look at the clock on my nightstand, finding the time to be past five. "It's probably Rick with Cora."

"Let me take care of it," he says.

"I want her to come home," I tell him. "I haven't seen her all day."

"Of course. I'll stick around and help with her. It's no problem."

I try to push myself up a little, realizing I'm still naked underneath the wrapped-up blanket. "You really don't have to do that, Logan. You've already done more than you should have today."

"Maybe, but I'm going for sainthood, so let me have this." He smirks as he pushes himself up to his feet. "I'll grab your clothes from the dryer while I'm down there." He had switched my laundry a couple of hours ago during a commercial break, and in my lethargic state I didn't argue, but I don't remember the last time someone has done my laundry.

"If Rick gives you any trouble, let me know," I tell him.

"I've got it taken care of," he says with a reassurance I can't understand. Rick is a dick. I don't know how many times I can recite this silently to myself, but he doesn't just give in.

I swear I hear laughing downstairs, but it must be my imagination. There couldn't possibly be anything the two of them have in common unless a devil and angel are somehow related, but surely that's not the case.

I hear little feet clomping up the stairs. She's moving around, so hopefully she feels better. My bedroom door flies open, and I'm still flat on the ground in a burrito. "Mommy?" Cora asks, obviously confused to see me lying in the middle of the ground.

"Hey sweetie," I say, reaching my arm out to her.

"Why are you on the ground in a blanket?" she asks.

I shove my hand under my face to look up at her. "I believe I caught whatever you have. How are you feeling now?"

She sits down in front of me, and her nose scrunches. "What is that smell? It smells like poop or throw up, maybe both."

I'm sure it's smelled like that in this room for the last three hours, and I've just gotten used to it. I can't imagine that Logan got used to it, yet he stayed. "Let's try not to worry about the smell. How are you feeling? That's what's important."

She shrugs her shoulders. "A little better. I'm kind of dizzy still, and my head hurts, but I want to go back to school tomorrow. Dad said I could if I don't have a fever in the morning."

"I'm so glad to hear you're doing better." And I'm so selfish for thinking that because she's better, I have a slight chance of being better tomorrow too. Maybe it's just a twenty-four-hour thing.

"Mom?"

"Cora ..."

"Why is Batman Beefcake here?"

I feel like whining and crying a little. Cora doesn't understand what it means to kick someone when they're down, nor would she think that's what she's doing right this second, but I'd rather not think of any form of Beefcake. "It's a long story," I tell her. It's the truth, but to be honest, I don't believe I really have a good explanation for why he brought me home at lunch and never left. It may be hard for her to understand.

"Good luck with that," I hear loudly from downstairs. It was Rick's voice. *Good luck with what?*

"Did Daddy take good care of you today?" I ask Cora.

She leans back onto her elbows and crosses her legs. She's such a mini-me. "Eh," she sighs. "He was on the phone all day, but Tiana braided my hair five times. It kind of hurt, but it's the only time she stops talking so I let her do it."

"Why isn't your hair in a braid now?" That woman drives me bonkers. I don't care if someone is good at doing hair, or calls herself a beautician, along with a fitness enthusiast, she should keep her hands off my child. Plus, I think one member of my family is enough for her to steal.

"I took it out. That's why she did it five times."

"I know, you don't like tight braids."

"I told her that, but she didn't listen." I roll my eyes, noting the extra pain it causes in my head. "Why are you naked?"

"It's part of the long story," I tell her. If she were older, my long story would be going in a bad direction right now.

"Daddy and Tiana were naked today too. Maybe it's naked day?"

"Um, what?" I'm hoping I just heard her wrong, so I'm going to let her say it one more time before I hunt my laundry down and head on over to castrate Rick's dick.

"Well," Cora says, letting her head fall to the side. "I was taking a nap, and when I woke up, I forgot where I was, so I got scared and ran to Daddy's room. I opened the door without knocking. It was an accident—" Crap, I don't want to hear any more. "But he was naked and so was Tiana. I think they were fighting or something because he was shaking her around against the wall, and she was yelling his name really loud. I told him to stop hurting her, and when he saw me, he dropped her."

"What?" I ask with exasperation.

"Yeah, she fell to the ground and screamed, then crawled into her closet. It was weird. Dad said he'd be with me in a minute and that I needed to go back to my room—did you know Daddy doesn't have a vagina like we do?" Dear God, I'm already sick to my stomach. Why must you do this to me today?

"Cora—" I can't do this.

"It's okay. Daddy told me that boys have a penis and girls have a vagina. It's not confusing. It makes sense now." I'm going to vomit again. Not because of this damn flu I have, but because I want to hurt that man. She's five. Five!

"Cora, sweetie, that's a lot of information for one day."

"You know what's weird, though?" she continues.

Tiana has one too? Oh, wouldn't that just answer all my questions!

"Laundry!" Logan says as he reenters the room with my laundry basket. "Nice and warm, right out of the dryer."

"Did you fold my clothes?" I ask him. I don't need to ask because they're neatly stacked in layers of organized clothing.

"Isn't that what you're supposed to do when they come out of the dryer? They'll wrinkle if you don't." He laughs at me since I'm the crazy one. He's folding his boss's laundry, and *I'm* crazy. I am crazy. I've lost my goddamn mind.

"Mommy, I was talking to you!" Cora snaps.

"I didn't mean to interrupt, Miss Cora," Logan says as he places the basket down on my bed.

"It's okay," she says with a smile, a smile just for Logan, not me. "So, Mommy, what was weird was that Tiana's boobies stand straight up on their own without one of those strappy bowls you wear. She doesn't need one of those, I guess."

I hear the wind fly out of Logan's lungs. "Cora," he says, "I think we should go downstairs and see what we can find in the kitchen to make for dinner while your mom gets cleaned up. What do you think?"

"I'm kind of tired," Cora says. "And my head hurts."

"I bet I know a way to make it feel better," Logan suggests. Maybe I should be concerned about him taking care of my five-year-old since

I don't know him very well, and he doesn't know her well either, but for some reason, I have more faith in his childcare skills than Rick's at the current moment.

"Really?" she asks with hope.

"Yup, I'm an expert at making headaches going away."

"A lot of flying balls to the head?" I belt out. I couldn't help it. The joke just rolled off my tongue without a second thought.

"Wow, cute and witty, who would have known?" He winks at me before scooping Cora off the ground, forcing her into a fit of giggles as he flies her out of the room.

My ovaries hurt almost as bad as my guts do now.

CHAPTER NINE

WEDNESDAY? IS THAT YOU? OR DID I SLEEP UNTIL SATURDAY, MAYBE? POSSIBLY? PLEASE, LET IT BE SATURDAY

Why does my face hurt? Why does it feel like I'm lying on sandpaper? With effort, I press my eyelids open, blinking a few times until the space in front of me becomes clear—dark and clear. Oh my God, what time is it? I've been asleep—on the cheap carpet Rick had to have—on my bedroom floor, the one good thing about throwing up on it. The door is only open a crack and ... Cora! "Cora?" I belt out, sounding like I swallowed a sharp piece of metal. "Cora?" I don't hear a thing. Shit. Shit. Shit.

I press myself up onto my knees. I'm still naked. What the hell kind of flu is this? Whatever it is, it's been eight hours, and I'm done with it. "You hear that, you shitty old body? I'm done. Mess with me all you want, go ahead ... try me." I'm delirious to boot. I get to my feet, holding the blanket tightly around me, and I spot a shadow of folded clothes on my bed. He folded my clothes. I almost forgot.

I feel around the pile, easily finding a silk pair of panties draped over the top. Come on, really? He couldn't at least hide them within the other clothes to make it look like he didn't see them?

I slip them on and then find a raggedy shirt and sweats. I'm dressed quickly, considering my body ate every one of my organs today. "Cora?" I call again.

What time is it? It's pitch black out. It must be late. Maybe Rick took her back. Why wouldn't anyone have woken me up? Why did I fall asleep? That's irresponsible. I was irresponsible today. I don't like it. I didn't even call work to let them know I wasn't coming back for the afternoon. I'm sure it doesn't look mildly weird at all that I took off with the temp and never returned.

Cora's door is partially closed, and I poke my head inside, searching for her curly ponytail that would be hanging off the side of her bed if she were sleeping in it, which she is.

Thank goodness.

I take a step inside, and I shouldn't be surprised to find Logan after everything he has done for me today, but there he is, sitting on the floor, leaning up against Cora's bed, asleep, with Cora's favorite book in hand.

Wow.

I tiptoe over to the bed and tighten the covers the way Cora likes, listening to her soft breaths whisper through her pursed lips.

"Hey," Logan utters under his breath. "You okay?"

I smile warmly and nod my head toward the door, afraid of waking Cora up. If she's up, she doesn't go back to bed. It's been her thing since she was an infant.

Logan and I make it out into the hall, and I close Cora's door the rest of the way. "I don't know how to thank you for everything you did today," I tell him.

He doesn't respond. He just smiles. I don't know what that means.

I never did shower again after the last time I projectile puked all over the place, so that's probably why. I likely have vomit chunks hanging from my hair.

"I should get going," he says.

"I should shower," I reply.

"You should." He laughs, but I sense it's not as funny as he's trying to pretend it is.

"I'm sorry for interrupting your day." I feel like I owe him that since he doesn't look too thrilled right now.

"Don't apologize, please. I'm glad I was here to help, really."

"I'm glad too," I offer.

"Are you feeling better now?"

"Enough to keep things under control here."

"Good."

We're in my hall, the lights are dim, and the tension is high. What the hell happened while I was taking a nap?

"I'll see you tomorrow?" I ask because if I'm judging the look on his face correctly, I think he might leave the state by tomorrow morning.

"Goodnight," he says in response.

"Okay." I feel dumb, embarrassed—no, mortified. What is going on? Or, what did Cora tell him is probably the better question.

"Thank you again," I say as he heads down the staircase.

He doesn't respond. Why? Why?

I already feel sick. I don't need to dread going into work tomorrow, having to explain a whole lot more than if I were just sick.

As the door closes downstairs, I turn for my bedroom, clipping my shoulder as I walk inside, but I hardly feel the pain shoot down my arm in comparison to the confusion buzzing through my head. This is why I don't nap. It's a good reason never to nap again.

The urge to wake up Cora and find out what happened while I was sleeping is overwhelming, so I'm stepping into a cold shower before I do something stupid.

Holy mother of—

"Mommy." There's a cold hand on my face. "Mommmyyyy."

"Cora, what?" I open one eye and roll to the side, finding it's six. It's six. It's time to get up and start the shit show. Shit show. Oh, no.

"Cora, sweetie, go and get dressed. I don't care what you wear today, but go get dressed and I'll come find you in a few minutes." What the hell is this? I thrash my covers off and run to the bathroom, making the base just as an explosion of crap erupts from the hollow insides of my body. Hell has landed inside of me. That's what this is. Did I sin? I don't know what the hell I did that was so wrong to deserve this.

Okay, it just keeps coming. Yup, we can stop now. Ugh, and now I'm going to puke. I can't sit here but can't get up either.

"Mommmyyy?"

"Cora, go to your goddamn room, and I'll be with you shortly. Shittttt."

"Why are you mad, Mommy?" I have my hand gripped against the cold sink, and my toes are curling beneath my feet. Sweat is pouring from every pore on my face, and my stomach has turned inside out. "Mommy?"

The doorknob twists just as another gush of wonder floods through my pipes. "Cora!" I scream.

She continues to open the door, and a look of horror and shock fills her face. "There's poop everywhere!"

"Cora get out of here, now!"

She doesn't move. She just wraps her arms around her stomach and lurches forward as vomit pours from her mouth.

That's all takes for the tears to start. I can't freaking do this. "I'm sorry," she says, quietly, while wiping her arm under her mouth.

The pain in my stomach eases for a moment, and it's enough time to clean up one mess so I can tend to the other.

It takes me a full hour to clean the bathroom, but by the time I'm done, I feel better. All the pains in my body have subsided, and another quick shower rinses off every memory of the last twenty hours of my life.

I find Cora downstairs in the living room, sitting quietly on the couch with her backpack. "Are you okay, sweetie?"

"I'm sorry," she says, again.

"Did you eat breakfast?" I ask.

"I had two granola bars, and I can buy lunch today."

"Okay. Let's get you to the bus."

As we're walking down the street, I recall my curiosity from last night. "Hey, Cora?"

"Yeah?" she says, shuffling the gravel beneath her little Ugg boots.

"Why was Logan in a bad mood last night when he left?"

She shrugs and doesn't lift her head. "Beefcake Batman seemed fine to me."

Ugh. Why? "Well, he seemed angry to me. Did you say anything you shouldn't have said, maybe?"

Cora looks like she's thinking about my question for a minute. "No, the last thing I remember him saying before I fell asleep was, 'I'd do anything for this life.' I don't know what he meant by it, though, and I was too tired to ask any more questions."

Clearly, the man is delusional, or was delusional. Who the hell thinks like that after witnessing what he saw yesterday. For the simple fact that I need to somehow face him today, part of me wants to call up all those nice men I work with and tell them to screw off because I quit. Except, I can't. I need money. I need to adult and be a mother and crap—well, I'll skip the crap. Had enough of that for now ...

We reach the bus stop just as I hear the rumbling engine echoing from the other side of the hill.

"Are you sure you feel good enough to go to school? You can't tell anyone you got sick this morning or they'll send you right home."

I kneel in front of Cora and look her straight in the eyes, seeing she still doesn't look right. She's a tough cookie. I'll give her that.

Cora places her hands on my shoulders. "Are you sure *you're* well enough to go to work today?"

"No, sweetie. No, I'm not."

"Then you should stay home in your jammies like I did yesterday."

"I wish I could," I tell her.

Missing a half day of work for being sick isn't my thing. The men in the office do it weekly to the point where I think they eat up more of their vacation time being sick than they do taking actual vacation days.

I kiss Cora on the head and watch her hop onto the bus as if nothing's wrong. I feel a little like death, which means she probably feels at least half of that since she's a day ahead of me. "Thank the cesspool at school for me," I mutter as the bus chugs by.

I move as quickly as possible back toward the house, spotting Rick and Tiana outside with their dog, Chicklette. How freaking cute are they in their bathrobes, walking a rat through their freshly sprinkled grass.

It's about time I find a back entrance into the house so I can avoid them whenever possible. Sometimes, I feel like they just wait outside to torture me—make me feel a little worse about my sorry life. That would be too easy for Rick, though. He could just call me up and say the words, "There's someone out there for you, Hannah Banana. Don't give up." It's been a year. I'm in my thirties. I've had a daughter. I have a full-time career, and oh, I live next door to my ex-husband and Princess Tiana. Mothertruckers.

"Good morning, Hannah!" Tiana shouts with her hand flopping in the air as if I were a long-lost friend she hasn't seen in years. "How are you feeling?"

"Fine," I grunt. "Thanks."

"Aww, Hannahbannana, the bug still got you down?" Rick coos.

"You know what, Rick?" I say, stopping halfway up my

driveway. "I hope you get this bug, and I hope it hits you like a sack of bricks. We all know how weak your poor little tummy is. Just wait."

"Oh, don't worry about Rick," Tiana says, cheerfully, "I've been giving him vitamins in his power drinks in the morning. His immune system is like 'pew pew,'" she says, making shooting motions, using her hands as pistols, like an idiot. "He has nothing to worry about." She smiles, flashing her blinding veneers.

I wonder what would happen if one of those things fell out of her mouth. I heard they usually end up filing the tooth all the way down to the nub or something before they attach them. So, there's a nub there somewhere, I bet. Oh, it would be so unfortunate if her nub was showing.

I don't have the stomach to continue this conversation, so I offer my fakest smile and head into the house.

I'm not sure how I'll make myself look human in the next fifteen minutes, but I pray I have enough makeup to do so.

It takes me less than one coat of lipstick to remember my car is at work. Logan is disgusted by me, or so it seemed … can't imagine why, and there is no way in hell I'm asking Rick for help.

I drop the lipstick tube into the sink, hearing the clang as it bounces against the porcelain. Why?

As if it were an answer to my answerless question, the doorbell rings. What now? Let me guess, Rick needs to come spit in my face? Maybe it's Tiana still jogging in place so I can watch her boobs bounce in synchronicity. It's hypnotizing, really.

I hobble down the steps while trying to get my shoes on at the same time. "Coming!"

Every stair is another small reminder of the hollowness in my stomach and the fire that might still be burning somewhere in that area.

I open the door and take a step back from surprise. I didn't think I'd see him here after last night, and certainly not with a smile on his face. "Logan?"

"Need a lift?"

"Well—"

"You have no car. I remembered at about four this morning."

"Right," I tell him.

"How are you feeling?" he asks. There's a definite switch in his mood. Maybe he turns into a jerk after dark or something. It's a common issue I've found in men throughout my life.

"I'm better, not completely cured, but I'm heading in the right direction, I think." If my stomach doesn't explode again today. "Thanks again—"

"Don't mention it. Really." Really. I got it now. I won't mention it.

"Did I do something to upset you?" You know, besides projectile vomit all over you and my house, among everything else I put you through.

"Not at all. Why would you think that?"

I laugh, trying to hide the nervous inflection I can't control. "You just seem—"

"Tired?"

Okay, maybe he's a jerk during the day too. Maybe I'm just being sensitive. I shouldn't care what he thinks anyway. I'm his boss, and he's already seen way too much of me.

"Let me just grab my bag," I tell him.

He stands at the door politely as if he has never been inside before. It's like yesterday didn't happen. I probably imagined the whole thing. Maybe my sandwich was drugged yesterday, or maybe that bitch at the coffee shop slipped something in my coffee. That would explain everything.

Let it go. Just let it go.

I grab my bag and head back to the door. After locking up the house, I find Rick and Tiana still pacing along their lawn. Does he even go to work anymore? Or is he a full-time caretaker for a miniature dog?

"Hey man," Logan calls out, waving at Rick. I guess I wasn't lucky enough to imagine that part of yesterday happening.

"How's it going?" Rick replies. "What a guy, picking up the leftovers." My eyes bug out of my head. Did he just say that?

"I forgot I left them here last night," Logan says with a chuckle.

Confused for a moment, I finally spot a Chinese food bag in Logan's hand. "They brought over some food for Cora and me last night since your fridge was empty."

Dear God, why does my life have to keep shitting on me? Please, make it stop.

I climb into Logan's truck without offering anyone another word. I just can't come up with anything of any intelligence at the moment.

"You two BFFs now or something?" I ask as Logan climbs in. Oh, it all makes sense now. That's why he's acting this way. Rick must have filled his head with made up shit last night. "What did he tell you about me?"

Logan starts up the truck and backs slowly out of the driveway, offering Rick one more wave before shoving the gear into drive. "He didn't say a thing."

"You're a liar," I tell him.

He looks over at me and grins. "Don't worry about it, okay?"

CHAPTER TEN

THURSDAY ... FRIDAY EVE. YEAH, WE'LL GO WITH THAT

If I had my car, I could convince myself that this was all just a bad nightmare, but I don't have my car. I'm in his car, and the nightmare is still alive. "Are you hanging in there?" he asks, halfway to the office. It's the first time he's spoken to me since we got into his truck.

"I'm fine," I respond in a way that mirrors his coolness.

"So, what's on the agenda for today, boss?"

We're all the way back there now. I shouldn't care. I should focus on the discomfort of having this completely out-of-my-league man sitting just a car seat away from me. It's not like I have a chance, had a chance, or ever will, so the nerves and whatever else is floating through my intestines right now should just go away.

"Um, just preparation for the event next week." I think I need to stop talking. It's suddenly apparent that speaking is only highlighting the internal battle between my organs, making their sore presence known.

"You look like you're pretty deep in thought over there."

I am. More than he knows. "I—don't know. I'm just trying to wake up, I guess."

"We have time for coffee," he says.

Coffee will loosen things up in my gut; not so sure I need that after this morning's blowout, but if I don't caffeinate, I'll have a migraine before noon. There is no winning. None. Tea, maybe that'll be the easiest on my stomach. I don't normally drink tea, but I've wanted to give it a try. I pull out my phone and start a Google search for, "Does tea cause the shits." I'm super classy this morning, but I need to get a direct answer to this question.

"No, tea does not cause the shits," Logan says, stifling a laugh.

I close my eyes slowly, twist my head, and look over at him. "How did you see that from over there?"

"Your text is quite large for a woman your age. I just glanced over, and there was your question. You don't need Google, you can just ask me." He's smirking, and while I enjoyed his smirk at one point yesterday, I'm not enjoying it right now. He's making fun of me and knows I'm worried about shitting myself.

"So, I'm at the point right now where I want to leave the state and cross out any chance of ever running into you again after what you've witnessed in the last day. That's how I feel. Except, I can't do that because I have a job, a daughter who can't leave the state without permission from her father, and a mortgage, which means I'm stuck."

"Why does this all bother you so much?" he asks, simply. I'm sure he'd be totally fine if I watched the bowels of hell expelling from his body yesterday.

"I'm mortified," I tell him.

"Why?"

"I wouldn't even want my ex-husband seeing what happened yesterday, and he watched me giving birth. That's why, never mind ... you."

"Have you considered that may be the reason he's your *ex-*husband?"

Did he just go *there*? He did. He totally just went there. "Excuse me?"

"I don't mean it in a rude way," he says, peering into the rearview mirror as he switches lanes. "It's just that ... if you're so closed off, maybe that put a barrier between you and Rick, you know?"

"From one divorcée to another, do you really think you should be giving me advice? Especially since I was cheated on and replaced by some Barbie bimbo, who can hardly spell her name. What's your excuse? Where did you go so wrong, Mr. Perfect?" I snap at him defensively.

He stalls, looks over at me, and swallows hard, before returning his gaze to the road. "I never said I was perfect."

"That wasn't the question."

"I know why my marriage went down the shitter. That's the difference between the two of us."

I reposition myself in my seat, feeling the heat rise through my neck and into the backs of my ears. "How do you have the nerve to make that kind of assumption after knowing me less than a week and having very few facts about my life to go on?"

"I've seen a lot in the last week," he says.

"So, you're blaming me for getting cheated on? I just want to make sure I'm understanding you correctly. I guess Rick is still as slick as ever with his greasy salesman spiels. I should have known you'd take his side when I heard you two laughing together yesterday."

"I didn't say that," he says.

"Then just say it, Logan. What have you figured out about me while watching me puke my brains out? I'm honestly intrigued." By the anger searing through each of my words, I doubt he believes I have any sort of curiosity about what he might say, but I do want to know where this crazy assumption is coming from.

"You don't want anyone to care about you," he says. "Just as men act like they don't want to be cared about, it's never the truth, so I can only assume you do want to be cared about. However, the big difference between men and women is that women still have a sense of nurturing even when pushed away. Men don't have that sixth sense, so if they think a woman doesn't want to be cared for, they may walk away."

I open my mouth to snap back with something, but nothing comes to me. No thoughts. No words. He just described me, but did he describe Rick's actions too? Rick never struck me as the type to want to feel needed. He's always been the one who has the needs and wants.

"I—" I still have nothing to say.

"Look at Tiana as an example," Logan says. "She clearly needs more attention than the average woman. I mean, I heard her tell Rick at least once last night that she needed some attention. I wasn't a huge fan of the baby talk that accompanied it, but I kind of thought … wow, it's nice to just be told what she wants instead of making a man play the whole guessing game. I can safely assume that Tiana is just easy."

I laugh because he hit the nail right on the head with that one. "That, she is, Logan."

He raises a brow and looks over at me briefly. "I'm serious. I mean easy as in simple, not high maintenance emotionally."

"Well, too bad for me, then. I am who I am, and if someone doesn't like it, they can go find another Tiana." I cross my arms, feeling defensive for the way I am, even though I don't care—I've never cared about what anyone else thinks.

"Look, don't get me wrong. I'm not saying you are the reason for your divorce, but I'm telling you it's okay to need help sometimes, and no one is going to judge you for it."

"Okay, thanks for kicking me when I'm down," I tell him. I don't want this conversation to continue. I'm even more uncomfortable now than I was when I got into the truck.

"For the record, I think it's hot when a woman can take care of herself, but there's still a time and place to lean on help when it's there. Sometimes we men need to be needed."

I let him help yesterday. I don't understand why he's being so pushy about this. I was helpless, as a matter of fact. Rick had to have filled his head with so much shit, I can't even process what he must know about me.

Did he just say it's hot to be independent?

I inhale sharply and set my gaze on the side window. "I'm like this for a reason. Everyone has reasons for the way they are."

"You're right," he says quickly. "and I'm pushy and forward, so because of that I'm taking you out on a date tonight."

I whip my head around. "Excuse me?"

"Yeah, I'm taking you out for a nice dinner. I might kiss you. I might even try to persuade you to do more, and I might break that sneering little look in your eye too."

I'm having a hot flash. Is that possible at thirty-three? "What?" I'm a little blunter this time, but seriously, what the hell is happening?

"Now's the part where I either say I'm kidding, or I reply with … is there a problem?" He clears his throat, pulls into the parking lot of the coffee shop, parks, and looks directly at me. "Which one do you prefer?"

What kind of question is this? Obviously, it's the latter half of his assumption—or whatever I'm supposed to call it. Obviously.

"Are you propositioning your boss?" I reply.

"Am I?" he questions.

Answer him, Hannah. "I could have you fired for this."

"Could you?"

"Yes," I snap.

"Then fire me."

"I liked you better before we had lunch yesterday. You were such a kiss ass."

"I can kiss your ass if that's what you like." I should slap him. How rude is he? Who says that? *Stop picturing him kissing your ass, Hannah.* "Although, it all depends on whether you get tea or coffee right now," he says with a chuckle, obviously amused with himself.

"Why did you pretend to be so sweet yesterday?" I ask him. Really, my brain feels like it might explode. Either he has multiple personalities, or he fooled me more than I've ever been fooled.

"I wasn't pretending."

"So, what is this?"

"I want you."

"Who says that?" I ask, throwing my hands in the air.

"A thirty-five-year-old man who knows what he wants when he sees it." How the hell do I respond to that? "Coffee or Tea? Or should I say, shits or no shits?"

"Tea," I snarl. The only reason I'm not going in with him is that I don't want anyone to see us together. "Here, let me give you money."

"Don't worry about it," he says, then closes the door before I have a chance to argue.

During the time I managed to graduate college, become a wife, a mother, and an ex-wife, I seem to have forgotten the girl I once was—the one who played mind-games with the guys who played hard to get until I lost interest. I was the one who never let anyone close enough to know what was going through my mind. Now, like the weak skin beneath my stretch marks, my thoughts can be penetrated without much force.

If Logan wants to play mind games. I can play too. The old me—and the real me is still here somewhere. I just need to relocate the parts.

The reminiscence of playing games brings my wandering eyes to my phone and Words With Friends, hoping to see a notification I might have missed from Dickle. My sweet Dickle, who I pushed away too many times.

There's nothing but a new game request from him. I open the game board, finding the letters spelling out the word, *sigh*.

I scan my letters, looking for anything I can respond to his sigh with. Rather than concerning myself with points, I use my "I" to add beneath his "H." His turn.

CHAPTER ELEVEN

AT LEAST IT'S THIRSTY THURSDAY. OR, IT WILL BE WHEN I GET HOME TONIGHT. ALONE. BY MYSELF. WITH A BOX OF WINE.

Other than a quick "Thank you," I keep my thoughts to myself as we cross the lot and park in front of the office building. The elevator ride is silent, despite the loud thoughts of a "Fifty Shades" scene that could be played out in here, and possibly with time to spare.

Maybe that's my game. I'm uncomfortable, so if I make him uncomfortable, I might not feel so bad. I look up at the numbers on the elevator, ticking by slowly as we chug up to the fifteenth floor, but we're only at five. He's watching the red digits too, which means he isn't aware of the thoughts buzzing around in my head. I can do this. I used to be so damn smooth.

I turn around and shove my hand into his chest, taking him by surprise as I pin him against the wall. I clench the linen material of his white shirt into my fist and press up on my toes before going in for the kill. A cold shiver runs through my core, leaving me breathless as my lips touch his. His body tightens, his breath catches in his throat, and his hands clench my shoulders.

I went way too far.

He pulls away and glares down at me with what looks like anger. "Are you freaking kidding me?"

I can't lose my confidence now. "What's to kid about? You said you wanted me. How was I?" It feels like the words of another—sharper—

version of me are coming from my mouth. Because this me—the one existing in my current state of mind. I don't even know if Logan was kissing me back, but his lips are like a ripe cherry that I could lick and bite all day. I haven't had those thoughts in—nope, never had those thoughts.

"Hold on a minute," he says.

With a hand still firmly holding onto me, he reaches over and hits the alarm button. "What are you doing?" Shit. I'm getting fired today. That's that.

"Did you just ask me how you were?" he asks with a guttural snarl.

"Yes, that's what I asked. Shut the alarm off, Logan."

Logan makes a sudden move and without an inclination of what's to come, I'm straddling his hips, in a skirt—thankfully, it's not a pencil skirt, that would have been an awkward tear. My back is pressed against the wall, and the vibration from the sirens are tingling through my back, but the sensation of his hardness is overwhelming as he places his lips back on mine. His tongue brushes against my lips, urging them to part. Coffee. It's all I taste on his tongue, and I want to drink him all in. His breaths match my own, heavy and out of control. Still pinned in an unmovable hold by his steel-hard body, his hands are free to comb through my hair. Holy mother of—this is hot. This is hotter than "Fifty Shades." He has muscles everywhere, and I just want to run my fingertips up and down his arms over and over as he continues mauling my mouth with gentle nips and sensual flicks of his tongue.

Don't stop. "Don't stop," I moan into his mouth.

"Hannah? Are you going to be sick again?" My eyes flash open, and I'm holding myself up on the bordering rail of the elevator wall, watching Logan stare at me from the corridor as if I were a loon. "Are you okay?"

"Yeah, why wouldn't I be okay?" I ask, trying to play it off as if whatever the hell I just did was normal elevator behavior.

"You just told me not to stop?"

Oh, dear heaven. "I think it was just a phantom wave of nausea," I tell him. Or a delusion of your lips touching mine in ways I can clearly only dream of.

"Yeah, that's normal. You'll be okay."

No, I won't. I'm not even wearing a skirt today. What the hell is wrong with me? Like I'd ever go after a man like that. Pfft.

"People are going to think it's weird if we walk in together," I tell him.

"People are going to think it's weird that your car was here all day and night, but you weren't," he adds in.

I brush past him and pry open my bag to look for my ID tag to scan, but he steps in front of me and presses his ass up against the scanner, holding it there until we hear the door unclick. *Cute.* No, that's hot. Dammit.

He opens the door and holds it open, waving me inside. Upon entering the office space, the only thing I see are half a dozen men poking their heads up and above their monitors, and Brielle with her mouth hanging open. She stands from her desk chair and trots over to me in her unthinkably high heels. "Hannah," she mutters through clenched teeth. With another quick peek over my shoulder, she smiles at Logan. "Good morning!"

Brielle is making a scene as she drags me along the row of cubes and shoves me into my office before closing us inside. "What in the world happened to you? Do you have any idea how many times I tried calling your phone? I thought you were abducted or something."

"Abducted?" I ask, lifting my brows with question. Who in the world would abduct me?

"Well, you went to lunch with ..." she shrugs and does a weird head nod toward the door, "you know."

"Logan?" I question.

"Shh," she says.

"Logan knows I went to lunch with him yesterday," I inform her.

"Then what?" she continues. "Huh? You're all pale and clammy looking. Something must have happened."

"Oh yeah, something happened all right." I take off my coat and drape it over the top of my bookshelf.

"You're not going to tell me, are you?" She's disappointed because I don't care to talk about vomiting all over the hottest man I think I've ever been within five feet of.

"I had the stomach flu, Brielle. I yakked all over the guy. He took me home, watched me puke again, naked at one point too, I should add in ... hot, right? Then he took care of Cora until she fell asleep. Oh, and now I have to face him every day for the indefinite future."

Brielle slowly squats down into the guest chair across from my desk. "Oh, my Blahniks, are you serious?"

"You think I'd make that up?"

"That is like the sweetest thing I've ever heard," she coos and bounces her feet. "Did he hold your hair and stuff?"

"Brielle—I'm absolutely mortified."

"He took care of Cora, Hannah. That's like—I mean, that's something." Every thought I've been trying not to think over the past few hours are now dribbling from Brielle's mouth like a leaky faucet. Maybe he stayed and took care of me and helped with Cora, but whatever it was yesterday isn't the same today. Or it's more. This is hurting my head, which already hurts. "Are you going to see him again?"

"You mean, when I'm not choking up chunks?"

"Well, yeah." She responds with true curiosity like I was serious.

"He asked me to go out with him tonight. I think he was joking, though." That's kind of a mean joke after being brutally sick for twenty-four hours. Who does that?

"Why do you think he was joking?" Brielle asks, leaning forward with interest as she presses her elbows into her knees. This is turning into another therapy session where I get schooled from a twenty-something-year-old on how to live.

"Come on, Brielle, really? Look at him. Look at me ..."

"Girl, you have some serious self-image problems. You're smokin' hot for thirty-three. You look like you're twenty. You could probably do something with your wardrobe, but you're gorgeous. Stop doubting yourself."

I look down at my cardigan and black dress pants. "What's wrong with my clothes?" As I'm asking, I admire her ensemble of navy blue, fitted dress pants and a white button-down shirt that's so fitted, it might explode into shreds with one deep breath. "I can't dress like you. I have a child, and hips, and—"

"Gigantic ladies," she continues speaking for me. Ladies ... boulders, same thing. "And your hips form an hourglass shape. Plus, I'd kill for your ass." *You don't want to see what that thing really looks like, honey. Trust me.*

I roll my eyes at her remarks and redirect my attention to my blacked-out monitor. I tap my mouse, bringing the bright-as-hell thing to life, and slouch back into my chair.

"That's it?" she asks.

"What?"

"Never mind," she sings while popping out of the chair. She opens the door and walks directly into Logan's cubicle. I watch, wondering what the hell she's about to say to him, but it's not as much about what she might be saying as what she's *doing*. What the hell, Brielle? She hoists herself up onto his desk, knocking over his pen cup. I can see the giggles and hear the reverb. Her hand is on his shoulders, and she's squeezing his tricep. She's got to be kidding me. This is so inappropriate. We're at work. I'm her boss. I'm his boss. This can't happen. I stand up, pushing my chair back a few feet, clearly a little more enraged than I should be. I make my way to Logan's cube in a nano-second and stare at the two of them like a mom—a mom with my hands on my hips. "This is completely inappropriate behavior for the office," I scold them, but it wasn't really Logan. It's Brielle.

"Have you felt this thing?" Brielle continues squeezing his arm. "It's like a rock. Did you pitch a lot?"

"I was a second batman—I mean baseman," Logan winks along with his answer. "But, that's history now." Logan seems mildly embarrassed by the show of—err—affection Brielle is giving him.

"That's so cool. I've always wanted to learn how to play baseball. Do you think you could maybe … teach me?"

My heart is throbbing in my chest, and my veins are filling with a surge of anger. "No, he can't teach you how to play baseball."

"Why not?" she argues, holding a mischievous arch to her brow.

"He's injured."

"No, I'm not," Logan responds.

Yes, he is. That's why he's not playing baseball anymore. "So, you lied? Because it's illegal to lie during an interview, you know?"

"I *was* injured, but I'm not now, so no, I didn't lie."

"Great, so you can show me how to play," Brielle pipes in again. "What are you doing tonight after work?"

My head falls to the side as I press my tongue against my cheek. She's freaking playing me like a toy right now.

What if he says yes to her?

I shouldn't care. They belong together, but she has a boyfriend …, I thought.

"He's going out with me tonight," I say, quietly.

"What was that?" Brielle asks.

"She said she was going out with me tonight," Logan repeats with a smirk.

"Will you both stop it," I hiss, looking from side to side. I'm just waiting for Nick or Taylor to walk up and add to the fun.

"Going out on a date with the boss.... You're totally in," Brielle tells him, offering him her fist to pound.

He pounds her fist and turns his chair away from us, centering himself back in front of his monitor.

I take the opportunity to grab Brielle's arm and drag her into the office, but not fast enough before we're stopped by Nick.

"Ladies, ladies, ladies," he greets us. "I have a proposition for you if you have a moment to spare?"

"What is it, Nick?" I ignore his chagrin and sit down behind my desk. Not that it stops him from entering, but at least Brielle is sitting in the only guest chair … which leaves the corner of my desk available. Of course.

"So, I have this vendor attending the event next week. His name is Fitz O'Brior."

"The CEO of GoGo Toys. Yes, I've heard of him, Nick."

"Good, good, so I need you to cozy up to him a little bit. You know, loosen your collar maybe, put a little makeup on. We need him to buy ad space for Q2." If he jiggles his eyebrows once more, I'm going to tear them off, one hair at a time.

Breathe, Hannah.

I hate playing this card. "Nick, first, I already have an appointment to meet with him. Second, have you heard the term sexual harassment? There are video training modules if you haven't. I can familiarize you with one … or ten."

"What are you talkinnnn' about? You can have a sleepover with the temp, but I ask you to do something for the business, and it's suddenly considered sexual harassment? Should I remind you of the company policy on interpersonal work relationships, Hannah?"

My blood is boiling. I haven't done a thing except upchuck a sandwich on Logan. "Nick, not that it's any of your business, but I haven't broken any sort of policy. Whatever assumption you may have, is purely for your own fantasy, so do me a favor and get your ass off my desk, walk out of my office, and use that brain of yours before you say something that utterly stupid again. Do you understand?" Brielle is pale, but with splotches of pink peppering her cheeks.

"You never have been much of a team player," Nick says, clearly in need of having the last word.

"I can't believe you just said all that to him," Brielle says.

"I've had it with the comments around here."

"Yeah," she says with a guilt-ridden grin. "I hear ya." She doesn't hear me. She loves the attention. I don't know why, considering every man in this office other than Logan is married, and/or middle-aged, and lacking social skills, but whatever floats her boat, I guess.

"Well, in other news, you have a date tonight. What are you going to wear?"

I close my eyes, trying to piece together how this all came about. I'm asking for trouble, but at this point, I don't think I have much to lose. "This?"

My eyes are still shut, but I can feel her stripping me with her blazing glare. "No, you're not. I'll handle it. Just smile and look pretty."

CHAPTER TWELVE

A THURSDAY SURPRISE—TOMORROW IS MARTIN LUTHER KING JR. DAY, WHICH MEANS THERE'S NO SCHOOL OR WORK... AND I JUST REALIZED THIS.

Picking Cora was like a mini vacation from my life, but now she's off to Rick's for the long weekend. Then, it's mission: *Make Hannah Look Hot*. First, I must find wine.

I step in front of my full-length mirror and try to position myself at an angle that makes me feel confident, but I haven't found that view yet. Another glass of wine will surely do the trick. A perk of getting divorced is the stress-starvation, which came with a complimentary SlimFast diet. Those twenty pounds brought me back to my pre-college weight, but what's underneath my clothes still makes me shudder.

My skin is dull, my eyes look as though they sag, and I think I'm getting frown lines. I try to avoid my reflection so I can ignore the voice in my head that reminds me I'm not *her*, and she isn't me. Yet, it's all I can see.

I pull my shoulders back and tousle my hair. The desperate thirty-three-year-old in me unclasps one more button, offering just a little more of a view. This is slutty, right?

"You need to get laid," Brielle says as she walks into my bedroom.

"Why are you still here?"

"To make sure you know how to put form-fitting clothes on properly." She shakes her head and walks up behind me, reaches around and yanks my shirt down way more than I'm comfortable with.

"If I take one wrong step, my bra will be on display."

"Right." She pulls my shirt away from my chest, looking down at my bra. I snatch the material out of her hand, but she saw enough. "No."

"I'm not changing my bra right now. He's going to be here at any minute."

"Yes, you are."

"I don't have anything nicer than this unless you'd prefer nursing bras. I still have some of those lying around."

She stomps her foot like a child and clenches her fists by her sides. "You are impossible."

"No, I'm a grown woman," I correct her. She's conducting an odd maneuver under her shirt, and I already know where this is going. "No, thank you." *As much as I'd like to wear the bra you've been showing off beneath your white blouse all day, I'd rather not.* She whips out a hot pink, lacy see-through piece of … tissue? That can't be fabric. "Find that at the dollar store?"

"Um, no, this is an eighty-dollar bra, so please keep it in one piece."

"It'll probably rip when I try to clasp the thing together," I argue.

She holds the thin fabric out to me, waiting. If I drag this out much longer, the doorbell is going to ring, and she'll pull another stunt like she did this afternoon.

I shuffle around under my shirt and detach the nude, supporting bra with comfortable straps, switching it out for the lingerie Brielle wears just for the hell of it. "Mmm, super comfy," I squeak. I look in the mirror and tilt my head to the side. "Um, I'm pretty sure I can see my nipples."

"Nah, you just know they're there, so you're imagining it," she says.

"I don't think that's how it works."

"It is, trust me. Adam tells me all the time." I'm waiting for the laughter to follow her boneheaded statement, but her face remains neutral.

"I'll just wear a sweater." I grab my black one from off the bed and slip it over my shoulders.

"Why would you waste such a perfect view with a frumpy sweater?"

"Because it's fifty degrees out, and my nipples will tear this new shirt apart—and I'm a mom." I glare at her through the mirror's reflection, and she looks away, checking out more of my attire. "At least those jeans are perfect."

"I haven't had purposeful holes in my jeans since the nineties," I tell her.

She ignores me and continues going down whatever checklist she's made up in her head. "Did you shave?"

"Obviously."

"Did you get a wax after work like I told you to?"

"I ran out of time."

"Hannah, no. What is the current situation down there? You better not tell me you have hip hugging, muffin-top controlling panties on right now."

"No, I'm wearing a thong," I mutter.

"A what?"

"A thong, Brielle. You know, the thread that tears up your ass crack all day?"

"What's under the thong?" she continues.

"What do you think is under the thong?" I counter.

"An unhappy little tree."

"That's it," I tell her. With my arms in the air, I walk past her and head downstairs.

"No, Hannah! I'm trying to protect you. You can't have sex tonight. Not until you remove the unhappy little tree. Logan isn't a forest ranger."

"Stop it," I shout. "Enough already."

"I'm serious, Hannah. No sex for you."

"Or what?"

"Or … or, I'll tell everyone in the office you slept with Logan."

I whip around, facing up the stairs where she's standing, carefully keeping her distance. "You better be joking with me right now. First, you won't know whether I *do* or not. Second, how could you say something like that?"

"Because. I'm trying to spare you. Logan isn't just some guy, Hannah. He could have any chick in this state, or in any of the bordering states for that matter. Hell, he could have anyone in this whole country, but for some reason, he's intrigued by you and your perm-a-scowl."

Wow. That's harsh. Even coming from the most honest person in the world, I wouldn't expect her to say something like that to me. "Real nice, Brielle."

"There's a difference between dating and being married for ten years." It's her closing argument just in time for the doorbell to ring. It's awesome that I can begin this night on *that* last note, leaving me to feel like I was just slapped across the face.

I open the door, finding Logan in fitted jeans, a black tee, and a leather jacket. His dark caramel hair is a short mess—sexed up and perfect. If I were him, I probably would have had sex with someone before coming here so I wouldn't feel so inclined to donate to this charity case of a washed-up mom.

"You look hot," he says, walking in, then past me.

"Thank you?"

"Is that a question?"

"Kinda."

"Well, you know how they say, 'There's no such thing as a dumb question?'"

"Is that how we're starting the night?" I ask.

"I guess so." He circles around the foyer, looking in the mirror for a quick second.

"Why did you want to go out with me tonight, Logan? Is this a joke? Do you feel bad for me?"

"I do feel bad for you, but it's not a joke."

"Oh, my grrr, okay, can you just go home, and we can pretend like this didn't happen?"

"No, I want to go out," he argues.

"Why? Please just save me the pity, and tell me the damn truth."

"Are you always like this?"

"Like what?"

"So … uptight?"

"No!"

"You have everything I want, Hannah. Is that so hard to believe?"

"I have what you want? What is that supposed to mean?" I'm verging on infuriated, trying to figure out what the hell his agenda is. If this weren't my house, I'd leave.

"Okay, folks, I'm going to take this brief intermission and sneak out before things get any more heated—or iced," Brielle says as she jogs down the steps toward us. "Oh, and one piece of advice—just bang bongos, already." Then she stops halfway down the stairs as if she forgot something. "Oh, wait. No, bongos tonight. Wait until the next night, yeah. Those are the rules, okay?" She shakes her head around as if she heard something loose rolling around in there, then continues down the stairs. *Bongos?*

Brielle is one for leaving with the last words, and those particular words are just the icing on the cake.

She slams the door on the way out, and now it's truly just the two of us here. That thought makes me anxious because I'm still wondering what it is he wants with me.

I cross my arms over my chest, feeling my shirt tug against the tissue bra I'm wearing. This is so stupid.

"You're gorgeous. You have your life together, even though you think you don't. You have a career and manage to care for your daughter better than most moms I see. You don't let people get too close because you're smart enough to protect yourself. You're mature, but a little immature. You're what I've been looking for in a woman, and if you add up all those qualities, it makes for a pretty long list. I feel like when I meet someone who gets all the check marks on my list, I shouldn't just waste the opportunity ... even if she pukes all over me." He hesitates before that last phrase, then adds it with a smirk, and a sparkle in his eyes I can't help finding a bit adorable.

I want to respond, but words aren't forming in my head. I make up some guy's crazy checklist? This must be another delusional daydream again. "I don't even know what to say."

"Thank you? I find you attractive too, and you're okay ... I guess." He speaks the words he'd like to hear me say, and maybe if I thought he was serious a moment ago, I would have said them instinctively, but I'm still hesitating. Maybe Nick and Taylor set up this practical joke to pay me back for "stealing" a promotion one of them could have had. I wouldn't put it past either of them.

"You know you're attractive. Why do I need to tell you?"

"Beauty is in the eye of the beholder, darlin'." I'm not sure what he means, but he's making it sound like he feels the way I do when looking at my reflection.

"I don't understand you," I tell him.

"Probably because we've only known each other a few days now."

"Exactly," I agree. "So, this is kind of quick to be going on a date, don't you think?"

"Considering people are in the habit of skipping dates and instead just meeting up for sex because a phone app said they're compatible, I'd like to think it was appropriate that I at least asked you out. What else was I supposed to do? Court you first?"

"Well—"

"Plus, you're sort of my boss, so before I steal your job from you, I want to say I slept with my boss." A smirk plays over his lips. He's kidding, but he's not kidding. He'd fit way better in the office than I have or ever will, even though it's a company running a mom magazine. "Plus, behind every product for a mom, is a great guy."

"Funny," I chide.

"You're smiling," he says. "So, I'm obviously a little funny."

"Okay, but you aren't stealing my job, so don't bother trying. I have the law on my side—the whole equality in the workplace thing."

"This has obviously crossed your mind already then, huh?" He's toying with me. He's trying to get under my skin ... or clothing. He's doing a fine job at both.

"If jerking cars around until your junk is grabbed isn't how you pick women up, is this your game? Antagonizing them until they fall to their knees?"

"No, but I like the way you think."

He's taking steps toward me, and I bet he expects me to take some steps backward in response, just to give him the power of control. I'm not moving, however.

The closer he comes, the more his cologne penetrates the air around me, and it's like a delicious-smelling salt, awakening every part of me. "Where are you taking me tonight?" I ask him, proving a sense of confidence I think he's doubting in me.

"I was going to leave it up to you since you seem to have an opinion about everything."

"I do have an opinion about everything. Is that a problem for you?"

He's in my bubble and staring down at me as if I were his meek prey. "I told you, I like that."

"Do you like standing in my space and staring down at me, too?"

"Tell me to move if you don't want me standing here ... this close to you." His voice has lowered to a whispering growl, and the vibrations echoing between the foyer's walls are triggering my nerves into a frenzied state of panic.

The words from Ryan Gosling in "The Notebook" ring through my head, "What do you want? What do you want? WHAT do you want?" I want to make out with a hot guy. I want that. I do. But he works for me, and it's wrong, which makes it so damn right. I could tell him, "It's not that simple," or "I have to go." For as long as I've been hearing Ryan Gosling's voice in my head and replaying that old-fashioned Southern scene in my mind, Logan's face is less than an inch from mine. Why am I thinking about Ryan Gosling when I have *this* man standing here? He's on the same level on the ovary-explode-o-meter as Gosling, and I'm being ballsy.

"I'm worried," I whisper.

He smirks as his faint breath envelops my lips. "That it won't be what you want?" he purrs into my mouth.

"No." I'm having trouble catching my breath, even though I haven't moved in minutes. "That it might be exactly what I want—precisely what I've needed—and ultimately, what I've never had."

"Well, in that case ..." His lips yield to mine in a seamless alliance of warmth and fervor as his fingertips press into my back, holding me hostage within his embrace. My heart drums against the inside of my chest, as shooting sparks of adrenaline fire down the center of my core.

A pause for air breaks the space between our mouths, leaving my lips tingling and a little numb. "I knew it," he says.

"What?" I croak.

"There's something between us—with us."

"Hot," is all I can mumble. Hot? Hot makes no sense. The kiss was hot, yes. Am I hot? Yes. Does he know any of this? I have no idea.

"Yeah," he groans. He gets it, I guess. His lips are back on mine, but this time we're moving backwards—my heels are nearly gliding until my back reaches the wall. His hips are pressed against mine, and he cups his hands firmly on my cheeks, inhaling sharply as he bites down on my bottom lip. Shit, I need more of this. I need him. I don't give a crap if I'm his boss or if he's my boss. I need to get screwed —now.

This is not a dream. This is real. Real. Real.

"Hannah?" The voice, the ear piercing, nails-on-a-chalkboard voice that I cannot stand, echoes through the cathedral ceiling within the foyer. "Oh, Hannah, I'm so sorry. I needed to get Cora's blankie. She can't sleep without it. Carry on with who you were doing—by all means. Just pretend like I'm not here." She literally walks by us as if we are no more than a piece of entryway decor that she admired for a brief moment. There was no knock on the door, no ringing the bell like we've talked about four million times. She just walked in, like I've asked her to stop doing.

Logan rests his forehead against mine. "Is this bad?"

I snicker. "Are you kidding? This is freaking fantastic," I tell him.

CHAPTER THIRTEEN

THIS THURSDAY-FRIDAY CAN KEEP ON GOING ...

"Am I taking advantage?" Logan asks as he tears my low-cut-for-nothing shirt up and over my head.

"No, you're solving a problem," I mumble between kissing and nibbling on his neck, wishing cologne tasted like it smelled.

"A problem?" He's breathless from carrying me up the stairs and fighting with a tight shirt, and tighter pants.

"It's been over a year," I admit, softly enough that I don't need to hear the words thunder in my head.

"A year is a long time," he says, freeing my pants from around my ass. His hands are warm, yet cool to the touch as they palm each cheek as if they're meant for gripping. He lifts me up, forcing my legs around his waist, and carries me to the bed.

He's a storm made of heated sensuality—soft and hard, and excited but reserved sensations, if that makes any sense. His movements are like a panther—slow, planned, and acutely accurate to achieve the imploring moans and whimpers emerging from my throat. I realize I'm the only one who's naked, and I need more of him.

I tug at Logan's shirt, peeling it slowly up his chest, admiring the ripples and ridges of his athletically toned and chiseled body. It's as perfect as I imagined. It's like I'm unwrapping the most awaited for gift on Christmas morning as I run my fingertips up and down the uneven surface, grazing the muscles with the tips of my fingers while admiring his bewitching craft.

With an ache between my legs continuing to grow, I reach for the button on his fitted jeans, unclasping, unzipping, and freeing his substantial boner from its constraints.

He presses my arms above my head, mounting me before lowering himself down. "Wait," I tell him.

"I don't want to," he says. His lips fall to my neck as his cock feathers against my thigh. My chest heaves with anticipation, but the coarse texture of his jeans are rough against my legs, enough to steal pleasure from the moment. I reach forward to tug his pants down more, needing him to be as naked as I am. "Stop."

"What's the matter?" I ask, concern filling my breathy voice.

He's holding himself above me with a look of intent, yet hesitation at the same time. Logan lowers himself and rests his head on my chest, bringing this encounter to an intimate moment rather than the heated passion we were sharing just seconds ago.

"Can't I just keep my pants on?" he asks.

Totally blindsided by his bizarre question, I can't help the snort exploding from within my nose. "You want to keep your pants on?" Laughter is still rolling in of its own accord, but seriously, what is this man talking about?

"Yes." He is as serious as a caged lion.

"Well, your jeans are a little rough to maneuver around—hey, so, why do you want to keep your pants on during sex?" Never have I ever just had a casual conversation about sex, right before sex, with a hot man who wants to have sex without removing his pants.

Logan sighs and rolls onto his back, placing his hand on his chest. "I told you I was injured and that's why I don't play anymore."

"Yes, you told me."

"I can't—" he continues.

"You can't ..."

"I just can't."

Okay, that's why he's interested in me. I'm the type of person who doesn't need a pretty penis to get off ... I've got nothing else.

"You can't keep it up?" Just taking a stab. Probably best not to say that out loud, however.

"Oh, no, I can—" he laughs, coyly, "I can keep it up, sweetheart." While mentally going through a dozen or so possibilities of what he can't do, he calls me sweetheart, and I melt a little, feeling the need to "aww" out loud. Although, I should note the fact that he was referring to me endearingly while assuring me he can keep his dick hard. What the hell is wrong with me?

"Okay, so you can keep *it* up, but you ..." I'm fishing here.

"It's just—," He grabs one of my pillows and smothers his face. After a long four-seconds, he tosses the pillow off the bed. "It's not pretty down there." Don't laugh, Hannah. Be an adult. Do not giggle. I exhale slowly to suppress the rumble working up the back of my throat.

I was right. "You have an ugly dick?" That was way louder than it needed to be.

He turns his head sharply, giving me a pointed look. "Is any dick pretty?"

"Well, what defines a pretty dick?"

"I don't know. Jesus, what kind of question is that?" he asks.

"I think a pretty dick is shiny, firm, smooth, and soft. On the contrary, it has no wild hairs, colors, or veins."

Logan presses up on his elbow, giving me either a "confused as hell" look, or a "Shit, that's what my cock looks like," look. "Wow," he says. "I mean, I didn't realize there were so many guidelines to having a pretty dick."

"Well, if any of the latter descriptions apply to you, you can always just tie a bow around it, and call it a day."

"No, I don't need to tie a bow around it. According to your standards, I have a pretty dick, I guess." He looks slightly amused and mildly proud, yet his pants are still on.

"Great, so what's the problem?" Oh, I know. Men are so sensitive about their asses sometimes, and I don't understand why. "It's natural to have hair on your ass. Is that it?"

"No, I don't have a hairy ass." Thank you, God. I couldn't do that again. Rick's ass has scarred me for life. I could braid the shit out of that lion's mane. Rick was what I once considered to be hot ... on the outside, at least, but then when the darkness was revealed, so was a whole lot of hair.

"Okay, I give up."

"Can we just cuddle tonight?"

"Cuddle? Like, spooning—spending the night in bed and waking up next to each other?" So, normally, I'd get down on my knees and beg a man like him to cuddle with me, but my curiosity of why he won't sex me is clouding my desire to be held in his arms. At thirty-three, I need sex, then cuddles. There's no rearranging the whole desire for events in that order, even if it makes me sound like a whore. I have needs, and they haven't been met, seen, heard, or thought of by anyone in over a year.

"I can go if you want," he offers, despondent expression and all.

"You need to just be honest with me because right now, I'm getting a complex." I tug at my blanket and cover my naked body.

"You don't need to do that," he says, grabbing the thick material from my hand.

"I don't want to be lying here naked while you're hesitant to take your pants off. It's weird. Don't you think? Especially after you saw me in my most vulnerable state yesterday." It's more than freaking weird. I'm not a model posing in front of an oil-painting class. Nor would I ever be chosen for such a job, unless it was for idolizing the effects of motherhood and how it wreaks havoc on a once perfect body.

"Tell me your wildest fantasy," he softly suggests.

Another loud laugh bucks from my throat. "I don't know, eating ice cream in a bathtub without a child screaming, 'Mommy?'"

"That's not the kind of fantasy I meant." I know what he meant. I don't have an answer because what the hell have I had to fantasize about lately?

Logan leans over to the nightstand and hits the light switch. "Never mind. Let me see if I can correct this fantasy issue." What? He just asked if we could cuddle.

Why are men so confusing? How in the world do they get away with calling women—

Oh. Oh, okay.

His hands are colder than I realized, and they're around each of my thighs, urging them apart. A breeze sweeps up the insides of my legs as movement encircles my body.

I don't have a moment to wonder what his plan is because his tongue is tracing a line up my right thigh but suddenly stops.

Did you wax? Brielle's voice echoes in my head. Oh no.

I place my hands on Logan's face and pull him up. "Cuddling sounds good," I tell him.

"What?"

"Just—let's take things slow." My dark hole is pruning at the moment, closing in on itself and pulsating with anger. I was just about to experience the most incredible moment of my life, and I didn't freaking wax.

"I can go slow," he says.

"From up here?" I counter.

His fingertips glide up toward my center, and I'm clenching my eyes and teeth in preparation for the recoiling of his hand when he meets the wooly mammoth I've allowed to grow in down there. I'm debating if I should stop him. I could ruin everything right this very second.

"You look like you're afraid this might hurt," he says. How can he see my face in the dark? I open one eye halfway, noting it's not completely dark in here because there's a car parked outside with the lights on. Lovely, let's shine some light on this subject.

"I wasn't prepared ..." I try to warn.

"Relax." That's what my OB always says. Don't say that. I even clean up down there for her. He scoots up, bringing his body parallel in position to mine, which comforts me a bit more. His lips are against my ear. "If you don't relax, I'll have to *make* you relax."

I don't think he's going to have a choice at this point. His fingers slip inside of me without pausing for a moment to acknowledge the situation down yonder, which allows my mind to slowly filter out all the terrifying thoughts, allowing me to focus on the warmth of his girthy fingers that are gliding in and out of me at just the right speed. Another finger joins the others, and I'm nearly climbing up the back of my bed, expelling moans so loud, the neighbors can probably to hear me. Asshole neighbors.

His thumb presses on my trigger, and my hips thrust against his hand, bucking wildly off the bed. "Holy shit. Holy shit. Holy shit. Yes. Don't stopppp. Right there. Yes, yes. Yes!"

Limp as a rag, I collapse like liquid into my plush mattress, riding the quivers that are running through every nerve in the lower region of my body. "Thank you," I cry out in the form of a plea as if he has solved all my world's problems with just his fingers.

"I almost got off just watching you get off," he murmurs.

"Let me help with that," I reply.

I slide off the bed, bringing myself to my knees. I pull his cock out of his unzipped pants and hold it firmly within my hand, noting it is as pretty as I described. He isn't stopping me, so maybe there really isn't an issue with his dick. We'll see, I guess. I just hope the zipper on his jeans doesn't do any damage. Usually, the pants are off for this part of the night.

With a firm grip around his shaft, I lower my mouth over the tip and lick gently while following my hand as it glides down his long, really long, wow, okay—dick until the tip hits the back of my throat. His hands tangle in my hair, and his fingers tighten and loosen with every flick of my tongue.

With a glance up at his face, I hope to catch a glimpse of his expression, but there's no more light filling the room, so I'm left with my imagination.

His grip grows tighter the faster my hand and mouth move around his cock, and growls scrape against his throat as his body moves in rhythm with my lips. Logan's hands find my face, and he squeezes gently. "I'm going to—"

"I suck him in a little harder, feeling the instant relief of warmth dribble down the back of my throat."

"Shit, Hannah, I don't even know what to say, other than that was probably one of the hottest moments of my life."

That's a nice compliment, and somewhat unexpected. "Thanks." I sound mousy, shy, and not like the woman who just sucked him off like it was my job. Nope because my job is to be his boss, but I'm better at getting him off.

And, I'd probably do it again.

CHAPTER FOURTEEN

IF IT WERE ANY OTHER FRIDAY, I WOULD BE GETTING READY FOR WORK, BUT INSTEAD ... THERE'S ANOTHER JOB TO BE DONE, AND IT'S NOT THE ONE I HAD IN MIND.

What is happening? What? I will my eyelids apart, trying to get a better scope of my situation, but I can't figure out what's happening. I can't breathe. Or move. It's still kind of dark, but I see sunlight.

Last night.

Oh shit.

That was nice.

I twist my heavy head to the right, finding Logan asleep with his arm draped over my naked chest and his hand cupped around my left breast. Maybe that's why I slept so well all night. Is having warm breasts the answer to a good night sleep? If so, I've been doing it wrong my whole life.

I move my legs around to get the blood circulating, and my bare toes run along the coarse material of his jeans. He's still wearing his freaking pants. Why?

I have to pee.

With an attempt to roll off the bed, Logan's fingertips seem to stick to my nipple, and he isn't any more aware than he was a minute ago. Yup, I'm pretty sure it's going to rip right off if I don't lift his hand. I wrap my fingers around his wrist and lift slowly so I can adorably tuck and roll like a sea lion—that's what I imagine I look like at the moment. Thank God he's asleep, and I can put clothes on before the daylight reveals the truth.

I tiptoe to the bathroom, grabbing a pair of yoga pants and a t-shirt from the pile that's still resting on top of my hamper from when Logan folded them the other day.

My feet hit the cold tiles of my bathroom, and I softly close the door while flipping the light switch. As I face place my clothes down on the counter and look into the mirror, I can only think that I look like a scene from a horror movie when the innocent character looks at their reflection to find a zombie in its place. I need to figure out how to deal with this situation before he wakes up.

A shower—that's the answer to all of life's problems. Hopefully, it doesn't wake him up. I slip in behind the glass door and crank the water up. The warmth erases some of my humility from last night, but as memories float through me, one by one, I realize I don't have much to be embarrassed about, except for the whole post-child body in comparison to his iron stealth.

I lean my back against the shower wall, drowning in the cascading water. How did I get myself into this situation? I have to see this man every day now, and he knows what this disaster looks like. As if I need extra reminders, I look down at the tattoo I got when I was eighteen. It was a small tribal circle with the symbol of life inside. Now, it looks like a child finger painted on my right hip with black ink. This is why marriage is supposed to last. "Through thick and thin." Well, Rick got the goddamn thin, and now he's left me with the thick part I was sure no one would want—but now there's a man who won't take his pants off, and I'm not sure whether to call it a win.

With exhaustion draping me, along with the steam, I close my eyes to clear my mind. Blindly, I grab the shampoo bottle and pour the liquid over the top of my head. I let it sit there for a minute before I weakly lather it through my hair that has grown longer than I've ever let it before. I've never been a short hair kind of person, but lately, I haven't had the time to blow dry and flat iron the kinky waves I have. Maybe it's time for a change. Maybe I need to make myself look twenty-something again. Brielle has been whining about me doing something with myself for the past year now, but I've been diligently tuning her out. She doesn't get it. Though, in all fairness, she is the one who gets laid several times a week.

Onto my next thought of why I'm up so early on a free day when I don't have a child to take care of. I'm busy burning out my thought engine already, I guess that's the reason. Does anyone else talk to themselves as much as I do? Does anyone just have a clear head for extended periods of time? Am I like, broken? That must be what this is. Maybe I need drugs. The head doctor did suggest it when I first started going to her after Rick double dipped. Oy.

I rinse the soap out of my hair and push the strands away from my face, feeling a freshness take over the gross layer I couldn't seem to shake yesterday. Everything will be okay. I just have to go with the flow.

A thundering bang scares the shit out of me just as I'm getting the last of the shampoo out of my hair, and some of the suds seep into my eyes. I turn in every direction, reaching for the handle on the door so I can grab my towel, but I stop when I hear a thud.

What the hell was that?

The shower floor is vibrating against the loud thuds following the crash. "Hello?" Then, the sound of porcelain hitting porcelain pierces my ears. "Logan?"

I poke my head out of the fogged-up shower door and peek with my one non-soap-burning eye, seeing the half-naked, stealth-clad man on his knees, vomiting. *Oh shit.*

For some reason, I can't move. I'm frozen, watching this all happen like an asshole. It's not like I can do much, but watching isn't nice, so I close myself back into the shower and bite down on the tip of my fingernail. What should I do? "Can I get you anything?" I shout out.

He answers with a gag, and the slop-hitting-water sound effect informs me he isn't done yet. I reach my arm out of the shower and grab the towel hanging from the rack. My lip is already curled into a snarl because I hate vomit more than I hate boogers and poop. I know parents are supposed to be used to all that, but my stomach reflexes don't agree. There hasn't been a time when Cora has gotten sick that I haven't felt the need to mirror her expelling situation.

I turn the water off and wrap the towel around my body, close my eyes, and pull in a sharp breath. *I can do this.* Man vomit is so much worse than child vomit, but he was there for me the other day. I can't be a total ass. He'll take the assumption of my divorce to another level if I don't do the right thing. I am a caring person.

I step out onto the plush bath mat and slowly approach him from behind. He's hugging the toilet with his head hanging over the bowl, and I place my wet hand on his back while kneeling beside him. I do my best to ignore the sight in front of us. That needs to be flushed, or we're both going to be vomiting. I reach over and flush, forgetting to move back in time to avoid the recoiling splash. Uh, no. *It's just a couple of drops, but I just got out of the shower.* Come on, really?

"I think I'm sick," he says with a groan.

"I'm so sorry, Logan. This is all my fault."

"It's not your fault," he says, looking over at me. His eyes are glassy and bloodshot, and his nose is running a little, yet the green hue of his cheeks brings out the blue in his eyes. Bastard. That's not fair. No one looks good while puking. No one!

He begins to shiver, so I get up and run to the bedroom for a blanket to wrap around him.

I return quickly and place it around his shoulders. "Here, is that better?"

"Thanks," he mutters while sliding back on his knees to push himself away from the toilet. I guess that position isn't comfortable, since he immediately lies down on the tiled floor.

"I know how awful this feels," I tell him. He looks up at me with puppy dog eyes, and I quickly assume he had his mother wrapped around his little finger with that look. "I'm sorry, Logan." I run my fingers through his silky hair that somehow still looks perfect after a night's sleep and vomiting. "Can I do anything?"

"Just sit here with me," he says in a whisper.

I look down at my wet towel. "Okay, sure." I sit down, leaning my back against the wall beside the toilet paper roll, and Logan scoots forward a couple of inches, placing his head on my lap.

I'm not sure why, but I'm looking around the bathroom, sort of wondering if anyone is watching this happen. While it wasn't evident last night when he was making me moan louder than I've ever moaned, right now with his head on my lap, I'm realizing how little we know about each other.

With his back in view, I notice a tattoo—two lines of text written in what looks to be Greek.

"What's this mean?" I ask, running my finger along the puckered skin.

Logan sucks in a short breath of air, and his hands tighten around my thighs. "It—" he swallows and pauses. "It means, 'We cannot learn without pain.' It's about something I lost, and it's a quote from Aristotle."

"Wow, how philosophical of you," I tell him, smiling a touch at the thought. I've had my assumptions about this man, but I may have had him all wrong. "So, what pain have you learned?" I know he was injured in baseball, but I think there's more.

Logan curls his legs into his stomach, and I watch the waistband of his jeans dig into his stomach. That can't feel good, but before I can suggest something else, he's pressing against me, reaching for the toilet.

It smells like the devil's feet in here, and I'm trying my hardest to breathe through my mouth rather than my nose.

"I think I'm dying," Logan grumbles.

"It's just the flu," I remind him gently, while running my hand up and down his bare back, which is burning up. "Come on, let me help you to bed."

I grab a face cloth and run it under the faucet before he stands up. "Here." I dab it over his face and flush the toilet. "It'll be okay."

He's staring up at me as if he just figured something out, but I can't imagine what could be going through his head right now. "Cora is a lucky girl," he utters.

I toss the washcloth into the sink and loop my arm under his. "Come on." He uses the toilet as leverage to get up to his feet but leans a lot of his weight on me too. Logan is not a small man—lean, yes, but those muscles weigh a ton. I manage to get him to the bed and help him under the covers. "I'll get you some water."

Logan grabs my wrist with a weak grip. "Thank you, Hannah." The bridge between superior and employee has been broken. We've taken a completely different path, and we'll need to figure out how to navigate through this one, but I'm willing to go that way because something feels different right now. Something feels good, despite the situation at hand.

I slip into a pair of leggings and a baggy t-shirt and jog down the steps toward the kitchen, just as the doorbell rings. It's way too early in the goddamn morning for company. Come on.

"Coming," I shout to whoever is rude enough to ring the bell before nine on a holiday or weekend.

I open the door, finding Rick, Tiana, and Cora standing on the front step. What the hell? "What's the matter?"

"I need you to take them," Tiana says. "I—I have plans today, and I can't deal with him when he's sick. Plus, I can't afford to get sick right now. I'll come back for him tomorrow night. Okay?"

My mouth falls open. "Whoa, whoa, whoa, hold on just a minute. You don't really think this is how things are going to work, do you? He's *your* problem now. You take care of him. I'll keep my daughter, though."

"No, no, no, I can't." She opens the screen door between us and shoves Rick inside.

"Titi, come on, babe. Why are you doing this?"

"Yeah, Titi, why are you doing this? Oh, that's right, you're *not* doing this," I tell her.

The sudden movement makes Rick fall to his knees, and of course, vomit. Cora is shrieking, holding her nose, and jumping around, making a scene. By the time I return my attention to the doorway, I see that Tiana is gone.

CHAPTER FIFTEEN

FRIDAY—IT'S THE NEW MONDAY, WITH A SIDE OF MAN-CHILD

Cora is circling around Rick like a bird ready to peck at a dead carcass on the side of the road. She's scratching her chin, and her forehead is creased with concern. "Daddy looks like he should be in a hospital maybe," she says. I contain my laughter while gazing at the adorable analysis she's conducting in her unicorn fleece PJs and piglet slippers. *And the perfect braid in her hair. Tiana knows she hates braids.*

"Cora, did Tiana do your hair before dragging your father over here?"

Cora runs her fingers down the length of her braid. "Yeah," she shrugs. "She said I couldn't leave the house with a bird's nest on my head. She's crazy. I don't have a bird's nest on my head. Do I?" She bends forward to show me the top of her head.

"No, sweetie, you do not have a bird's nest on your head. Tiana is just a little confused about her priorities."

"Priorities?"

"Your father should not be lying on my floor right now. He should be at his house, with Tiana taking care of him."

"But he's sick, and you're the mommy, so …" Cora still doesn't completely understand how this works. Apparently, she thinks I'm still responsible for taking care of Rick, just like I take care of her, which makes me wonder what she thinks about Tiana. For all I know, she probably thinks Tiana's Rick's shitty babysitter. Might as well be.

"Hannah?" Logan croaks from upstairs. "Are you still getting some water?" Shit! How can all this be happening?

Rick lifts his head two inches from the ground and looks up at me. "He slept over?"

"Really? That's what you're concerned about right now?" I respond in a pitched howl.

"He is out of your league, sweetie," Rick manages to sputter.

"Out of my league? You're living with a beautiful woman who is, oddly enough, attracted to a meathead. Except, it isn't odd at all when you think about how much longer she can stay in the U.S. without getting married, right? You think it's cute that she's a little ditzy sometimes. She's a freaking genius, Rick. You're the dumbass. And since you're lying on my floor in a puddle of vomit, I really don't think you should be insulting me right now. Not a smart choice."

Without another thought, the anger rages through my body, and my foot instinctively comes out from beneath me and splashes him with his own vomit. "Mommy!" Cora scolds.

"It's just a form of affection, sweetie," I assure her.

"Oh, yeah, that's what Daddy says to Tiana every night when I'm falling asleep."

"Well then, Daddy deserves a taste of his own medicine, don't you think?" My teeth grit, and this time instinct isn't fast enough to keep up with my desire. I kick more of the puddle into him, coating his face this time.

"Come on, Hannah, what the hell? I'm sick."

"You should have thought it through before you let your Barbie doll deliver you here in your current condition. This is not a shelter for wayward, sick, jackass ex-husbands. In fact, if you expected me to take care of you when you were sick, there is a whole list of different choices you should have made in the past."

"Uh oh," Cora says.

"What's uh oh?" I say, my head snapping over to Cora as I finish my rant.

"He's turning green like The Hulk again. This is what happened earlier. Mommy, do something! Daddy feels sick!"

"Oh, no you don't. You're not puking on my freshly cleaned floors. Get up, now."

"I can't move," he groans.

"Cora, help me." I grab his arm, and she grabs the other. I know she won't be pulling much weight, but the downstairs bathroom is just a few feet away. I pull as hard as I can, happy that there are no obstructions between the hardwoods and the bathroom's tiled floor. Just as I manage to get him into the bathroom, he starts bucking like a cat with a fur ball. Ugh. I will care for someone I like, but to watch someone I despise puking, no thank you. "Do it in the toilet," I tell him.

He pulls himself up with his arms, leaving his legs limp and flat on the ground behind him. "Give me a break, Rick. Man up."

As I walk out, I hear the splash in the toilet, followed by more groaning. Karma, asshole.

Off to the kitchen I go to get a glass of water for the other patient. Was I this bad yesterday? I guess I was.

"Cora, stay with Dad and keep an eye on him. Or just wait outside the bathroom in case he needs anything."

"Okay, mommy, I'm on duty. Get it?" she laughs.

"I got ya," I tell her with a snicker.

I retrieve a glass from the cupboard and fill it with water before jogging back up the stairs. As I make my way into the bedroom, I find Logan hanging half out of the bed, one foot on the floor and the other under the covers. "That doesn't look comfortable."

"I can't move," he moans.

"Well, I brought you some water," I say, trying to sound more composed than I feel. "You should drink some, so you stay hydrated."

He looks at the glass for a long second. "Hannah?" He squints one eye as he glances up at me. "Do you have a straw maybe?"

"A straw?" I question.

"Yeah, so I don't—I can't move."

I almost want to give him a second to tell me he's kidding, but by the pathetic look on his face, I don't think that's the case. "Um, yeah, sure, I should have a straw. I'll be right back." I set the glass of water down on the nightstand and head back downstairs to the kitchen.

Rick is still groaning or moaning—I can't tell the difference between the two sounds. Funny, how I always found that to be quite a turn on … err … definitely not so much now. At least he's still in the bathroom, though. Cora is leaning against the wall outside the hall bathroom, holding her head as if she has a headache. "Are you okay, sweetie?"

"This is exhausting," she says. "Do you know that Dad sounded like a crying dog in the middle of the night last night? I wanted to tell him to grow up, but I figured I'd get in trouble."

This child is one hundred percent me. "I shouldn't be saying this, but you're right," I tell her. "Daddy probably caught the flu you had, but he's acting much worse than you did when you were sick. You see, when a man gets sick, it's kind of like the world is coming to an end. They don't handle it very well, at all."

Cora looks utterly confused by my brief explanation about the male species. "I thought men were stronger than women, though?"

Oh dear, I thought I taught her better than that. "Physically, like their muscles … yes, a lot of them are stronger than women. However, women can handle more pain and discomfort than men. That's why women have babies and men don't." This isn't a great lesson to be teaching her, especially with a lot of my opinion thrown in right now, but she needs to be aware of what the male brain considers to be true. Plus, I'm still mad, and I need to lash out at Rick and his entire gender right now. I'm not exactly objective about this situation.

"I wondered why women were the only people to have babies. Daddy said it was because women need something to do when the men work."

If my eyes could pop out of their sockets, they would have by now. Cora is unaffected by the look Rick causes my face to contort into. It's nothing new to her, but right now, I'd like to kick him in the nuts, then the stomach again. He deserves that and more.

It takes everything I have not to say anything to Cora in response to what she said. Instead, I place my hands on her shoulders and offer a smile through gritted teeth. "Can you find a straw for me, sweetie. I'll be right back."

I huff and inhale a few times before making it to the downstairs bathroom where Rick has made himself comfortable. "Women have babies so they have something to do while the men work?" I snarl, hardly moving my lips enough to enunciate.

"What?" he chokes out.

"You heard me."

"Ugh, Hannah, I was kidding."

"Cora didn't think you were kidding. What the hell is wrong with you? She's a girl who will eventually be a woman, and that's what you want her to think? You want her to end up with a womanizer like you?" I realize I'm being louder than I should, considering Cora is in the next room, and Logan is upstairs, but this man has crossed yet another line, and I am totally losing my cool.

"I'm sorry, Hannah, okay?" He drops his head back into the toilet bowl.

"No! It's not okay! While you were at work, I sat on this floor alone for twenty weeks straight, puking my brains out. It wasn't because I needed something to do while you were flirting with your secretary. Every doctor's appointment you missed was another opportunity you lost out on, the experience of seeing your daughter grow from a tiny seed into a full-size baby. I watched life grow within me while you watched every woman's ass at your office. If you want to call that a woman's job, that's fine, but just realize, you have dug yourself even further into the pig pen. You are so dirty and vile, there's no chance any woman would want to live with you forever, no matter how many smoothies she feeds you."

Wow, that felt good. "Geez, Hannah, take it easy, will you? I'm dying here."

"Good, get the hell out of my house because I have a man upstairs I'd like to tend to."

"You can't be serious," he argues.

"I'm as serious as you were the day I called to tell you I had food poisoning at thirty weeks pregnant. I needed you, but you said you were too busy to come home. What were you doing until eleven that night?"

"I'll go," he concedes.

"Now."

I turn to find Cora with the straw, standing directly behind me. I close my eyes and instantly regret everything I just said. Not because it wasn't true, but because despite everything I want to say to Rick, the motherly instinct inside of me still wants to preserve Cora's innocence. I want her to look up to her dad, even if he is a dick.

"Why were you so mean to Mommy?" Cora says with tears in her eyes. Her words trail off as she runs up the stairs with the straw in hand.

"Thanks a lot, Hannah," Rick says while pushing himself up to his knees.

"For telling our daughter the truth?"

"She wasn't the mistake. You were," he says.

Really? This dirtbag has the nerve to say that when he's totally imposing on me and at my mercy right now? It's the last thing I need to hear before I can't bear another moment in such a close proximity to him. "A mistake? Finding someone whose life revolves around you for ten freaking years was a mistake? Rick, you don't know a good thing when you have it. Your girlfriend just kicked you out of your own house for being sick. Go ahead and tell me again that *I* was the mistake."

He pulls himself up to his feet and drags his limp body to the front door. How does this man still make my chest ache, even when he makes my blood boil? Why do I have to be a good person and have feelings for all people, good and bad?

Rick nearly falls against the door and presses his head against the finished wood. The back of his neck is dark red, and I can tell he has a fever. He always turns red like that when he's sick.

"Oh, for goodness sake, let's go." I take his arm and pull him along through the kitchen and into the family room—a room I haven't spent any time in since I was part of a family. It has felt off limits. Cora plays in her bedroom or mine, and that's where we spend our time. There doesn't seem to be a purpose to feeling alone in this big, empty room, but at least there's a pull-out sofa for unexpected guests.

I prop Rick up against the wall and pull the bed out. Cora reappears, looking forlorn, but nevertheless, wanting to help, as usual. She knows the drill with company since Mom and Dad drop by once every couple months, so she goes to the closet and pulls out the bed in a bag. She drags the plastic bag along the floor until she reaches the side of the couch. "Thanks, sweetie."

I make up the bed without much care and help Rick over, with even less concern. "Thank you," he mutters.

I close my eyes and shake my head. How does someone walk away from their significant other when they're sick? I want to ask myself, but karma kind of answers my question. He's basically getting what he asked for with the choices he's made. However, if it is karma having her way with Rick, how did I become the helping hand once again?

I suddenly remember I came down here for a straw, and I have no clue where it ended up in the last few minutes, so I grab another on my way back upstairs.

One day after dealing with my own flu, I'm somehow running an infirmary. I've barely recovered myself. I'm not ready to take care of not one, but two full-grown, sick men. I hike back up the stairs and find Logan peacefully asleep.

"The world works in mysterious ways." Mom has always repeated this old quote to me, thinking it would solve my world's problems. Nothing has ever felt like much of a mystery until now, though. None of this makes sense.

I scoot down against my nightstand, keeping my gaze set on Logan and his peaceful, man-tasizingly beautiful features that belong on Prince Charming, though I'll bet Prince Charming never came down with the man-flu. If he had, they could never have lived happily ever after. In any case, with the out-of-control disaster Logan and I have unfortunately found in common these last few days, I haven't given myself the chance to analyze this man who I was so eager to get into bed with last night.

Before Rick, I vowed never to date the same kind of guy twice, so I took notes about each date, boyfriend, and relationship. Thinking about it now, it was probably a little Type A of me, but I didn't want to forget about the lunatics, possible serial killers, and obsessive stalkers in my past. They all had traits and qualities that could tip me off in the future if needed.

Rick, good old Rick fit none of the qualities and traits in my notes, and after my fair share of dating, and whatevers, I figured I had enough data to draw an intelligent conclusion.

Turns out I was wrong. How could my judgment be so bad, despite my efforts to choose a good guy?

I knew from the moment I became pregnant with Cora that I needed to take a closer look at those notes and continue making notes on my relationship with Rick. I suspected there may be a future where I'd need a list of qualities to avoid in a person. Maybe I should go on a hunt for that list, though I'm afraid it would leave no available men for my future.

"Hey," Logan grumbles.

"That was a quick nap," I tell him, offering an empathetic smile. "I brought you the straw."

"I was wondering where you disappeared to."

I should probably let him know about the situation downstairs. "Well, Tiana dropped Rick at the door like roadkill, then took off."

"Huh?" he asks while rubbing his temple.

"Rick has the flu too, but Tiana didn't want to be anywhere near him or his moaning and germs, so she was kind enough to drop him off here so I could deal with him."

"But, you're divorced, I thought."

"I am," I assure him with a sigh.

"I don't understand." He seems irritable, along with his other crashing symptoms. Not that I wouldn't be irritated too, but there isn't a better way to explain this situation.

"That makes two of us, Logan. I don't want him here. He's not my problem. I'd be happier if the man moved an hour away, honestly."

"Does he know I'm up here?" Logan asks.

"Yeah, I told him. I have nothing to hide. I'm a single woman with the freedom to do as I choose."

Logan tries to smile, but it almost looks like there's a force tugging his lips into the opposite direction. "Oh no."

"Let me help you." I try to lift his dead weight from the bed.

"No, it's not that," he says.

"What is it?" I'm still awkwardly trying to pull him off the bed.

"I have to get out of here," he continues.

"Well, you're in no condition to drive, and I'm happy to take care of you until you're better." I'm not sure I want to guess why he suddenly needs to leave.

"You don't understand. This isn't right. I have to go."

"Logan?" It's Rick. I'm not stupid. "Please tell me what Rick said to you the other night."

Logan drops his head into the pillow and stares up at me. "Hannah, I don't think you want to know."

CHAPTER SIXTEEN

MAYBE FRIDAY COULD JUST TAKE A DUMP ON ME TOO
...

"Did he tell you I'm crazy? Psycho? Nuts? Won't stop until I have what I want?" Yup. That all just unraveled from my tongue.

"No," he grumbles. "I wouldn't go that far."

"Well then, he should have warned you." I need to stop. I don't need to show off this side of me—this angry, hateful side that Rick forced me to be. It isn't who I really am, who I was, or who I want to be.

Logan squeezes his hands around his head and presses his fingers into his eyebrows. "Hannah, I don't have the energy to figure out what you're talking about, but I do need to get moving."

"No," I snap. *Easy, killer. Sounding a little desperate.*

"I can't stay, okay?"

"Fine, go," I tell him. "I'll just go ask Rick what was said."

"Please don't do that." Logan rolls onto his side and clutches his stomach. "I think the room is spinning like one of those damn, carnival tilt-a-whirl rides. The room isn't moving, right?"

"No, it's not."

Logan's fingertips dig into the mattress as if he's holding onto it for dear life. "What the hell is going on?"

I place my hand on his back and softly caress the length of his spine. "Hannah ..."

"Do you want me to get you anything for the road? A trash bag and some water?"

"Hannah ..."

"What is it?" I ask him.

"I've never wondered what it might be like to have a hard-on while feeling like I'm standing in the middle of an earthquake after drinking my weight in tequila. Do you know men have trouble getting it up when they are that intoxicated? The human body isn't meant to handle so much action at once. Yet ..."

Oh, I'm not sure what I've done to cause that. "'Yet,' what?"

"Can you stop stroking my back with your fingernails. It's nice, but—"

"Oh. Oh! Sorry. I mean, I'm not sorry, but at this particular moment, I'm sorry."

He rolls back to his original spot, possibly with a change of mind as it seems. Maybe he just realized there's no way he's able to drive at the moment. "If you need me to drive you home, I can."

His focus struggles under his apparently heavy eyelids. "Can I ask you something?"

"Okay ..."

"Is it true you're a perfectionist?"

I can't fathom how that could be a concern of his right now. "Why do you ask?"

"It's something I need to know."

He's sick as a dog, asking me if I like things to be perfect. Is it a bad trait if I do? I don't bother people with it.

"I don't know—sometimes, I guess."

"Sometimes, or like OCD—all the time." My level of annoyance is growing alongside the pressuring questions, which strictly regard my personality—something I can't control. I have two sick men in my house, neither of whom lives here, both expecting me to take care of them, yet they both seem to think this is the time to criticize me? What the hell?

"I like things in order. If something is broken, I like to fix it. I don't think it's an issue."

"What if you can't fix something?" Where the hell is he going with this?

"I don't know. I would probably do what anyone might do and replace it?"

"Wrong answer," he says with a clipped intonation.

"I don't like mind games. I can tell you that." That came out snippier than I intended, but what the hell?

He drops the back of his arm across his forehead. "Do I feel hot to you?" I'm so frustrated with the interruption. I want to know what this is all about.

Instead, I lean forward and place the back of my hand over the lower part of his forehead, then his cheek, like I do with Cora. "Yes, you're warm." I hand him the glass of water with a straw. "I'll go grab you some Advil, okay?"

He groans, then sighs, softly. "Do you have any of that liquid stuff. If I try to swallow anything solid right now, I'll probably upchuck."

I inhale slowly before responding, needing a moment to maintain my composure and brace myself for this continuing situation I'm in. "Logan, this is making me crazy. Why do I feel like we're on two different playing fields? Does that make any sense to you? It seems like you have some kind of advantage or insight into my life and yet, I'm totally in the dark about yours." I already know I'm not getting anywhere with my questions, but I have a right to know what kind of person he has me pegged as. "Plus, five minutes ago, you were hellbent on leaving, and now you're drilling me about perfectionism one-second, and then needing child's cold medicine—enough to fill a man's grown body—the next. Give me something to go on here, will you? Maybe a reason to put up with this shit? When I was sick, and you were taking care of me, I don't think I returned the favor by acting rude and ungrateful."

Logan stares past me toward the window with a hazy look in his eyes like he's pondering the meaning of life, or possibly just trying to ward off another round of nausea.

"Let's just say, I'm not perfect."

"And?" That doesn't clarify anything. "What's that have to do with the way you're acting?" These riddles and clues aren't bringing me to any logical or decent explanations. It's something south of the border. That's about all I can figure.

"Never mind."

"Okay, let's start with something easier." I sit down on the edge of the bed and place my hand gently on his chest. "Why did you want to leave after I told you Rick was downstairs?"

Still no effort to make eye contact, but he looks like he's about to say something, I think.

His arm lowers to his stomach and his lip curls. "I'm going to die, aren't I?"

"Nope. No, Logan, you're not going to die."

"Mom, I need you!" Cora is shouting for me from downstairs. I can only imagine what's going on down there now.

"Don't leave," Logan says pleadingly.

"Oh my gosh, I can't handle two sick men at once. What is it? Spit it out."

Why did I say that? At a time like this, no one in their right mind would say spit it out to a sick person who's lying on freshly cleaned sheets.

He certainly spits it out, though. All over those clean sheets.

"I'm so sorry," he mutters.

I pull the blanket off and roll it into a ball before tossing it to the ground. "He said he doesn't want me anywhere near you," Logan confesses as I'm grabbing a spare blanket from the closet.

"Rick said that?" I'm not surprised. He didn't want the divorce. He just wanted to cheat on me. I think it's called *having your cake and eating it too*. Yeah, Rick thought the *too* was spelled *two*. Being an asshole is one thing. Sleeping with another woman is a no-no in my book. Rick did everything in his power to stop the divorce proceedings, so it took an extra-long time, making everything harder than necessary. Then he moved next door in hopes of making me feel jealous and crazy as he moved Tiana in with him. It hurt like hell—that's the worst part. Even when he was an asshole, I still loved him. I loved him, but I'm not stupid. "He hurt me every single day for years, and he still thinks there's a chance for us. I told him it will never happen. It's the truth, Logan."

"I have no right getting involved," he says. "We just met, and you have a history with him and a little girl."

"And you don't have any history or baggage?" I counter.

"Oh, I do, but my ex-wife doesn't live next door to me. She lives in another state now."

"I can't control the fact that Rick moved in next door to me. What am I supposed to do, Logan? Uproot my daughter so I can secure a second chance at love? She's the most important thing to me, and everyone else will always come second. It's a fact of my life—a fact anyone will have to deal with if they're with me. We *did* just meet, so I won't be offended if whatever interest you had in me has vanished. It happens." I offer a smile because what else can I do? This is my life. I made my bed, and I will lie in it ... *just not right now*.

He nods his head and wipes at his mouth, making sure it's clean from the latest spewing episode. "I'm sorry," he says. "I shouldn't have brought up any of that. It's none of my business, and you're right about Cora."

"I'm sorry we couldn't have a chance, even if I am your boss, and it's totally inappropriate."

"What do you mean?" he asks, as lines furrow deep within his forehead.

"I'm not going to hold any of this against you. You're a single man making a move—a bold one—with your new boss. I'm flattered, but you're out of my league by a long shot, and this life I'm living isn't one you need to bear the weight of." I laugh because it's true. He's so far out of my league, I can't believe I'm lucky enough to say Logan Grier puked in my bed.

"That's not what I mean," he says. "Rick can go screw himself if that's how you truly feel. I just didn't want to chance stepping into the middle of a family reconciliation. That's what he was going on about, that and some other things ..."

"Wow. Nope, there is definitely no family reconciliation in our future. None." I'm honestly taken aback. "So—"

"I'll take my pants off next time, then." He smirks and groans as he rolls onto his back.

"There will be a next time?" I scratch my fingers gently down the length of his arm, playing along with his words.

"I guess we'll see where the flu takes us," he says with a humming sigh. Logan crosses his arms behind his head, revealing a whole lot of vomit beside the pillow.

"You should start with taking a shower," I tell him. "I have to clean the sheets."

"Yeah." He looks down, disgusted at the mess he's lying in. "Oh, man."

Logan carefully drags himself up and out of the bed. Oy. He's wearing the vomit like it's another layer of clothes. "Uh, I should wash everything," which will leave him naked up here in my bedroom.

He looks down, and his cheeks turn pale. "The sight of this is making me feel sick again."

"Okay, let's get you into the shower." If only he weren't sick while I'm telling him to get into my shower, I might be a whole lot happier.

I wrap my hand around Logan's bicep—his rock hard, holy-shit-is-that-bone-or-steel bicep—and guide him toward the bathroom. I'd like to think I'm helping hold up a portion of his weight, but I don't think it's possible. He's a rock.

Once I get him into the bathroom, he falls against the sink, holding himself up with his elbows as he stares at his reflection with an expression that looks like he's about to start a fight with himself.

I reach into the shower and turn the knob, then test the temperature of the water in the palm of my hand. "Okay, all set. Can I have your clothes?"

"I—I'll take care of that and hand them to you in a minute. Do you mind waiting in the bedroom?"

"Oh, okay, sure. Are you going to be okay?"

"Yeah, yeah, I'm fine."

I know this is wrong and completely inappropriate considering how sick he is, but I kind of need to know what the big deal is in his pants. His cock is fine. Like—definitely—fine, but there's something I'm obviously missing.

I leave the bathroom and wait outside the door, listening to groans as Logan's clothes fall to the floor. Another minute passes before a hand shoots out from a small cracked opening in the doorway, and his clothes are dropped in a ball at my feet. I want to bust in there right now and just find out what he's hiding, but that's low. Low, low, low—and I know I can't do that.

I take the soiled clothes and bedding downstairs to the laundry room off to the back side of the kitchen. "Babe?" Rick calls out.

I laugh. He didn't just refer to me as "Babe," did he? He couldn't possibly be delirious or delusional enough to say something stupid like that.

With a stiff breath, I let the comment pass by and move on to the laundry. Once the soap is in and the button has been pressed, I feel an urge to lock myself in this tiny room and take a nap. I'm still not feeling great, and it's sort of like I was only allowed one day to be sick with the flu. Next time I get sick, I'm somehow checking myself into a hotel and not leaving until I've made a full recovery. I should probably consider scheduling that time into a calendar too.

Reluctantly, I reopen the door to the infirmary and head for the family room, where Rick is still whining about something.

Cora is seated at the edge of the pull-out, watching some YouTube chick play with Play-doh. *What is this crap?*

"Did you need something?" I made sure not to leave out any snark. "I can call Tiana if you miss the boob. Is that what it is? You need a bubba?"

"No, mommy. Tiana said she can't just make milk appear like other women can—from her—." Cora points to my chest. "Those things." Think, then speak, Hannah. I have tried my hardest to stop talking shit about Rick or Tiana in front of Cora, but with the current extenuating circumstances, I just can't stop it. I'm an awful mother sometimes ... awful. Yet, I can't stop laughing until I realize what Cora just asked me.

"Wait, wait, wait. Did Tiana tell Cora—our five-year-old—that she can't make milk ... you know like a mother does? Please say it's not true, Rick. Please."

Rick presses his fingers into the sides of his head. "Gawd, Hannah, she was listening outside the door. What do you want from me?"

"Are you planning to have another child with her?"

"I don't know," he groans. "It doesn't concern you, though."

"Oh, it doesn't? Hmm. So, how exactly does it concern *you* that Logan is upstairs? You obviously felt the need to insert yourself into that topic."

Rick shudders with laughter. "You're kidding me, right?"

I grit my teeth and nod. "No, Rick, I'm not kidding you."

"Do you even know who Logan Grier is?" he asks.

"Yes, he played baseball in the major leagues. I'm sure it's a big deal to you."

His laughter grows a little louder, and it's becoming infuriating. "Let's try this again. Do you know who Logan Grier was, and still is?"

I'm not playing into this with him. I know what he's up to now, and Rick Pierce will stop at nothing to win a point or competition. "Yeah, I do. Now drop it."

"So, you're okay with that whole ... situation?"

I almost ask. Almost, but I refrain. "Sure am."

"Interesting," he says with a curious grimace as he scratches at his chin.

"I just thought you wanted something different."

It's taking everything I have not to bite the bait. "It's none of your business."

Rick holds his hands up in defense. "You're right."

"I know," I argue. Like a child.

"Well, in case you're just saying you know, but you really don't, and I sort of have an inkling that you don't, you might want to watch ESPN Zone on demand and search Logan's name. Not sure how his whole situation works, but I think it's safe to assume you don't know Logan's whole story, even if you think you do. Let's just say, Logan is single and good-looking for a reason, Hannah."

My nausea is slowly returning, with a side of a racing pulse. Shit. What am I getting myself into?

"I know everything, so stop interfering with my life and go get back to yours with your girlfriend who will stick by your side through sickness and in health—oh wait, scratch that first part." I point to the door. I've had it. I don't care how sick he is. He's too much to deal with, and he is not my problem anymore.

"Hannah, come on," he whines. "Can't I just have some soup first? Tiana can't cook, and you know soup is the only thing that makes me feel better."

Wow. There was honestly a time when this childish whining made me feel wanted and needed. I would drive to the ends of the earth to make him feel better when he wanted to act like a man-child. Now, these sounds are like nails on a chalkboard. After the way he's treated me throughout the last few days, he wants me to make him soup. Unbelievable.

"Your fever must have spiked because you're out of your goddamn mind."

"Mommy, don't use God's name in vain. It's just soup. I can make it for him."

In moments like these, I experience an internal battle with myself about why didn't I know Rick for who he truly was before I married him and had Cora. Then, the other part reminds me I wouldn't have Cora if it weren't for this bastard. What the hell is wrong with my bumpy-as-shit life path? It's like the universe hiccuped when it was creating a line for me to follow.

"Cora, go to your room, please."

"But Daddy said he needs me."

"Daddy needs to grow a pair—never mind, go upstairs right now. It's not up for debate."

"Daddy needs to grow a pair—" Rick laughs. "You're funny, Han."

"Get out of my house, now."

"Just one cup of soup?" He places his hands together and pleads silently.

"Go call your girlfriend, from your house, and tell her you want some goddamn soup. I'm not your wife. I'm not your anything, and don't mistake me for someone who wants to ever fill that role again."

For years, I couldn't stand up for myself. I let him mentally abuse me in ways I didn't realize. He broke me down, made me feel like nothing, and he thinks that with just a charming smile and wink of his eye, he can weasel his way back into my life when his sexy little girlfriend can't figure out how to turn on a stove.

"I'm sorry, Hannah," he says, turning onto his side.

Sorry, that's funny. This man does not know the meaning of an apology. "It doesn't matter."

"Come here," he says, waving me over.

I know this move too. This is where he butters me up, puts his arm around me, and asks me what's *really* bothering me … as if it's not him.

"No, get out."

I don't feel a thing this time—not like last time I had to say this to him. Not like when I found him and Tiana in our bedroom while Cora was eating breakfast alone downstairs. *When a business trip ends a day early, and you want to surprise your husband, call first, especially if you're married to someone like Rick.* That's what I learned. That's what he's taught me—to walk on eggshells and always be cautious.

Rick pushes himself up and tosses the covers to the side. "Okay."

"I can open the door to make it easier for you." I twist my head to the side and smile. It's very callous of me, but he deserves to know this side of Hannah.

"You really don't give a shit about me anymore, do you?"

"Aw, Ricky, was this a little test? Were you just trying to see how much I still care about you? Does it help you sleep better at night? You know, knowing I'm next door weeping and wallowing over the loss of our marriage? Because—," I touch my finger to my lips since I'm trying to stop smiling, which feels unstoppable as I get this all off my chest. "That's not what's happening. I'm over you. I'm over us. I don't care if you live next door or in another country. Other than our custody arrangement, you're dead to me."

"Shit, Hannah. Don't stop there. Tell me what you really think."

"Oh, I'm done. That *is* what I think."

"Ouch." He stands up from the pull-out and sighs. "I'm not going to lie and say it doesn't hurt to hear you say that." What is he expecting to hear from me? "Things aren't going well with Tiana, you know."

"What were you expecting? You're fifteen years older than her. She can have any man she wants, and at some point, even the biggest gold-diggers figure out it isn't always worth it in the end."

There's a possibility I said too much. There's also a possibility I don't care. Rick looks hurt—like the rug has been pulled out from beneath him, and I can't care.

I don't care. I actually feel a small sense of relief.

There is no part of me that should care.

I'm stronger than this.

CHAPTER SEVENTEEN

SATURDAYS WERE FOR SLEEPING IN ... BUT NOW IT'S FOR FINDING A CURE TO THE MAN FLU WHILE PARENTING AN ACTUAL FIVE-YEAR-OLD.

"Mommy," Cora whispers into my ear. "Mommmmy. It's pancake time."

"Cora, it's time to let me sleep for a little longer," I groan and roll onto my opposite side. "I'll be down in a little bit. Go watch TV."

"I can't. Daddy and Beefcake Batman are watching A Peen Zone."

That perks me up. The last thing I want is those two men conspiring against me. Not that I think Logan would do that, but Rick is so manipulative and deceitful, he could get a car salesman to buy a car for him.

I rip the covers off and let my feet fall to the floor as my usual morning dizziness takes me with it. I have to stop popping out of bed. "Yay! Pancakes!"

"Cora, what have Daddy and Logan been saying to each other?"

Cora climbs onto the bed and slips into my warmed spot. "I don't know, ball stuff."

"Ball stuff?"

"Yeah, I guess baseball stuff. You know, one ball strike and you're out?"

"That's not how the game goes," I tell her as I search through my drawers for clothes.

"It is when Logan plays."

"I think you're confused," I tell her.

"Nope. I'm not."

"Okay." I pull on a pair of pants and my Saturday's finest white t-shirt. "Come on, let's go."

Cora jumps across the bed until she flies into my arms. "I'm glad you're up now. There's too much boy stuff down there."

"You have no idea," I tell her with a poke on her button nose. "Who let Daddy in this morning?"

She shrugs, and I squint an eye. "It's kind of nice having Daddy here, isn't it?"

No, no it's not. "I'm glad it makes you happy," I tell her. Who the hell let that man back in the house? It took me a full hour to shove him out the door last night with his puppy dog pout and droopy eyes. I felt like the biggest a-hole in the world, but no. I'm not going backward. It's all just a game until he wins, then it's back to the good old times. I've done this way too many times to be fooled again. Now, he's trying to befriend a potential interest in my personal life.

I'm imagining the two of them sitting on the couch with beers in their hand before nine in the morning, but there's one part I'm confused about. How is it that the two of them go from sick as hell to awake before me and shooting the shit like it was a pre-planned arrangement?

What I wasn't prepared for was the sight in front of me, however.

The sofa has been pulled back out into the bed formation, and the blankets are strewn across the top with Logan and Rick tucked in tightly.

"What is this?" I ask them.

"We're dying," Logan says, sounding as if he thinks he's telling the truth.

I'm still staring. I can't think of anything worthy to respond with. They're dying. Together.

"Why are you back here?" I ask, holding my glare on Rick. "I think I was clear about you leaving last night, and I didn't give you an invitation to return."

"He's pretty sick, Hannah. Not that he should be *here*, but, seeing as I know how he feels, you should cut him a little slack, maybe? This is a bad case of the flu, like it's bad. To be honest, I'm not sure how people are making it through this without hospitalization." Logan intervenes. I'm not the slightest bit surprised by this. Maybe I should be, but I'm not. My life is a big joke, and it obviously always will be. I just had the same goddamn flu!

"Why are you back here, Rick?" I ask, ignoring Logan.

"Tiana kicked me out last night, so I let myself in with the spare key that was under the doormat," Rick says.

"And I was up at three, sick to my stomach. Your bathroom ran out of toilet paper, so I went downstairs to find more. Rick showed me where it was, and we got to talking."

"How sweet," I grunt. "Rick, you can't stay here. Tiana's going to need to find somewhere else to dump you."

"Hannah," Logan interrupts. "Just give him a break for a few. He feels like shit—I get it."

I bite down on my bottom lip to stop myself from saying something I shouldn't say with Cora around, but I can't resist saying something. "Um, you know I had the same flu, right?"

"It obviously wasn't the same," Rick says. Leave it to Rick to make that comment. It seems Logan might be smart enough not to say such a thing.

"Of course," I play along. "Your flu must be worse than mine was."

"Do you have anything bland we can eat for breakfast?" Logan asks. "I can get it."

"We?" Seeing them curled up in bed together, all I can think is that Logan and Rick are now dating, so that's fun.

"Us," Logan says, pointing back and forth between him and Rick.

I'm still stuck staring at the two of them, trying to figure out my next move. I pivot and leave the room, heading right for the front door. I grab my coat and step into my Uggs on the way out, then cross the lawn over to Rick's house.

I try the doorknob first but it's locked, so I reach under the front mat and retrieve their spare key. Rick is the one who left the spare key to my house under the front mat. I forgot it was there. He clearly hasn't changed his ways. Doesn't he know it's the first place anyone would look?

I unlock the door and walk inside. This house is the same layout as mine, except it's mirrored. "Tiana?" I holler on my way to their *broken-family* room.

I poke my head into the kitchen, but I'm not surprised to find it empty. She can't cook. She can only make green smoothies. I look from side to side as I near the family room, but that room is empty too. I have no issues hiking upstairs since she just walks into my house unannounced. "Tiana?"

I open their bedroom door and peek inside, finding her sitting on the edge of her bed, painting her toenails while watching a talk show. "What are you doing?" I ask her. "Didn't you hear me calling you?"

"I did," she responds.

"So, you just ignored me?"

"Yup." There's a snippiness to her response, so I can guess where this conversation is heading.

"I heard you kicked Rick out?" It should be none of my business, but Rick has made it my business.

She swivels around and faces me with her eyes jutting out from between her thick, black lashes. "He said I kicked him out?"

"Yes." Now, I'd like to leave and unstick myself from this situation.

"Do you know how many times that man has called out your name during our lovemaking?" Gag. I'm going to gag. I don't want to hear about their lovemaking or anything of that nature. Visualizing that would most likely make me want to puke again.

But he's called my name out while doing this pretty little hussy.

"No, Tiana, I wouldn't know how many times that's happened, but I can assume it was only because we were married for quite a while. A name just gets stuck in your head sometimes."

"Hannah," she says in her Cuban accent. "He doesn't want a temporary fixture in his life. He wants his wife. He was just having a mid-wife crisis."

"Mid-life," I correct her.

"What—ever. He's over me. I'm old news. I can't cook or clean, and he's sick of my smoothies. I have nothing to offer but my body."

Breathe. In and out. Breathe. "Well, I don't want him back, so make it work," I tell her, keeping my face clear of all emotions.

"You think I haven't tried?" she argues. "This isn't something new." I think this might be the most serious conversation I've had with this woman, and I'm starting to empathize with her, rather than hate her.

"I'm sure you're just going through a rough patch. All couples have them." If someone would have told me five years ago that I'd be persuading my husband's mistress to hang onto him, I'm not sure what my reaction would be … well, other than poisoning the shit out of him so I could watch him suffer.

"Look, he's needy right now. I'm trying my hand at this whole dating-after-a-divorce thing, and Rick has to get out of my house," I tell her.

Tiana stands up, towering over me with her five-foot-eight-ish stature. "So, this is all about you, is it?" She's kidding. She has to be kidding.

"Opposed to you for a change, yes," I tell her. "You wanted him badly enough to break up a family, now do something to keep him."

"Dios Mio, Hannah, are you that blonde? I'm here on a work visa. I didn't know Rick was married when he started pursuing me. He wasn't wearing a wedding ring, and he certainly didn't mention you or Cora. How was I to know?"

They met at work. She was teaching some yoga class during lunch to help Rick's company gain a better work/life/health balance. I knew Rick was going to yoga, and I assumed why he was going, but I had no proof, and he kept Tiana to himself for quite a while before I found them.

"When you found out he has a daughter, it didn't cross your mind that he was possibly married?"

"No!" she shouts. "He said you left them." Unbelievable. She's seeing everything so clearly now, and I wonder how long this has been settling in her head. Still, not my problem. She found out I didn't leave and still stuck with Rick, so I don't care a whole lot about her reason for staying.

"Well, as you know now, we were, in fact, still married."

"Yes, I know," she replies, casting her gaze past my face.

"So, you're here on a work visa, like you just said." I repeat, knowing little about her story—just that she came over here from Cuba in search of work when the border laws were lifted.

A nervous look flutters over her eyes. "Yes, so?"

"Shouldn't you be figuring out how to marry him? He's your ticket to staying here, isn't he?"

"Who said I want to stay here in your country?"

Me.

"You're right. I shouldn't be insisting that you do anything beyond what is going to make you happy." I don't even know what I'm saying or doing anymore. All I know is, I still have to go back and deal with Rick, who is doing everything in his power to kill my chances with Logan. That is if my chances aren't already dead.

"Rick was making me happy, but something changed. He must have gotten bored of trying to please me," she says. "I'm pretty sure he thinks he has a chance to win you back, and that's what he's trying to do."

I sit down next to Tiana on her bed and take her shoulders with my grip. "I told him it wasn't happening. It's not happening. He hurt me, and I will never forget it. He needs to move forward, not backward."

"He's jealous of that baseball player, but I don't know why. It's not like he's the whole package," she says with a tickled laugh.

"What are you talking about?" I ask.

"Oh." She covers her mouth and realigns the natural bow in her lips. "Nothing."

"Fine, well if jealousy is the problem, I'll just go back over there and rub it in his face."

"Rub what in his face?" Tiana asks, seemingly confused.

"Logan."

"Can I watch?" she asks.

"Only if you take Rick back home with you."

"He's the one who left," she reminds me.

"Well, be the one to make him come back. I'm sure there's some kind of trick you can use." My eyes fall on her tight, cotton shirt. "Here." I tug the collar down a few inches, exposing more of her voluptuous D-cups Cora is apparently enamored by.

She looks down at her chest and grins. "That should work." Tiana stands up with a hint of confidence and a smirk.

I follow with hope. "Oh, one last question before we head over there?"

She stops in the doorway and turns to face me. "Yes, Hannah, these are real. So is everything else on my body, but thank you for the compliment."

"What? How? I—" Cora. Why did she have to inherit my big mouth, of all things?

"Your daughter does not have a filter and cannot keep secrets." She wags her finger at me and continues to the stairs.

"I'm glad we talked," I tell her as we walk out of the house.

"Yeah, we'll see." I've never tried to like her but depending on how today goes, we'll see if our camaraderie will continue.

The second I open the front door of my house, I hear Cora screaming, mixed with a variety of other noises. "What the hell is going on in here?" I run toward the family room, bewildered by the sight in front of me.

CHAPTER EIGHTEEN

ALL THE MEN ARE DYING, AND I JUST WANTED TO SLEEP IN ON THIS LOVELY DAY OFF ...

"What in the world is going on?" Logan is on all fours and Rick is hanging over the side of the bed, rubbing Logan's bare back. No one answers me, but then Logan starts making some awful noise that sounds like a cat with a hairball.

"Dry heaves," Rick finally says. "Hang in there, buddy."

Dry heaves? Logan had soup and crackers last night and kept it down, so I'm having a hard time thinking he'd be dry heaving right now.

Tiana walks in, and I turn to find out why she was so far behind me. Her arm is outstretched in front of her, her eyes are squeezed tightly shut, and her other hand is over her nose and mouth.

"What are you doing?" I ask her.

"I can't handle the vomit."

"No one is sick right now," I tell her.

She peeks through one eye, scoping out the area. "Then why is he sitting like that?"

Can't I just say the words "man flu"? Then everything will make sense.

"Tiana," Rick says as he clears his throat.

"Rick," she replies. "I want you to come home." There is so much emotion in her sentence, I can hardly keep myself from choking up. *Not really.*

"Tiana, come on," I grunt quietly.

"Rick, I want you to come back home with me. You don't have a life here with Hannah anymore. I'll make you soup, or try to, whatever you want."

"You said you don't cook," Rick whines like a child.

"I never cooked before I came to the US, Rick. You know that. My mami always did the cooking." Tiana has a story beyond being the mistress with perfect hair, a perfect ass, fake tits, and Botox-injected lips. There's a chance I was wrong, but I will not say it out loud. She is still the reason my husband left me, but if it wasn't her, it would have been another hussy.

Damn hussies.

"I bet," Rick begins. "I bet Hannah could show you a thing or two." Rick has this soft, sweet smile tugging at his mouth, and I have the urge to see if it would peel off. I'm not freaking teaching her how to cook.

"Or!" I chuckle, sardonically. "I have a better idea. Why don't you pull up YouTube and search for cooking lessons? Cora could probably teach you how to do that."

I almost forgot about Logan, who is still on all fours, looking like he's preparing for his next contraction. I kneel and help him back up to the bed.

"I'm so weak," he says. "How long have I gone without food?" His words are hardly audible through his parched throat.

I glance down at my watch. "It's been approximately nine hours since you ate. Nine."

"It feels like an eternity."

"You're really not feeling any better at all?" I ask him.

"Yeah, man, I'm starting to shake this thing, I think," Rick says, rolling back into the center of the pull-out.

"Maybe you should take me to the hospital," Logan groans. Crap, am I being that big of an asshole? Is something really wrong?

"That might be a good idea," Rick says. "He's not doing well."

"What am I supposed to do with Cora?" I ask Rick. It's his weekend, but up until last night, he couldn't hold himself upright, and we all know how Tiana feels about childcare.

"I—I'll take care of her," Tiana says. "I'll do her hair and makeup. You know, girl stuff."

Cora's looking at me from across the room with big eyes. I know she doesn't like when Tiana does her hair. She said she tugs too tight.

"Sweetie, I need you to go back to Daddy's house so I can take care of Logan for a bit. I'll come get you as soon as I can, okay?"

Cora folds her arms over her chest and juts her bottom lip out. "Fine, but I'm not getting dressed. Today was supposed to be a pajama day."

Rick moans as he stands from the bed. "Come on, princess. It's still a pajama day. I'll even give you a ride to my house." Cora runs and leaps onto the bed, gaining height before making the next jump onto Rick's back.

This is the part that kills me. He's a good dad when he's around and not working. He loves that little girl, but he screwed everything up, and that makes me hate him.

Rick leans down beside me so Cora can give me a kiss on the cheek. "I love you, Mommy."

"Bye, baby. Have fun," I tell her.

"I hope you feel better, Logan," Cora says.

"Thanks, kiddo." Logan whimpers, falling backward into a pile of pillows and wrapping his arms around his stomach like he's in pain.

Tiana smiles at me as if she's broken down one of my barriers. I'll let her think that for now, but I don't forget that easily.

The house is empty except for Logan and me, and I'm watching him for a moment, gauging his level of discomfort. "You really want to go to the hospital?" I ask.

"I think so. I don't know. Everything hurts."

"What does everything consist of?"

"My head, stomach, back, neck, legs, and arms." Yup, I guess that's everything.

He's on his side, so I make my way around the bed and climb in so I can rub his shoulders. Maybe if he relaxes a bit, some of the pain will subside. I didn't have any pain when I was sick, so I'm not sure if he has the same thing.

I press my fingers into the muscle of his shoulders, then knead the areas with my fists. Almost instantly, I feel some of the tension in his body subside, and his head falls deeper into the pillow. "That feels nice," he mumbles.

I continue massaging his shoulders and back until my hands become weak. As I pull away, I hear his breaths lingering softly. He's asleep.

I want to curl up and join him, but I'm wide awake and focused on the TV replaying parts of a baseball game from last night.

The sight of baseball reminds me of this little secret Logan has been hiding inside his pants. What kind of injury would be so traumatic it caused him to both retire, and fear taking his pants off?

I look down at his legs that are tangled up in the sheets, suddenly wondering where he got those sweatpants from. Before I think too much, though, my lip snarls because I know exactly where they came from. Logan is wearing Rick's sweatpants.

Please, make this stop.

Rick is a bit larger in the waist than Logan, which means the sweatpants must be loose on him.

I shouldn't do this.

I should know what I'm getting into, though.

But, he's asleep, and this might be considered some kind of necrophilia crap.

Though, I'd just be taking a look.

Then I could tell him I saw it, and it's no big deal, and he doesn't have to hide anymore. It sounds like the perfect solution to this problem. Whatever the problem is.

Logan's quiet breaths are a bit heavier now, verging on a slight snore. He's out cold. I roll off the other side of the bed, careful not to make any sudden movements or shake the mattress. I crawl around the side of the pull-out where I'm face to face with the lower half of Logan's body. He's curled up on his side, so I'm hoping it will make it easier for me to get a good look.

I slip my fingers gently beneath the waistband of his pants and pull them away. There isn't much restriction since the pants are, in fact, loose. I create just enough of a gap for me to see what's going on.

Okay, so first … why wouldn't you be wearing boxers or briefs when wearing another man's pants? I'm not complaining because it's making things easier at the moment, but really, what would make a person want to do that?

I've already familiarized myself with his impressive ballpark sausage, but I haven't met the ballpark itself. I reach down carefully to push his fella to the side, and as soon as I touch it, it pops up like a watchdog protecting its bones. I guess that's one way of revealing what's beneath the curtain. My gaze trails down the length of his leg, finding no scars or any other obvious disfigurement. So, what is the big deal?

Oh. Ohhhh. I tilt my head to get a better look at what I'm seeing. Oh, wow. That's a big scar and a lot of loose skin. Oh no, poor Logan!

"What the—what are you—why would you? What is wrong with you?" Logan asks with a growl slicing through his throat. I fly backward, shocked that he's awake, and mortified that I've been caught because I have no type of explanation I can follow this up with.

"I'm sorry," I offer. "It's just that Rick seemed to know, and Tiana was making weird comments. It's like I was the only one who didn't know what you were hiding down there."

Logan sits up, pulling the pants tight around his waist. "You probably are the only person who didn't know, Hannah. It was all over the goddamn news for a month."

"Your love sack was all over the news?" *Did I just say that out loud?*

He nods his head and bites down on his lip. "Wow. I guess I should have just assumed you'd be like all the others. I actually thought I was lucky because I met an attractive woman who hates sports."

"I didn't mean to insult you. I say weird things when I get uncomfortable, and right now I'm uncomfortable."

"I'm the one missing a ball, Hannah. I'm not sure why that would make you uncomfortable."

Gee, I don't know. I had my hands down your pants and was studying your anatomy while I thought you were asleep. No biggie. "Does it hurt?" What the hell kind of question is that? This obviously didn't just happen last week.

"No, the accident was over a year ago."

"I—I don't know what to say." And I can assume that's not what he wants to hear.

"Well, let's just get this out of the way first. The doctors said I'm most likely shooting blanks, so babies are out of the question."

I don't recall mentioning the topic in the week I've known him, or even considering the idea of a second child once in the past four years. Cora is more than enough for me to handle right now. I'm grateful for her, but I'm not jonesin' for another baby. "I'm sorry, I didn't think I was giving you that vibe, not that we were at a point where that should have been discussed. In any case, I wasn't planning on having any more kids, so hopefully, that thought wasn't going through your head about whatever was going on between us."

"You don't want another child?"

I shake my head without a thought. "No, Cora is my world, and maybe I'm selfish, but I don't know if I have more room in my heart for a second child." I hadn't considered the topic after leaving Rick. It's not like I've dipped my toes into the dating scene much this past year, and whatever I did experience never went past a first dinner. In the back of my head, I figured most men would be happy to hear I wasn't looking to settle down as quick as possible so I could pop out some more kids before I'm too old.

"I wanted a baby," he says. "I wanted a family—the full package." I'm going to assume he intended that pun, but I'm ignoring it.

He wanted a baby. "I thought you said you had a baby …"

He points to his back, where I saw the tattoo, and my heart immediately begins to hurt. "Stillborn. Sierra Grier, five pounds, three ounces, and a full head of blonde curls. It destroyed my marriage. Then, to add insult to injury, my accident happened, and the dream of a baby for both my wife and me was more or less gone. That's when she left me. There, that's my story. Now you know everything. The injury forced me to retire early, and I've been sitting on my ass for over a year doing nothing. I needed something to fill my time, so I got a job."

"I am so sorry," I tell him. His story has me on the brink of tears, and I feel terrible for acting so ungrateful in the form of exhaustion with Cora. He must think I'm horrible. Being a single mom has been the hardest thing I've had to deal with, but I recognize that it's nothing in comparison to a surviving a stillborn baby, and everything that came after it.

"I held her for a minute before she was taken away. I have that."

"Logan, I don't know what to say." I don't. Life is cruel and unforgiving, and it's not fair what he's gone through and is still probably going through. I inhale sharply and look up at him through my blur of tears. "You don't have to hide anything from me. We all have our scars, pasts, and haunting memories. I've convinced myself over the past year that the only thing that matters is what I do today, tomorrow, and every day after that. There are other ways of obtaining your dream, but broken hearts leave scars, and not even time can fix that sometimes. We just have to find the good parts of life to fill in some of the gaps."

"Yeah, what you're saying is everything I've thought," he says. "I had too much time to think, though. It wasn't a good thing."

"I can't imagine time alone to think helped."

"Hannah, it's like my man-card has been taken from me."

"Because of a silly missing ball?" That doesn't make him less of a man.

He looks at me like I'm crazy and missing some part of his point. "Well, yeah."

"But, I mean, it makes your one ball special and unique, you know?" I say it with a straight face. I think it was just the first thing that came to mind. I'm a mom, I try to make everything better. It's my job.

He's looking back at me with the same straight face, waiting for me to crack up or follow it with something else, but that's all I should say. Nothing good will follow, I'm sure.

"Are you serious?"

"I'm as serious as a bag of uncracked nuts."

Logan throws his head back and folds his arm over his face to cover his smile and laughter. "You really don't care about this, do you?"

"Everyone has their thing or lack thereof. I do care about your baby. That's different, but your ball … I don't think you should focus so much on it."

He peeks out from under his arm. "Are you done?"

"Yes, but how are you suddenly not in pain anymore?"

He recovers his face, followed by a groan. "I feel better."

"You felt better last night," I tell him.

"Yeah, and then I remembered I said I'd take my pants off when I felt better."

"Do you know what you're making me sound like right now?"

"A sex addict?" he replies with a grin.

"It has been a long year," I sigh. "I'm not an addict, but you showed interest, and I had hope."

"So, that's all you want with me? Sex."

"No." I want it all. I want a mutual feeling of care and love with a man. I want someone who doesn't need to go looking elsewhere for a good time when I'm at home waiting for them. I didn't realize it was a lot to ask for, but clearly, it is.

"What do you want?"

"I'm not sure, but this living alone as a single mom crap sucks. It's not my thing."

"You're doing a great job if it's any consolation."

"Pfft. You can't tell that after a week of knowing me."

"I'm a good judge of character," he says.

"We'll go with that. So, what now, Logan? Where do we stand with each other?"

"TV?"

I climb up on the bed and slip under the covers with him. "Hey?"

"Yeah?" he replies.

"If you're feeling better, why were you on all fours when I walked in the house?"

"Uh—" I don't know if I like the reason for his pause.

"Spit it out …"

"Cora came downstairs, and Rick and I were shouting at the TV—we were watching a recap of the game from last night. She called us out on being sick."

"So, you tricked my daughter into thinking you were still sick … by acting like a dying cat?"

"Yeah, I think I scared her a little."

"You scared *me* a little."

"I never said I was a good actor."

"True. Okay, next question. What happened to your ball?" I'm just going to throw it out there. "Or, should I Google your name?"

"I must say, I'm a little surprised you haven't already Googled my name. You strike me as that crazy type." I *am* that crazy type, but with the stomach flu and man flu all in one week, I haven't had much time to do my typical man stalking.

"You have me pegged wrong," I lie.

"Go ahead and Google me. You'll have all your answers and more."

CHAPTER NINETEEN

SUNDAY IS FOR BALLS ... ERR

Logan decided to go home yesterday as I was opening the Google browser. I don't need to wonder why, but he is the one who suggested I go look. He told me he'd see me at work on Monday, so I didn't say a whole lot because I was caught off guard. To be fair, he was at my house for almost two days, so maybe it was just time for him to go. It didn't take me long to realize I don't have his phone number, and he doesn't have mine. Therefore, our unorthodox date that lasted way too long must have ended up being one of *those* kinds of dates—one where we pretend it never happened when we run into each other—or in our case, see each other at the office tomorrow. This could be an interesting, and awkward, week at work. What was I thinking? Maybe the flu virus I had impaired my ability to make rational decisions. Yeah, that must be it.

It never fails, the one day my house is quiet, I'm up by eight and ready for a full day of errands and Sunday have-tos. Why can't I sleep in? I really need the rest, but my brain is in overdrive.

After debating it all afternoon and night yesterday, I still haven't decided whether I should I Google Logan or just let the story slide. My imagination is already doing a number on me, so I'm kind of hopeful that what I'm assuming happened is a lot worse than what happened, but I know there's only one way to find out the truth. It's inevitable that I'll eventually look, so I might as well get it over with.

I sit down at my desk up in my loft and wait for the laptop to boot up. I have my fourth cup of coffee of the day, a blanket, and quiet, the perfect components for taking the time to reflect on this past week of my life. Last Sunday, I was hustling around to get the grocery shopping completed, laundry done, and the house clean. My life was normal and lame as it always has been. If I knew what the week had in store for me, I might have called out sick from work for the week.

"Come on, hurry up, you damn laptop."

My fingers stumble across the keyboard as I type his name into the search bar and watch the little circle thingy spin while it searches the Internet for a lost ball.

Pages and pages of Logan Grier pop up, and I can't imagine how I managed to miss hearing about this. There are articles and videos on all the major news and social media outlets, including Facebook and Twitter. I'm a loser.

I open the top link since it's apparently the most popular, and I'm greeted by this headline:

CHAPTER 20

ONE FOUL BALL FOR ANOTHER

Ouch. Don't they know the athletes will see these stupid headlines? Assholes. I'm guessing *they* all still have their balls intact.

> Last night, at the top of the ninth inning, Logan Grier was up to bat when a slider pitch came in at eighty-five miles per hour. It looked as though Grier was preparing to let it fly, but didn't decide in time. The ball made contact with the bat and ricocheted off of his right foot before bouncing directly upward into an unfortunate bodily location. Grier was knocked out cold, clearly not protected properly by his gear. He was quickly carried off the field on a stretcher, and we are still waiting on a final diagnosis of his injury, but at this time, things aren't looking good for Grier and his career.

There's footage. I don't know if I can watch. My muscles are hard as stone right now at the thought of what happened. I'm aware I don't have that body part, but I know how sensitive that area is for men, and the thought of being hit there in those dangling parts makes me cringe.

Like any car accident, though, I can't stop myself from clicking play.

As Logan walks up to the plate, I notice a look on his face I haven't seen before. I can't tell if it's pride, or maybe just a different kind of happiness. It's hard not to admire what he looks like in his uniform, the way his pants hug his muscles, and the bands on his wrists accentuate his dark tanned muscles. I can only see one side of his profile, but it's pretty much the definition of perfection. He's covered with some of the reddish dirt from the encircling field, and it accents his appearance like a halo. Wow, he looks amazing. The pitcher throws the first ball, and Logan prepares to swing but stops. His forearms tighten, and his hand grips the bat a little tighter.

How could I not have ever been a baseball fan? *It just got a lot hotter in here.* This Logan is completely different from the Logan I know right now. Not that I know him well, but it's like he's two different people. The crowd is screaming his name, and the video switches to the stands where the crowd is watching, enraptured. They love him. Here I am, not knowing who the hell he really is, and he's been staying in my house for two days. Maybe because I wasn't drooling all over him, he found me intriguing.

The announcer begins talking about the pitcher winding up, and—I can't do this. I can't watch him get hurt. I won't be able to un-see it, and it's all I'll be thinking about the next time I see him.

I hit pause and close out of the search engine. My mind is everywhere but mostly centered on how life managed to bring Logan and me together in such a peculiar way. I mean, it all started when he got assigned to my office as a temp. Then he wanted to have lunch with me. Nothing was coincidental. He had intentions, but what were they if he didn't want me to know his secret? I love how men think women are so confusing, yet I've spent more time scratching my head over the men in my life than those men have probably spent scratching their balls. It's not right.

I head down to the kitchen, grab my phone off the center island, and text Brielle. I don't usually send her messages on the weekends, but I need to know if she knew about Logan. Maybe I'm the only one in the world who didn't know who he was or what happened to him. The whole "living under a rock" thing I've been doing since Rick and I divorced doesn't always bode well for me.

Me: Hey, have you ever watched a baseball game that Logan was playing in?

I'm not surprised to see the dots flickering immediately. Brielle lives on her phone, even when she should be working. I told her she should get the thing surgically adhered to her palm.

Brielle: Who hasn't? LOL

Me: ...

Brielle: Hannah, really? You didn't know about Logan?

Me: No.

Brielle: So, you saw it?

What does it look like? I've heard it looks like a flat tire. Poor Logan.

Me: I'll see you tomorrow.

Brielle: Lame. Byeeeeee.

I'm circling the downstairs feeling completely out of my element, just as I remember I'm leaving for a trip in two days. It totally slipped my mind, and I'm nowhere near prepared for this expo.

CHAPTER 21

NOTHING LIKE A GOOD CUP OF MONDAY MORNING TO GET YOU MOVING ...

I'm sitting in the parking lot with my coffee mug from home. I'm a little early, but rather than go inside and get to work on all the shit I have to get done before I leave tomorrow morning, I'll just take a few extra breaths as I watch snowflakes falling from the dark sky.

I decided to avoid the weather channel this morning in fear of what they'll say is coming. I wasn't ready to face it. However, the sky is basically black, and I can pretty much assume what we're all in for. School will be canceled in three hours because no one knew a storm was brewing, and we need to make sure everyone gets home safely before the buses can no longer get up hills.

Rick will be too busy to help, and the world knows he had Cora for an entire day and a half. That's like an eternity for him, and he needs at least a day's break before he's forced to parent for the rest of the week while I'm gone.

I'll also have to figure out how to clear a path in the driveway tomorrow at five in the morning so the airport shuttle car can pick me up. There will be delays flying down to Orlando, and I have a layover in Chicago, so there's that excursion to look forward to. So yeah, cheers to you, fracking, dark sky. I hold my mug up and tap the windshield. FML.

I kick my company's door open without a care that I am not dressed professionally today. I'm probably getting fired anyway since I molested the temp in his sleep. Is that a felony or just a slap on the wrist? In any case, today called for knee-high boots, holey jeans, and a flannel blouse.

I swing the glass door open and barrel through the foyer like I'm on a mission. If I get fired, I don't have to come to work anymore. I won't be able to pay my mortgage, which means I'll have to sell the house, and between unemployment and child support, an apartment will work out nicely. I'll be away from Rick, and there's a whole lot less cleaning to do in a smaller place. I can do a little freelance editing and marketing, and bam—life is perfect. Why haven't I done this before?

I walk past Brielle's empty cube, Logan's occupied cube, and close myself into my office. I toss my coat onto the guest chair and drop down into my seat.

In an attempt not to destroy my day today, I answered some emails yesterday afternoon, but with the event tomorrow, my inbox is full again. Somehow, I'm supposed to prepare to leave while also answering every minor question in the world. It would be awesome if we had a facts and questions page on our website, rather than tossing all the questions to me. Plus, sales can't be bothered. They're too busy planning for their parties and dinners.

A blur walks past my door, and I can't see what it is because the glass has ripples to make sure no one can see anyone having sex inside when the doors are closed. Seriously, I do wonder if that really happens in offices. It must. If not, there's no real purpose of having windows that aren't see-through.

A tap on my door startles me a bit because I'm trying to figure out how two people would have sex in an office this size? It doesn't sound like a good time. I think the utility closet would probably be a better option.

The door opens even though I didn't invite anyone in, and Logan is standing in front of me in a pair of gray slacks and a white button down. "Do you have a minute?" he asks.

Without waiting for an answer, he closes himself inside my office before I say anything. "I'm sorry for leaving on an awkward note like I did. I realized when I got home that I didn't have your number, so I figured it was a sign that I should just keep quiet until today."

I shift my weight around in the chair because I'm super uncomfortable. I didn't think he would bring this all up so quickly, or at all for that matter. Men are usually experts at avoidance, but he must not be one of *those* men. "You have nothing to apologize for. I was out of line," I tell him.

He looks down and drops his hands into his pockets, and I notice his hair is perfectly styled with product, which I find hot because Rick never knew how to take care of himself. I had to do his hair before he left for work in the morning, or he'd leave with it sticking straight up in the air.

"Yes, you were kind of out of line," he agrees. "However, I should have been upfront with you before things got as far as they did on Thursday night."

"It's none of my business," I tell him, feeling ashamed of my behavior. I most definitely owed him this apology at the very least, plus I'm sure I screwed everything up.

"Is the video as bad as everyone says it is?" He hasn't watched it? I guess I probably wouldn't want to watch myself go through that either, but I also don't understand the people who enjoy watching their own sex tapes. I'd end up critiquing myself, and it doesn't sound like a healthy situation.

"I don't know," I tell him.

"You didn't watch?" He seems surprised that I had the willpower to stop myself from watching his incident.

"I couldn't. I saw you step up to the plate, watched the first ball fly, and my heart started to race. You have a lot of fans, huh?"

"I did."

"Anyway, I shut it off. I couldn't fathom watching you go through that, and I'm positive I don't ever want to see it, so I'm glad I stopped."

"My friends watched it over and over. I didn't understand why they wanted to, and it was all they would talk about, so I cut them out of my life. I cut everyone out of my life, actually. I don't want to keep reliving that damn accident, but it's a part of me now, and rather than just living with some stupid scar, I feel the need to warn people, so I don't have to deal with the aftermath over and over."

"People? Have there been a lot of people since your divorce?"

"Just a few who 'wanted to see it for themselves.' That hurt. One girl actually got up and left in a fit of laughter before we—you know."

I recoil at the thought. Who the hell would act that way? *Who the hell would try to look down a man's pants while they're asleep?* "I guess I'm no better."

"You didn't run away. I did." He does have a point there. "I'm kind of like a bull in a China shop sometimes. It's like I haven't figured out how to make this dating shit work, and I just go at it full force."

"That's kind of hot," I tell him.

Logan's face brightens with a blush, which I'm sure matches my own complexion. "Wow," he mutters under his breath. "So, this whole —you're my boss, thing—what do we do about that?"

"Frankly, Logan, I don't give a fluck." His eyes widen in response to my statement. "I was wondering why you came in dressed all cute and sexy today." I might have put a little effort into my outfit. However, I also somewhat expected Logan to avoid my presence.

The door to my office flies open. "Oh my Blahniks, I'm so sorry I'm late." Brielle puts her coffee cup down on the edge of my desk and tears her coat off. "It was a crazy morning, you have no idea." The number of times I listen to her tell me how crazy her mornings and nights are, and she doesn't have a pet, child, or spouse, makes me want to laugh sometimes, but I refrain like the adult I'm supposed to be.

"Morning after pill again?" I ask.

"Han-nah," she hisses. "No."

Logan scratches at his chin, obviously uncomfortable with where this conversation is likely going, but surprisingly, he turns toward the guest chair, moves my coat over the back side and takes the seat.

Brielle looks over at him with amusement, and she better not say a word. "No, so after we um … remember I told you about that guy, Fray, last week?"

The threesome. I completely forgot I gave her that amazing advice. "Of course, how could I have forgotten? How did it go?"

"Wow, so it was way better than I ever expected … like I highly suggest everyone try it at least once." I instantly remember Logan knew what she was talking about last week because he emailed me to fill me in as she was asking my opinion. I'm not always a super good listener when it comes to Brielle's stories, so he caught onto that quickly. He's bright red, looking toward the wall, probably ready to burst into laughter. His eyes are even watering a little, which makes me want to laugh too.

"I'll have to take that under advisement," I tell her.

"So anyway, because I was so accepting of the 'activity,'" she air-quotes, still under the impression that Logan is clueless, "Adam asked me to marry him this morning."

Act surprised and excited, Hannah. You can do it! "Oh, no way! Let me see the ring!" Was that good? I'm a horrible actress. She's known him six months, and he needed a threesome to figure out that he wanted to marry her? That's not good. Not good at all, but if I tell Brielle my thoughts on the situation, she'll just fly into his arms. She's not one for listening to advice, except the threesome, of course.

She lifts her hand up and looks at her empty ring finger. "Oh, yeah, he doesn't have one yet, but he said he's been saving up for months, and he should have enough money soon to get me the one I want."

"Oh, you guys have gone ring shopping? I didn't know that." I'm thinking she would have mentioned that at some point.

"No, but I told him what my dream ring is, and he wrote it down, along with my ring size, so hopefully, I'll soon be a promised woman." She does a little jig and circles around to what must be a tune in her own head. "I'm so excited. We're thinking about a spring wedding."

"Oh! Well, hopefully, he has the ring by then," I say. *Oops. Too sarcastic.* She's mad. She'll get over it in like three-seconds, but I should have kept that to myself.

"Maybe another threesome will move things along with the ring a little faster. You know how men are," Logan says.

Okay, now my mouth is hanging open. I can't believe he just said that. She's going to think I told him, when he just overheard her talking about it last week. "You told him?" She squawks at me.

"No, of course not," I tell her while holding my glare on Logan who now knows he shouldn't have said anything.

"Oh, I overheard you," he says.

"Yeah, right. I was in here when I told her."

"The walls are thin," Logan argues.

Brielle looks over at Logan with flames in her eyes, and my heart pretty much just stops pumping blood. Please, don't say anything. Please, please, please. "Okay, I have to get some work done today because we're probably getting plowed with snow, and of course, we're leaving first thing tomorrow, kids," I announce.

"I'm older than you," Logan reminds me.

"I know, I know. Just go work or something."

"I have so much I could say to you right now," Brielle tells him, narrowing her eyes.

"Baseball fan?" Logan asks. I'm kind of flattered he didn't assume I ran to her, even though I did.

"I was when I was dating my last boyfriend."

"Congratulations," Logan replies. "And yes, it looks like a flat tire. Happy now?"

Brielle jerks her head back, and her mouth twists into an uncomfortable, sneering glower. "No, that's terrible. I'm so sorry."

"Don't be," he says.

Brielle grabs her coffee and quietly leaves the office. "The flat tire thing is a thing?"

"Thanks to the Sunday morning newspaper cartoons, it's a thing. I think there are t-shirts out there that say, 'Logan's got a flat tire and no spare.'"

"That's crude and distasteful," I tell him.

"It's fine. The number of puns I've heard have really given me a new sense of appreciation for all the dickheads out there."

A horrible snorting sound wrenches through my throat as I fold over laughing. "Oh, stop." I'm going to pee myself, for real.

"Want to share a car with me tomorrow morning? They told me to book one, but I saw you already have one coming to pick you up. Plus, snow is coming, and I can help you out."

I know what this all means. It means I still haven't gotten a wax job, it's snowing, and Logan's ready to have his flat tire blown, which means ..., "Uh, yeah, that would be great. We can order out or something. Can your stomach handle pizza yet?"

"I think I'll be okay with that," he says.

"Um, can you start printing out the event-labeled files I have in the shared folder? I have a quick errand I need to run for tomorrow. If anyone asks, tell them I'll be back within the hour."

"Sure thing, boss."

He needs to stop saying that. It sends my mind in completely the wrong direction.

CHAPTER 22

ON THE COUNT OF THREE, HOLD YOUR BREATH ...

"Where are you going? Is it for tomorrow? Do you need help? I'll come, and we can take my car, okay?" Brielle says while grabbing her coat.

"Uh, I—I don't need any help with this errand. You should probably see if Logan needs any help with collating the papers he's printing off."

Her arm drops to her side, coat and all. "You're asking *me* to go help our temp? I knew it. I'm out. This is why you have a temp. You're trying to replace me. Why wouldn't you just tell me the truth, and why would you want to replace me with yet another penis around here?"

I reach forward and grab her shoulder. "Will you relax? I'm not trying to replace you. On the contrary, I have recommended you for a promotion, which is why I've been weeding through temps."

"Oh my God," she says with a gasp. "Are you serious?" You'd think I just told her she won a million dollars. "What's the position?"

"Marketing Manager 1. I think you have potential ... to do a good job."

"What's that supposed to mean?" She looks entirely too confused to make me think suggesting her for the job was a good decision.

"Did you finish the call list for the expo?" I ask her.

"Actually, yes. When you were out sick last week, I stayed late and finished it up." Maybe I stand corrected.

"What about the website updates I sent you last week?"

"Done."

"Well, then I guess I made the right choice," I tell her as I try to sneak by, attempting to avoid her offer to tag along.

"Wait, I'm still going to come with you." Did she miss the whole part where I told her to help Logan?

"I'm fine, really. I just need to get this done and come back."

"Get what done?" she questions.

I close my eyes and scratch my forehead. "Could I please just sneak out for a few minutes?"

Brielle slips her coat on and follows me out the door. "I'm still your assistant, which means whatever you're doing, I can somehow help, I'm sure."

Once we're outside of the office, and in the elevator, I look at her and shake my head. "I'm going to get a quick wax. I'm not sure I need assistance with that."

"Hell yeah, you do," she says.

"I'm pretty sure I can walk in and lie down on a table without help."

"What kind of wax are you getting?"

"A regular one?" I raise a brow at her, wondering why she cares what kind of wax job I'm getting.

"No, I mean, are you getting an all-American bikini touch up, a full bikini, a French wax with a landing strip, a Brazilian wax with a triangle trim, a Brazilian with a deserted island, a love heart, or just a full-blown Hollywood glow?"

I'm staring straight ahead, watching the buttons light up one by one as my body becomes cold. She has to be kidding. There can't be that many options. The last time I got waxed, I simply requested a bikini wax, but now there are evidently quite a few more options. How could so much have changed during the last ten years of not caring about my hairstyle down yonder? "Um, I hadn't really thought of it."

"Well, what do you think Batman likes?"

"Uh—"

"Wait, wait, wait." She's waving her hands in front of her face as the elevator doors open. "How did you know about his flat tire unless you guys ... I thought you had already rounded those bases ... if you know what I mean?" She makes this throaty sound in her voice as she talks about bases as if we're in high school, or like it's a secret she's trying to be inconspicuous about.

"Brielle!" I snap.

"What? You're the one who texted me about the flat tire. What was I supposed to assume?"

I decide not to say another word until we're out the main doors, walking through a heavy, wet snow that has accumulated a half inch since I arrived at work this morning. "He started to ... you know, but then I remembered I hadn't gotten waxed, so I changed things up."

"Oh, so you did bang him?" I love how she sounds relieved to think that was the case.

"Why are you so invested in me getting nailed by Logan?"

Her car lights flash in front of us as she unlocks the door. Failing to offer a reply to my question, she scurries through the snow in her heels, while trying to skip between the snowflakes so her hair doesn't get wet. I make my way around her little red sports car and slip inside. I know how she feels about my mom-van, but it's probably a hell of a lot safer in snow and ice. Thankfully, this place is just two blocks away.

"It's not that I'm invested in you and Batman putting the *p* in the *v*, but let's be honest with ourselves. It's been well over a year since you've had your butter churned, and Logan looks like David Beckham with salt and pepper hair. He's hot, Hannah. These opportunities don't just come around all the time after you're thirty. You know that."

If I haven't already gotten in trouble for molesting the temp, I wonder if I would get in trouble for slapping my assistant. "Thanks for your honesty ..., and how the hell would you know what 'opportunities' women over thirty get?" I snap back.

"Whoa, I'm just assuming. Geez ..." she rebuts. Even though she doesn't know how hard it really is to find a single, hot man in his thirties, it is, and it's nice to have someone like Logan interested in me. I'm still not sure why he is, but I guess a lack of self-confidence can cause beer-goggles, or a willingness to settle for a downgrade.

"Plus, why do you think I'm about to go through the pain of having every hair torn off my lady bits? Just for fun? No."

"Oh, so you have decided to go with the Hollywood glow?"

"What does that even mean?"

"Hair or bare, duh," she says, playfully.

"Like, completely bare?" I question.

"Don't you watch porn?"

I laugh because I think she's kidding, but I'm quick to see she is not. "No, Brielle, I have a five-year-old, which doesn't leave me a lot of time to watch porn."

"So, you don't … you know, make yourself happy?"

"This conversation is so not appropriate to be having with my assistant."

"Which means you don't," she says, dryly, while pulling into the spa's parking lot.

"Brielle, I make myself happy."

"With a vibe, your hand, shower hose, or another kind of household object?"

"Please stop." Another household object? I'd have to throw it away after. I'd rather not think about people using household products. You just never know what you're touching in someone else's house, I guess. I'm going to be thinking twice before I touch anyone else's salt and pepper shakers from now on, though.

"Ah, you're a handy girl. There's nothing wrong with that. You do vibe though, right?"

I groan because I'm not answering these questions. "Do you order yours from Amazon because I've wondered where they came from and who has touched them before me, but I suppose I'd wonder that no matter where I buy it. I always give it a good rinse first. You do that too, right?"

"Stop."

I continue pushing away the subject as she pulls into a parking spot. "Does yours have a name?"

"Please don't go there," I tell her. If she can't hear the pleading in my voice, she's either deaf or doesn't care.

"Mine is Eggerman," she says with a smile, like she's in love with the thing.

"What the hell? Why Eggerman?"

"Well, it's kind of in the shape of an egg, and I like eggplants, and men, so, it just fits, you know?"

"That's insane, Brielle."

"No, it's not. It's completely normal to name your vibe. One of my friends I went to college with had one named Shermanator. Honestly, that's the best vibe name in the entire world."

"Shermanator? Like, from American Pie?" I laugh because that's creative. I'll give her that. I can't remember the quote exactly, but I remember Sherman calling himself some kind of sex god.

"Yes, like American Pie. So, you have one, right?"

I open the door. "Yes, Brielle, I have one, plus some others. I'm single and lonely as hell. Give me a break, will you?"

She steps out of the car too and meets me out front on the curb. "Okay, well you'll feel a lot closer to whichever is your favorite if you give it a name. What color is the one you use the most?"

I open the door to the spa and walk in, trying to brush her off my shoulder. "Good afternoon," an older woman at the front desk greets me. "How can I help you today?"

"She needs a Hollywood glow, stat," Brielle speaks for me. The thought of going completely bare makes me cringe, but maybe that's what Logan likes. He's probably been with a lot of women. Well, before the incident. Hopefully, he didn't catch a peek at my current situation. I think I stopped that in time.

"Follow me," the woman says.

I unbutton my coat, slip it off, and hand it to Brielle. "Thanks."

"Enjoy!" Screw you.

"Please take off everything from the waist down. Here is a sheet you can cover yourself with."

"Thank you, I'll just be a minute," I tell her. I don't think I've ever been to a spa where a seventy-year-old woman is a waxer. She must think I'm a whore, unless this is the treatment women commonly request.

"Oh, do you want your friend to come in and hold your hand?" the woman asks as if it's a normal thing to do.

"Oh, no, no, no, thank you. I'm more of a modest type of gal."

The woman's eyebrows rise about a half inch. "Modest, huh? Well, you won't want to be very modest when I'm through with you." She winks. *She just winked at me.* Oh God, she winked, and she's about to strip me clean. What the hell! "My name is Mary, in case you need anything." She offers me a cute, wrinkly smile before leaving me alone in this quaint, relaxing room with soothing music before I'm massacred. The irony.

I take off my pants and panties and pile them up on the stool in the corner of the room. Oh, this is just lovely. It's like I'm at the OB, but this is going to be way worse, I suspect.

I climb up on the table and wrap the thin sheet around my bottom half. "I'm ready, Mary," I shout.

I hear Brielle laughing hysterically in the hall, and it stresses me out. I just want to get this over with, and she's out there chatting this woman up. This is why I wanted to come alone.

Mary re-enters the room and takes a pair of knitting-circle-like eyeglasses off the prepping counter and slides them on. "My eyes aren't what they used to be, and I need to see what I'm doing. Don't want to wax the wrong part off!" she says with a hoarse laugh.

She finds that funny? "Wait." I push up on my elbows. "Is that possible? Can fragile parts be torn off?" Like Logan's ball. I guess it wasn't torn off, but things are delicate down there. "Is there any danger to this?"

"Oh, no, dear. That's just a little esthetician humor." Fabulous. How nice to be in the company of an old, funny pube-snatcher.

I lay back down and hear her gloves snap into place. "I'll be quick, honey. Don't worry."

"Thank you." But I am worried.

The hot wax is spread in a thick coat down one side of my lady bits, and I close my eyes in preparation for the next steps. The cloth adheres with the assistance of the lady's palm, which is so weird. There's an old lady's hand on my crotch. I'm going to be traumatized when I leave here. "Your friend told me to remind you about figuring out a name for your vibrator. I think it will be a great distraction," she says.

I'm going to kill Brielle.

The first rip comes, and I feel the need to scream a line of obscenities at old lady Mary, but I bite my lip instead.

The next layer is applied, and I do what she suggested and begin the consideration of vibrator names. The cloth is on, and I'm trying to think. Think, Hannah. Think. Muffin-beater? Ow, mothertrucking ow. Ow. Camel-pole? No, that's weird. Ummm, oh, Mr. Wiggles! No, no no, no. Oh, there's wax all the way in there. "Oh my, I might need two rounds on this section, so I'm sorry in advance," Mary says, interrupting my train of thought.

Am I abnormal or something? Why act surprised? It's a vagina, lady. Come on. It's perfectly normal. That's what you're supposed to tell me. Maybe I should name the vibrator Norm? Norm is good. No, Norm isn't good. Why am I even thinking about this? Why am I doing this? Holy mother of—no, that feels like it was a part of my body that should still be there.

I'm doing this because of Logan, the Beefcake Batman. All this pain for a man. Well, if that's the case, I might as well name my vibrator after him. Batman, it is. I've made a decision.

Shittttttt.

"This is the worst part, so just think about whatever name you've come up with. Ready?"

There? She's putting wax there? Why the hell would she be putting wax— "Mothertrucking, Batman, nooooo!"

"I'm sorry, dear, but we're all done now."

"No, I'm so sorry. I didn't mean to scream at you." I am humiliated. I can't believe I just screamed that out loud, and I'm sure Brielle heard.

"Oh, trust me, I've heard far worse."

"Let me just clean you up really quick. You might be a little puffy for a few hours, but you should be ready to get on that saddle by night time." I hate myself. I hate everything about this hour of my life. Why did I think this was a good idea? I feel like my vagina is on fire, and her little dabs from a wet wipe are doing nothing to soothe the burning sensation, nor did she hit every forsaken area. Whatever, I need to get the hell out of here, now.

"You know, we do have a laser option available. It may be something you want to consider in the future." I would probably laugh if I wasn't trying so hard not to cry, but I don't think I could ever lie on a bed like this again and ask for a repeat of what just happened I feel somehow violated, like the last of my remaining innocence was just stolen by Mary.

"Thank you, I'll take that into consideration."

"Take your time getting dressed, and I'll meet you out front."

I sit up, and it burns. Shit, does it burn! I swing my legs off the side of the table, and it burns. I stand up, and it burns. I'm burning inside and out, my asshole too. I'm on fire. I need to sit on ice. I need to kill Brielle. If slapping doesn't get me fired, killing her sure as hell will. Why would someone intentionally get this done more than once? Every bottle of body wax I've ever purchased explicitly says it should be used on the outside of the body only. Wax should not be anywhere near the inside of my body, yet there it was, all the way up there, and back there, and up and back there. I have been mutilated. When that hair grows back, I'm going to feel like I'm being stabbed by a thousand tiny needles all at one time, and God knows how many days in a row that will last.

It hurts to lift my legs. Everything hurts so badly. I now have a name for my vibrator, but I don't think I can get near myself with Batman, never mind Logan's Batman. I'm going to need to tell him I have a sunken ship inside of chapped lips.

CHAPTER 23

MAYBE A LITTLE ICE MIGHT HELP … NOPE. NO, IT WON'T

"Women do this every day, Hannah. I think you're overreacting," Brielle has the nerve to tell me.

"I need ice," I tell her.

"The burn will be gone by the time we get back to the office. Seriously, everything is going to be okay. You've been waxed before, haven't you?"

"Yes, but for maintenance, not for a deep cleaning."

Brielle leans back into her seat and focuses on driving through the wet snow. "At least she was fast, right? We've hardly been gone forty-five minutes."

"True. If anyone asks, we were shipping a couple of boxes down to the expo, and I needed your help getting them into the mail center."

"Did anyone see you walk out?" she asks.

"I doubt it."

Stepping out of the car and into the snow proves to be far more painful than when I left the spa, despite Brielle telling me I'd feel better by time we got back. Umm … *no,* Brielle. You were wrong on this one.

"Are you feeling better?" she chirps as we cross the parking lot.

I must be walking like I have a pole up my ass, just to ensure none of my effected parts rub against each other, so I don't think she needs to ask me. "No, Brielle. No, I'm not feeling better."

"Really?"

I choose not to respond, and I also choose not to speak to her throughout the elevator ride. I'm not blaming Brielle for what happened since I intended to get waxed, but I never would have opted for the package deal I got if it wasn't for her.

"Am I walking funny?" I finally speak just as we're about to enter the office.

"Just a little, but I'm sure no one will notice."

I do my best to fight the pain and scurry by Logan's cube, in fear of him calling me in, since there's no way I can stand right now.

Of course, I try to sit, but um, that's not working either. I was able get into the car seat, but sitting down in a right angle is not working. The burn has subsided, but now I feel like I'm tearing open. This can't be normal.

I sit sweating for more than a few minutes, kind of just waiting for the pain to go away or at least recede, but the tearing sensation continues to increase, and I don't know what I can do for relief.

I need to get a closer look at this situation, so I rush through the office, walking like a penguin, and make it into the—thankfully—empty bathroom. I lock the stall and drop my jeans. I just had to wear jeans today. Of course.

I place my hands on my hips and twist as far as I can to see my back end, and now the ripping, pulling, and burning is all happening at the same moment. Are my ass cheeks glued together? That can't happen. No. She's a professional. She has to have a license—not that I looked, but she must, right?

I grab each cheek and slowly try to peel them apart, but um, yeah, that's not working. Oh, dear. Oh no. Noooo. No, no, no.

My heart is beating in my throat, and I'm sweating through my shirt. I don't know what I'm going to do, or what I can do, for that matter.

I don't have my phone, and I can't just start screaming in here. Dammit to hell. I pull my pants back up and waddle back through the office, stopping in Brielle's cube. "I have a situation."

"Are you okay?" she asks. She's concerned this time. I can see it on her face, probably because she can see it all over mine.

"No, I need you to be quiet when I tell you this, but my ass cheeks are waxed together, like dried and stuck. I'm a human, freaking candle without a wick, Brielle."

Her mouth drops open, and it looks like I may have to catch her eyeballs in a second too. "What?"

"I'm not repeating it. You heard me," I tell her. "What am I supposed to do?"

"Ladies, ladies, ladies," Taylor says as he blocks the opening of Brielle's cube, cornering us into six square feet of open space. "How is all the prep work going for the event?"

"Great," Brielle pipes up. "Everything is just about done. We might even be able to get out of here early today." On the contrary, I haven't gotten a thing done in preparation for this week. I don't have any handouts or speaker notes prepared. I should have had this done last week, but everything has gone nuts, or nut. Nut. Why?

"Perfect. I was meaning to tell you that there is an attending vendor for a breast pump company looking for potential ad space. His name is Keith Champ. Hannah, I'm going to need you to turn up the charm with this one. Take some time and buy him a drink or two. Maybe even share your experiences about breast-pumps."

I don't know when I placed my hand on the side of my face or when I fell against the wall of the cube, but Taylor has managed to shock me yet again. He has no filter, and basically no brain. I've reported him to Human Resources so many times that I'm sure he has dirt on Human Resources since I've never seen him receive so much as a slap on the wrist for the crap he's pulled. Brett has sent him home a few times for the things he's said, yet here we are, talking breast pumps.

"Taylor, despite knowing *what* my job is this week, telling me to charm a vendor and talk about my experiences with breast pumps is highly inappropriate. You do know this, right?"

Taylor scratches the back of his head, then pushes his black-framed glasses up his nose. His glasses are prescription-free, their sole purpose to offer him an intelligent appearance. "Uh, Hannah, do I need to remind you that you spent an entire year in one of our offices pumping milk out of your breasts? Do you know how inappropriate it was to have to listen to that day after day? We didn't even get to watch. We could only listen. Now that, that is inappropriate. So, since we've been through *that* annoyance, I think you can do the company a solid this week. Am I wrong?"

"Yeah, man, you're wrong." Logan walks up from behind the cube wall I'm leaning on. "I just heard that whole thing." Logan is visibly enraged. His face is a dark shade of red, and his top lip is slightly curled to one side. "Get the hell out of her cube before I do something far worse than what Human Resources would do."

I can't lie and say I don't love having someone stick up for me here. It's been years of battling this crap on my own, and I've gotten nowhere. Last year at the expo, Taylor asked me to set up a kissing booth, along with assuring me that he and Nick would be the first in line. That same trip, I got calls at midnight with requests to visit their hotel rooms for a late-night rendezvous as if I were some paid prostitute. Each situation was reported. Each situation was ignored. No proof, no story. It's nice.

"Logan, don't bother trying to explain anything to him," I say. Can this situation get any more complicated right now? What I urgently need is to figure out how to re-split my ass cheeks apart from each other before I die of pain, but instead, I'm talking to the world's biggest pig.

"Aren't you just a temp?" Taylor asks Logan. "I'm sure you have some papers to be collating somewhere else, don't you?"

Logan takes in a deep breath, and his chest puffs out in response. He places his hands on top of the cube walls, now locking Taylor into this tight space with Brielle and me. "I don't think you should be talking to me that way."

"Temp, go away," Taylor says through unnerving laughter.

"His name is Logan Grier," Brielle tells him. I know why she added the Grier in, and now I'm watching Taylor's expression contort into utter humiliation. He had no idea.

"Wait a minute. You're Logan Grier, as in MVP of 2015, and the Logan Grier who was nearly castrated in front of over a million people?"

He had to throw that in there? Obviously, Logan was more than talented and a top player, yet his final moment on the field is what he's remembered for. How does he walk around with confidence like he does? No wonder he got gun shy with me the other day.

"How many Logan Griers do you know?" Logan asks Taylor.

"Just you," Taylor says with amazement. "I can't believe I'm standing in the presence of a baseball god."

"Taylor, I'm going to ask you to apologize to the ladies and move on with your day."

Taylor lifts his arm and squeezes his shoulder while stretching his neck in each direction. Then, he looks at me and babbles something before hightailing it out of the cube. "I think I've waited to see a look like that on his face since he started here five years ago. Thank you," I tell him. *Now if you only you knew of a way to separate my ass cheeks, I might fall in love with you right here and now.*

"You're just all sorts of amazing, aren't you Logan?" Brielle asks him with a wink. "Maybe you have more tricks up your sleeve to help our poor Hannah out today." Brielle winks at me as if I didn't ask her very nicely to keep her mouth shut about my situation.

"How can I help you, Hannah? Is everything okay?" I specifically asked Brielle not to react to my situation so I could avoid it being announced, and instead, she hints about it to Logan. She couldn't just wait two minutes for him to leave the cube. Unbelievable. Nope, it's believable. This girl cannot control her mouth.

"Ah, I think I'll just go handle the problem myself," I say, looking between the two of them.

"What's going on?"

"Nothing, it's fine, really. It's just girl stuff, no big deal."

"This isn't girl stuff," Brielle chirps. "This is a serious issue, Hannah. We may need to go back to see that woman. She can fix this."

I can either waddle out of here, or I can sink to the floor and scream out in pain—neither of which will make this any better.

"Seriously, what's going on?" Logan asks. There's more force behind his voice this time, which I find to be a turn on, but also very upsetting because I'm aware he's about to find out what I did this morning, for him, and what the outcome was, which will not benefit him in the least at the moment.

I love how Brielle can bring it up so casually and then look at me like a deer in headlights afterward as if it were a total accident. *It's not that hard, is it? To think before you speak?* I want to ask her.

More sweat is percolating under my skin, and I'm burning up. Nothing has gone smoothly—ha ha—with Logan, and I was so hoping tonight would go well, but this all seems to be a bad joke that's on repeat. First, I puke all over him, and now he's about to find out that my ass cheeks are waxed together because I needed to do a serious weed hack before he came anywhere near me again.

I think it's been about two full minutes since anyone has said anything, and there is no way for me to slip out of this cube.

"Logan, I can't ..."

"You can't what?"

"Her butt is glued shut," Brielle says as she slaps her hand over her mouth. Why do people do that, like it's involuntary? The human mind *can* control what is being said.

Logan laughs, and I know that *is* an involuntary reaction, but I think he's only laughing because he thinks Brielle is joking.

"It's not a joke," I tell him. My face probably matches my whole nether region right now.

"How is that possible?" Logan's disposition straightens out, accompanying a more serious tone.

"Wax. Our poor girl is like a human candle right now, and we don't know how to fix the problem."

Logan closes his eyes and presses his hand over his face. "Hold up, you had the inside of your ass waxed?"

"Yeah, Logan, it's called a Hollywood glow, so obviously, many people do it," Brielle says in my defense.

"Just because you hear Hollywood does something does not mean it's common," he corrects her. "And have you done this sort of thing before?"

"No!" I'm quick to blurt out. "Never. It was her idea." I'm pointing to Brielle like I'm in fifth grade because it's just the easiest way to handle the repercussions of my stupid decision, and she did insist on the Hollywood Glow.

Logan looks to be chewing on the inside of his cheek as I've seen him do a few times now while thinking intently about something. "Wax melts, so we have to reheat it somehow."

"When did this become a 'we' thing?" I ask. No one is coming anywhere near my ass.

"Can you heat up your ass alone? I mean, all the power to you if you can, but I'm not sure I'd have the capability of doing such a thing."

"Heat up my ass?"

"How else are you going to melt the wax?"

This is getting worse by the second. "I think I should just go back to the woman who did this."

"Here, I'll take you," Logan says.

"I'm not prepared for the event tomorrow, not at all. I still have hours' worth of work to do."

"I have it all under control," he says.

"How? I didn't go over everything with you."

"What else was left?" he asks.

"I don't even know right now. I can't even think straight with the pain I have down there. And I have to figure out how to get this fixed before Cora's school calls with an early snow dismissal or something inside of me tears."

"Can you do whatever is left from home?" Logan asks. He's beginning to look more concerned than I feel, which is making me a whole lot more nervous.

"Yeah, I suppose I can."

"Give me two minutes," Logan says.

He walks off toward the offices, and he's on a mission I'm not sure I want to know about. "What the hell, Bri?"

"I'm sorry. I'm so sorry. It slipped. I didn't mean to say it, but it just blah— It blurted out of me, and I couldn't stop it."

"Thanks, Brielle. Let it be known, I have all intentions of storming out of your cube because I'm pissed, but I'm not sure I can move."

I reach into my back pocket for my phone and realize I don't have it on me. I went to the bathroom in such a panic, I left it on my desk. I've been worried about school getting canceled, and I have no clue if they tried to call or email. Shit.

"Help me up," I tell Brielle, reaching my arm out to her. I'm in an odd squatting position against the wall, and the thought of moving seems like the worst idea ever. "Actually, don't help me up. Could you go get my phone off my desk? I'm worried the school tried to call."

Brielle scurries off in her four-inch-heeled boots and slams her hand down on my desk while making contact with my phone. It's never hard to figure out where that girl is with the amount of noise she makes. She has it back to me in a matter of seconds, and I'm relieved to see the school hasn't tried to call. I should just check the damn forecast already.

"Folks," Alan says from outside his office. "Can I have your attention for a minute." Everyone in their cubicles turns to face the corner office. "I know most of you are leaving in the morning for the expo, but the snow isn't expected to stop until about midnight tonight. So, in hopes of everyone getting home safely and having everything in order for the morning, I'd like you all to go home now and finish up whatever remaining work you have remotely. I'll be accessible all evening through email, so please take extra caution while driving home." All I heard was, blah blah blah, I don't want the company to be sued, and work all night so you can be exhausted in the morning when you're digging out your driveway in preparation for an airport transfer.

Logan returns to Brielle's cube with my coat and a box of papers. "Let's go."

"Did you just do that?"

"Oh, you, and your cute little tight-end, I have a certain finesse with my words. Haven't you learned that yet?"

"Tight-end?" I repeat. "Really? Don't you think it's a little soon to be making jokes, considering I'm still suffering right now?"

"Don't yell, you might split the seam," he chuckles, obviously having fun with this situation, at my expense.

"While you're making jokes, I need to figure out how to drive home, and I can't sit, so please have some empathy."

"Empathy?" he laughs. "Should I remind you about my 'flat tire'? Imagine sitting on that thing for the first two months."

Fair point. "Come on, I'm here to help you," Logan continues. "We'll get you fixed up. Think of it as a butt lift. It's training your muscles to stick together and be perky."

"Are you saying I need a butt lift?" My butt isn't flat, but it doesn't stand up all perky and crap like Tiana's does because it blew up like a freaking balloon when I was pregnant, then deflated.

"That wasn't what I was saying," Logan corrects my thoughts and adds a smile for good measure. "Where is this wax place?"

"Just down the street," I tell him.

"Hawaiian Breeze Spa?" he questions.

How does he know ... "Yes?"

"Oh no, did you happen to get waxed by Mary?"

"Logan, how do you know so much about Hawaiian Breeze Spa? And Mary, for that matter?"

"Let's just say ... I know her."

CHAPTER 24

IT'S STILL MONDAY, ALSO KNOWN AS THE MOST MORTIFYING DAY OF MY LIFE. TAKE TWO

"You know Mary?"

"I know Mary," he repeats.

"How do you know her?"

"Mary used to work for my team. She was fired and relocated to the suburbs. Then she opened up a shop."

"I'm sorry, what exactly did Mary do for a bunch of baseball players?" I'm holding myself up against the railing in the elevator, hoping the bouncing doesn't do any further damage.

"We waxed stuff. It's really not important," he says.

"Yeah, it is kind of important. What did you wax? Now that you've brought it up, I need to know."

Logan glances over at me with a raised brow and a smirk. "How about you use your wildest imagination and go with that." This man is turning me on with just a look and the words coming from his mouth.

"So, you all just took turns getting waxed by Mary?" I know I'm pushing, but it's distracting me from my situation. "Like, was she in the locker room and you all just stood in line waiting for your turn?"

"Hannah," he says sweetly. "I'm more than happy to help you today, and even happier to spend time with you tonight, but I'm a little less excited to talk about anything that has to do with baseball, or the life that accompanied it." He had to throw in that card just to make me feel guilty enough to stop asking questions.

"Fine. I'll stop for now, but don't think this is over yet."

"On a scale of one to ten, how much pain are you in right now?" he asks.

"Are you a nurse or a doctor?"

"No, but I spent enough time with them to know how they gauge pain. Considering you've been through childbirth, I have an idea what to base your pain level on and whether we should go directly to the hospital or back to the spa."

"I don't want to go to the hospital, and I have to be free to get Cora off the bus. That's if they don't cancel school early. The ER will take hours since I won't be on their top list of emergencies."

"This *is* kind of an emergency. What if you have to go to the bathroom or pass gas?" These thoughts hadn't crossed my mind, nor did I want them to because now I'm sitting here wondering what's going to happen if either of those two situations come up before I'm repaired. Will I just explode? This is serious.

We walk—I hobble—outside into the snow that's piling up to several inches at this point. I hear the plows, which is good since that means they're planning to keep up with it. I also hope that means they aren't planning to let school out early. "I really don't know how I'm going to drive like this," I tell Logan.

"Well, let me drive you to Mary's first, and then after that, we'll come back for your car." Minivan. You can say it, it's fine. I'm not embarrassed by it. I can make a minivan look hot, even with my candlestick ass.

"Okay, so my next question is about how I'm going to get into your monstrously high truck?" We shuffle through the snow and up to the passenger side of the truck. He opens the door and scoops me up with what feels like little effort. "This really hurts."

"Did you do this for me?" he asks quietly.

I close my eyes because he's staring at me with the most adorable smile I've ever seen on a man, and I'm melting, which would be awesome if I meant that literally. "I did. I wanted to give you what you're probably used to being with."

"That's ridiculous because you have no idea what I like or what kind of women I've been with."

"Well, Brielle appointed herself as my waxing mentor, and I was also basing it on my own experience because I know for a fact that's it's horrible to get a pube stuck in your teeth."

Logan jerks his head back, and a small gust of snow blows off the top of his head. "How in the world did that happen?"

"He was covered from base to ... like, halfway up. I was trying to show off my skills, and all of the sudden I felt like there was floss in my teeth. I told him I didn't feel well and made him go home. End of story."

"First, I don't think that's normal. I mean, I've unfortunately seen my fair share of dicks in the locker room, and I don't believe I've ever seen someone with that much pubic hair. Second, I can see why you might be scarred."

Okayyy, enough about my history with bad dates. "Anyway, here I am, and I'm waxed shut."

"I have a feeling you'll laugh about this someday," he says with a soft smile.

"I have a feeling I'll still be crying about this someday, but I'd like to go with your theory for the time being."

"I think it's adorable that you cared enough to do that during a snowstorm and when you have a lot of work to get done. You must really like me, huh?" he says lightheartedly, giving me a gentle squeeze.

"We survived the man flu, and we're still speaking to each other. I think that should answer your question on whether I like you." I try to laugh, but it hurts.

"I didn't think I was that bad. Compared to other times I've been sick, I think I kept myself under control for the most part." He's calling that controlled? Oy.

"Logan, you needed liquid Advil ..."

"So?"

"I think we should start over and pretend like this last week never happened. What do you say?" I offer.

"I say we do that after we figure out how to tear your ass apart."

"Right." I tried to forget my current predicament for a moment, but now I remember why I'm scooped up into this man's cradling arms.

He curls me into his chest slowly, careful not to cause me any pain. "I really do like you," he mutters quietly, under his breath.

With the snow falling around us and his warm body blocking out the frigid wind, I completely feel the exact same way. I'd tell him so but his lips are moving in toward mine, and I let my gaze linger on his face for an extra second, enjoying the sight of his dimples up close, noticing the faint freckles on his nose. As he moves closer to me, the scent of his spicy cologne mixed with the fresh snow forces my eyes closed just as his lips touch mine. He must have been chewing gum or had a mint recently because his breath is cool against me and strikes my lips with chills colder than the wind around us.

He's a slow kisser and apparently likes to take his time moving from my top lip to the bottom, then covering all the parts in between. The tip of his tongue swirls around mine, leaving a cool sensation in its trail.

I'm lost in the moment, forgetting about everything else.

The connection between us is more than it's ever been, more than I thought it was. I feel something deep inside that makes all the wrong seem right.

He hugs me to him a little tighter, and suddenly I know that I'd love to be his for as long as he'll hang onto me. I'd even stay out in this cold snow in his arms with my ass cheeks glued together for an eternity, if life paused like this.

My heart thaws despite the opposing elements, and my pulse is erratic, speeding at a pace I haven't felt in many years. Logan has brought me to a new place that I want to continue to exist in. I'm ready to feel the happiness I've avoided and yet missed, at the same time.

When he pulls away, I struggle to catch my missing breaths, and each one burns against the cold air surrounding us. With a light kiss on my nose and my forehead, Logan slides me into the truck and lowers the seat back a bit, so I'm in at an angle. "How's that?" My senses are too overwhelmed for words right now, so I nod with a bashful smile.

I close my eyes throughout the short trip, trying to focus on something else, but the only thing I can think about is that kiss and the one from the other night. This man knows his way around a pair of lips, a talent I might have enjoyed later in other areas as well, but now I'll probably have to wear a diaper or something—so much for a distraction.

The crunching of the snow beneath the truck's tires becomes louder as we pull into the lot, and I tighten my fists, preparing for even the slightest jerk as we come to a stop. I've never thought about how much I use my butt muscles, but it's a lot, which makes me wonder why I don't have an ass of steel.

"I'll help you out," Logan says as he steps out of the truck. He's halfway around the front of the hood when I watch him take a sharp left toward the front door of the spa, followed by his hands cupping over the glass door so he can look inside. He stands there for a few long seconds before twisting toward the truck and giving me a look of dread.

I know what the look says. It means they closed early because of the snowstorm, and I'm completely screwed. Shit! I'm leaving for Florida in less than eighteen hours. Logan makes his way back to the truck and releases a breath of exasperation as he closes his door. "Don't worry. I think I know how we can fix this."

"Hot water?" I question.

"No, that won't help. Let me just run into the grocery store really quick." Thankfully, the store is in the next plaza over, but I still don't know how I'm going to manage to drive home. I can't move my foot up and down over and over. It will kill me.

Logan is quick with his trip into the grocery store and returns with more than one bag, which makes me wonder what else he got, and if he needs multiple items to deal with this situation. Maybe he doesn't have one solution, but a few to try. I'd rather go with a sure plan if that's an option. Beggars can't be choosers, though.

"What did you get?" I ask as he switches the gear into reverse. "Don't worry. Just know I have a plan to take care of you, okay?"

I feel kind of sick right now. Are we ever going to get a chance to interact under normal circumstances? "What about my car?"

"It'll be fine in the parking lot until we return at the end of the week. No one is going to tow it, and I've seen that a couple of cars in the lot haven't moved since I started working there." My instinct tells me it's a bad idea to leave my car there, but my ass is saying something different.

The snow is coming down super hard too, and the van has never been great with more than a few inches on the roads. They may be plowing the main streets, but I'm sure the backroads and my neighborhood haven't seen so much as a shovel yet.

It takes much longer than usual to get home, but I'm thankful for Logan's four-wheel drive and skidding skills. We pull into the driveway, spotting Tiana in her yard with their stupid little dog. She's wearing a fur coat, pink Uggs, and a Burberry scarf, with her hair loosely tussled up in a purposefully messy bun. I think I know her well enough to assume she has only fixed herself up today to take the dog outside in her "casual snow gear."

"I don't want them to know," I tell Logan. I'm sure he already assumed, but I just want to make sure it's at the forefront of his mind.

"Of course, I can understand that," he says. "Let me help you, though." He hops out of the truck, and I open my door at the same time, so I'm not acting like some priss who needs her door opened, as well as needing to be carried inside.

Logan helps me down into the snow, and I somehow need to figure out how to either lift my feet or use enough of my muscles to shuffle against the snow. "I can't move," I tell Logan, who's waiting for me to walk ahead. He reaches into the truck and grabs the bags, then slides an arm around my back and opposite hip. He lifts me enough so it looks like I'm walking on top of the snow. If Tiana peers over, she'll surely know something is up, though. *Please don't look over here.*

We make it all the way to the front step before she turns around with her arms wrapped around her chest. "Oh, hi!" she shouts over. "Just taking Chicklette for a tinkle." A tinkle. Who talks like that? I reach into my pocket for my key and unlock the front door, now staring at the one last step before we make it inside. Logan stands still for the moment, waiting to see if I make a move, but I don't because I can't figure out how to lift either of my legs without the tearing sensation resurrecting. "Is everything okay, Hannah?"

"She just sprained her ankle at work, she'll be fine. Nothing a little ice can't fix."

"Oh no, I can look at it for you. I had to take first aid during my yoga certification class. Do you want me to look?"

"No!" we both shout at the same time. That doesn't seem weird or obvious at all. "Thanks, though." I don't think our exasperated response was helpful because she's looking at us like we're lunatics. Whatever, it's the same way I look at them all the time.

Finally inside, Logan closes the door and locks it, then helps me over to the living room couch. I haven't spent so much time in this damn room in forever, and now I can't seem to escape it. I don't think I'll ever have a good memory of this end of the house. "I'm mortified," I tell him.

"My ex-wife had to put ointment on my ball sack scar for a month.

While she did that, she curled her lip in disgust and touched it with a Q-tip as if she were touching a piece of dog shit. It was pretty much the highlight of my adult life," he says, sarcastically.

"Can you dim the lights first. I don't even know what my ass looks like in broad daylight, and I don't think I want you to know either."

"Hannah, I can handle whatever it is, okay?"

"What are you using to ... fix ... this?"

"Warm coconut oil," he answers. So normally, I would think that sounds amazing, and kind of sexy hot as well, but I'm sure this occasion will ruin the idea of hot oil for me.

"Just lie down on your stomach and try to relax."

The last time I heard that I slapped Rick's dick. That went over as well as this is probably going to go.

CHAPTER 25

THERE IS NO COMING BACK FROM THIS ...

"Is it hot?" I ask him while he's preparing the oil.

"Not scalding, but very warm," he responds.

"Is it going to hurt?"

"You've given birth. I think you'll be okay," he continues.

Logan slides a towel beneath me since I'm on the couch. "All right, I'm going to slide your jeans down," he explains.

"Logan?"

"Yeah?"

"Don't talk like you're a doctor."

"I'm sorry." He clears his throat. "Hey baby, I'm about to rip these nasty pants off of that sweet ass. Now, don't go putting up a fight about it or I'll have to get rough, and you don't want that, do you?" His voice is low, guttural, and raunchy as hell.

"Logan?"

"Yeah?"

"Don't turn me on right now, either."

"Sorry, sorry." He clears his voice again. "I should probably just not say anything then."

"Yeah, that's a good idea." I place my face in the crook of my folded arms and close my eyes in hopes of daydreaming about another place and time.

Then, I feel the warm, satisfying oil coat my butt cheeks. I imagined this feeling a lot worse, but I'm also sure the worst of it isn't over yet.

"For the record, you have a hot as hell ass, even with it glued together," Logan whispers into my ear. His words are like the tip of a feather, sending shivers down my spine, which I shouldn't be thinking about. I find myself feeling a strange mixture of embarrassment, gratitude, and arousal.

The palms of his hands connect with my bare, overly sensitive skin, and I flinch. "I'm going to massage the oil in so it breaks the wax apart. Try to hold still." His voice is in its normal gruffness, which is still not making this easier, but I can't tell him to stop talking again. He's helping me in a way that I wouldn't have been helped today if he didn't volunteer.

There isn't any pain like I'd been expecting, or feeling for that matter, but there's a crackling sensation, which I think is a good thing.

"It's starting to work," he says.

"It is?" My excitement is muffled by my sleeve, but I hope he's not blowing smoke up my—yeah, that's not happening.

"I need a little more oil." Oh, for the love of shit. All the muscles in my frontal region are tight and throbbing. I can't be getting excited about this. I should just be thankful it's working.

More oil drips slowly down the crevice, and his finger follows. My breaths quicken and my chest uncontrollably heaves up and down. It's obvious enough that he can't ignore what he's doing to me.

His fingers continue to massage the affected area, working his way into the dent he's slowing melting. Logan climbs over me and straddles my body as he continues working the wax in, and I'm doing everything in my power to keep my body from moving on its own or wavering against his hands.

"I'm so close," he tells me in a honeyed voice. "Almost there."

"Me too," I mistakenly blurt out.

Oh crap. That was out loud.

He laughs quietly. "Don't get ahead of yourself. I need to clean you up a bit, but then you should be as good as new."

"Seriously? It's gone?"

"Juuuuust about." He runs off to the kitchen and the cool breeze from his motion makes me want to pull a blanket over my backside, but I'm still scared to move.

Refusing to look up from my arms, the shuffling footsteps return, and a new wind with the scent of his cologne fills the air around me.

A warm cloth is pressed into the crevices and dabbed along every square inch of my rear. Nothing hotter than being wiped by a deliciously hot man who was once interested in me before this shitty situation.

"You're clean."

No, I. Am. Not.

He slides my jeans back up to where they belong and runs his hand soothingly along my back. "Feel better?"

"Yes, but humiliated. However, that seems to be our thing."

"We have a thing. That's better than nothing, right?"

"It is." I push myself up, testing out the use of my ass, and it's like nothing ever happened, except the slightly raw burn from the wax. Everything seems to have calmed down, and I feel much better. "I don't think we'll ever be able to look at each other normally again." I'm saying this more on his behalf than mine. I know he's embarrassed about his situation, but I didn't have to wipe his ass.

"Probably," he says. This sucks. I had hope. I shouldn't have had hope. I knew Logan was a long shot for me. I'm not his type. I'm washed up, not-so-perfect, and busy caring for a daughter. I'm sticking with my thoughts that he could have any woman he wants, even with a flat tire.

He presses his hands into his knee and stands up, letting out a slight groan. "Are you okay?"

"Yeah, my back sucks. I'm fine, though."

"I've heard athletes' bodies hate them after they quit playing."

"Whoever you heard that from was right."

"Maybe you should still be playing," I suggest.

He laughs like I told a good joke, but I was serious. "That's funny. I'm thirty-five. Even if I didn't have my accident, I wouldn't be playing for much longer anyway. Getting back into it now would take too long, and I don't have enough time left to get back to the place I was at."

"Do you still love it?" I ask.

"Always."

"You should coach, then. Do that instead of temping at a woman's magazine."

He presses his hands into the small of his back and leans into them. "Are you firing me, boss?"

"No, but you're meant for better things in this world."

"So are you, you know?"

Now it's my turn to laugh. "Right. I don't even know what I'm capable of besides changing a diaper, cleaning up vomit, and packing a lunch. My job is mindless, and I'm surrounded by a whole lot of stupidity, as you witnessed today."

"What's your dream, Hannah?"

I lean into the couch and release a long exhale, remembering back to about a year ago when the only thing I wanted to do was lock myself inside, homeschool Cora, and have everything delivered to my house. While I know that's not a permanent solution to anyone's life, it would be nice for just a week.

"Don't laugh."

"Never," he agrees with a grin.

"I want to lock myself inside this house, make it look like no one's home, and hide from the world. I want to sit in yoga pants all day, eat what I want, and watch as much TV as humanly possible."

Logan takes a seat next to me on the couch. "That does sound like a dream come true, but that won't keep you happy forever. Trust me. You'll be bored in a week. I tried it."

"Then, just a week of quiet and solitude would satisfy my desire."

"Sounds good, Hannah." Logan stands up and grabs his coat off the reclining chair in the corner. "I have to get going. I forgot a few things I need for the trip tomorrow."

My heart pounds angrily against my ribcage as I come to the unfortunate realization that I truly scared him away. How could I not have? How did it take this long? "Right, yeah, the trip." I'm not asking him if he's coming back. I don't want to know.

He finds the remote under his coat and turns on the TV for me. "Here, relax for a bit before Cora comes home."

"Thanks, but I have to finish up my work."

"Right." Logan has this switch. Things are great, and then they're gone. I don't get it.

He slips his coat on and waves at me before heading for the door. *A wave.*

He kissed me just an hour ago, and now I'm getting a wave.

"See ya," I tell him, trying not to sound completely heartbroken.

When the door closes, my mind goes back to the place that tells me I need to get the hell out of this miserable state and far away from everything I've ever known before, but it takes less than a second to remember Cora is my permanent anchor to this area.

While I don't need to be living in this house or next door to Rick, going much further won't do anyone any good. I'm stuck because of that man, and it's the worst feeling in the entire world.

I grab the blanket from the top of the couch and wrap it around myself, hugging it tightly to release some of the tension in my chest. Tears threaten the corners of my eyes, and I know once they start, they won't stop. My eyes are like two bottles of Champagne ready to explode, and it's been that way for a year since I told myself I was no longer allowed to feel sorry for myself.

I need to rally, get my shit done for tomorrow, pack, and move on with my life. It is what it is. I chose this path, and now I need to live with it. Alone.

I stand up, feeling only a slight ache in the muscles that were clenched for way too long. At least I can avoid squats for a couple of weeks after that workout.

I turn the TV on to the music station and crank up the volume to the loudest setting. I have two hours before Cora comes home, and I'm getting everything done.

I head through the foyer toward the stairs, and the front door flies open, scaring the shit out of me, which isn't funny because that unfortunate situation wouldn't surprise me at this point. Logan is standing on the front mat, covered in snow, looking like a hot, grizzly mountain man. "Did you forget something?" My voice is less than enthusiastic, but I don't know how I should sound right now.

He barrels toward me, and his shoulder collides with the soft part of my stomach. My legs are in the air, and I fold over him like a sack of sand. He's trekking up the stairs with me in tow, and I'm in shock.

I close my eyes from the swaying motion below me, and I don't reopen them until I feel the plush contour of my bed cradle my weight. Logan is tearing his clothes off faster than I've ever seen another person undress, and I'm staring with awe. Holy crap, he's hot.

I wonder if Mary waxes his chest, because it's so bare, it's shiny. Maybe it's sweat, or maybe it's just his natural glow.

I'm almost expecting him to stop when he works his way down to his pants, but he doesn't slow down. His pants are off and the only thing left is his black boxer briefs, which do little to conceal his magnitude. Oh, geez.

He falls on top of me and maneuvers the buttons on my flannel shirt with simple flicks of his fingers, and since he's already versed in removing my jeans, there's no hindrance there.

His hands cradle my head as he works his lips against mine forcefully, passionately, with only small breaths escaping in between the brief seconds it takes us to switch positions. His cold fingers slide under the hem of my panties, and it causes a frenzy of pulsating thrills. His hands slide the thin material down my legs until they fall to the ground.

I debate whether to return the favor or give him the time he needs to remove the last article of clothing between us, but less than a second passes before his briefs are off and lying with mine on the ground.

The blankets are torn from below us and billow down slowly as his body melds against mine. All of him is against all of me, and I'm waiting for the moment to end as I wake up. This is unreal. He's unreal. He's like this sublime specimen of a man, and I refuse to close my eyes and miss even a second of what's about to happen.

He grabs his cock and thrusts into me. There isn't resistance, only a warm welcoming. His lips relentlessly work down my neck, then to my breasts. He gently brushes the scruff of his short beard against my nipples, causing them to pebble in response to the stimulating sensation.

His length hits me in the right spot almost immediately, and I know this isn't going to last long for me because I was almost there just a half hour ago. His jaw tightens, and his eyes close as he pumps in and out while soft groans roar in his throat. "I have imagined this for an entire damn week, but I didn't think I stood a chance with you," he mutters.

"Me?" I cry out.

"You're goddamn perfect."

I want to tell him it's nothing in comparison to what he brings to the table, but that's too much talking for the moment.

"Logan, I'm—I'm close, I don't know how much longer—"

He drives into me harder, and just as I think my body can't hold on any longer, it's like I rebound, and the incoming wave of rigorous blasts keeps building.

As I'm teetering on the edge of a cliff, Logan's teeth graze the skin of my neck like he's hungry for me, and it's the final push that forces my body to release and give into the combustion of a million exhilarating sensations. "Holy shit, holy shit, Logan, oh my—"

"Come for me, baby. Don't let it stop."

He's still riding in full force, and I'm grappling the sheets so tightly my nails might tear through the fabric. It's like an endless loop of orgasms as he spills into me.

Drops of sweat fall from Logan's chest and dribble onto my breasts, acting like tiny triggering aftershocks that rock through my body.

Never. It has never felt like that for me ... more intense than I imagined.

Logan collapses most of his weight to the side of me but lowers his chest to mine. His fingers comb through my hair, and he smiles as if he just won a twelve-inning game. "I thought you left. I thought I scared you away," I tell him my thoughts from a half hour earlier.

"Nah, I was playing with you. I was going to make you sweat it out a little longer, but it's seriously shitty outside."

"Is playing hard to get your game?" I laugh softly, but he had to know he was stirring me up.

"I just needed to set the mood after your incident." Clever. I find it mildly humorous he thought to do that ... because separation was obviously needed between the humiliation and hotness.

"Do you actually have your things for the trip tomorrow?" I ask him.

"Of course, I do."

"So, you just knew I was going to agree to let you sleep over tonight?" Am I that transparently desperate?

"I had no idea if that would be the case or not, but I wanted to be prepared if you happened to agree."

"Are you homeless?" I'm not sure why the question spills out of my mouth, but I've just realized that I have no clue where he lives. Yet, he's been here way more than any other man I have casually dated for just a week, and we haven't even been on a real date. This is ridiculous. What *am* I doing?

"I am not homeless. I live about twenty minutes from here."

"House, apartment, condo?" I question.

"A condo in a high-rise on top of a mall."

"You live on top of the mall and haven't invited me over?"

"I was thinking, after we go out on a first date, I'd invite you back to my place."

Questions are pouring into my head. I think I've been simply infatuated with the idea of this former pro-athlete and his perfect package.

"Why are you really working as a temp?"

"I was bored."

"Why not take up a hobby?"

Logan turns on his side to face me and props his head up with his fist. "Honestly?"

"I'd prefer that," I tell him.

"A friend told me if I wanted to meet a woman, the best place to do it would be in a corporate office."

I feel a little shaken by his statement. His only intention for taking a temporary job was to meet someone. I guess someone should have warned him it was slim pickings at the office he was being placed at. "I guess you got the raw end of that deal."

"How so?" he asks. If he's playing me, he's playing me good right now.

"Well, you had a choice between Brielle and me, and unless you're a one in a million type of guy who isn't into the Miss America look-alike, why set your eyes on me?"

Logan looks taken aback by my comments, but I probably appear the same way because I'm confused and not so sure I like what I've just heard. "First, Brielle isn't my type. She's exactly like my ex-wife, and I've been avoiding the Brielles of the world since my divorce."

"So, you're looking more for the washed-up, motherly brand?" That sounded kind of bitchy, but seriously, how am I supposed to believe that any guy would choose me over Brielle, and why is this just now crossing my mind? I need a good smack on the back of my head.

"Is that how you see yourself?" he asks while sitting upright. "Can I just tell you something? Your sporadic comments here and there about your looks and how I shouldn't look at you in the light, all that crap, I've heard everything you've said about yourself. Now, I don't know what you see when you look in the mirror, but I see this brilliant woman with a strong personality and gorgeous features."

"Logan, you don't have to do this ..."

"Jesus, Hannah, quit being so obnoxious for a second."

I guess I've met my match. "Hey, I'm not being obnoxious. That's rude."

"Then, quit it. Yes, you're a mother, and I think that's amazing because it's something I wanted to watch in life—a woman I love, mother our child. On top of that, you're a single mom with a douchey ex-husband, yet you wake up every morning and put one foot in front of the other like every other schmuck in that office, but you do it with grace and confidence. I've already told you how hot I think that is, so if you don't believe me, I'm sorry, but I'm glad as hell I got placed in your office because otherwise, I may never have met you in person. You know, there was this little voice in my head when I laid eyes on you that said, 'Dude, you did the right thing. She's something'."

I'm at a loss for words, and I'm not sure I understand everything he just said. This type of thing doesn't happen to me. I end up with crappy men because I've been the shallow one who goes for looks rather than a personality. Granted, I was in my twenties when I had that mindset and ended up in a ten-year marriage with Rick, but I blame myself for not being smarter back then. "I'm not fighting it, and what do you mean by, you may never have met me in … person?"

"Stop what-if'ing it," he says. "Live, Hannah. You deserve to do that for yourself."

"No one has ever said any of that to me," I tell him, briefly forgetting my question about meeting me in person.

"Even with all that Words With Friends you do?"

"How did you know—"

A smile perks at the corner of his lips. "I've been known to play a few games. Actually, it's funny. I started talking to this one chick who was a total workaholic and too busy with her daughter to agree to one simple date. Three times I tried to meet her, and she just kept canceling."

I close my eyes, and my heart flutters into a fit of erratic thuds. "You." *Dickle15.*

"You are a tough one to nail down."

"You took a temp job—"

"So I could do it the old-fashioned way … yeah."

Wow. Whoa, I am speechless. Should I be creeped out or flattered? "That's kind of a creepy thing to do," I tell him.

"I thought you might say that."

"And you're telling me after we slept together," I remind him.

Now, I'm back to the "why me" part of this. A hotshot who could have anyone tricks me into meeting him.

"Online dating sucks, especially while playing the millennial version of Scrabble. I wasn't sure I could go back and try things the old-fashioned way, but I wasn't ready to give up. I'm sorry if it was wrong and deceitful. I should have been honest up front, but things spiraled quickly, and it kept getting harder to come clean."

I may have a panic attack. I slide out of bed, taking one of the sheets with me, and close myself into the bathroom, needing a minute to think.

CHAPTER 26

DICKLE. WHAT IS A DICKLE?

Logan is Dickle15. Dickle15 is Logan. That's why he stopped talking to me. I've been sending him messages throughout the week, getting no response, and he's been here all along. I'm not sure I'm capable of digesting this.

I've been sitting on the toilet seat cover for twenty-five minutes, staring at the speckles within the tiled floor. It's creepy, right? I should be against this behavior. He joined a company to meet me. That's borderline stalkerish—it's something Brielle would do. I did tell him where I work, so that was my mistake. He never specified his career to me, and I never pushed the topic. I also did cancel our dates, but it was because I was scared of meeting any more creeps online, and now, here I am.

What would I be teaching Cora if I went along with this type of behavior? Granted, she may never find out, but I'm trying to teach her to avoid men like him.

Cora. It's almost time to get her.

I step out of the bathroom and grab my clothes from the floor, finding Logan staring out the window from the bed. He hasn't moved an inch since I went into the bathroom. "I'm sorry," he says.

"I have to go get Cora off the bus."

"Okay, I'll get my stuff together and head out."

"Just wait, okay. I need more time to think. I'll be back in a few minutes."

I dress quickly, avoiding eye contact with the perfect-looking man in my bed. That's my problem. Perfect-looking men.

I run out of the bedroom and down the stairs, throwing my coat on and slipping into my snow boots, leaving the laces loose and hanging to the sides.

The winds are almost unbearable, and the snow is blowing sideways, directly into my face. It's hard to see, it's so bad. Why didn't they close school earlier? There's easily half a foot already.

I reach the bottom of the short hill and pull the hood of my jacket down over my face to block out some of the snow.

Somehow, by the grace of God, the bus is on time, and Cora jumps off the big step with her usual perky smile. I never should have let Logan in the house before I knew him well enough to let Cora get mixed up in this.

"How was school, kiddo?" I ask her, trying to hide the pain in my voice.

"It was boring. We couldn't go out and play today."

"You wouldn't want to be outside in this for too long. Trust me," I tell her.

As we walk closer to the house, she notices Logan's truck in the driveway. "Logan is over?" she asks with excitement—excitement I'd rather not hear.

"He is. He had to help me with something for work," I lie.

"So, he's not staying again?"

"I'm not sure right now, sweetie." This blows. I should have known something was up. Life doesn't just happen the way it happened. He was so wrong to do what he did. It was deceitful, and I promised myself I'd never end up with someone like that again, not after what Rick did to me.

We walk inside, and Cora shakes the snow off her body and tosses her boots to the side. I follow suit, then hang everything up and place our wet boots on the doormat next to Logan's.

"Beefcake Batman!" she shouts. She runs into the kitchen as if she knows exactly where he is.

"Miss Cora," he says with a smile I can hear. "How was your snowy school day?"

Cora chatters more about her day in thirty-seconds to him than she did with me on the three-minute walk home. I hate that she likes him.

I hate that he's good with her. I hate that I let him into my house with Cora home, now that I know what he did.

"Can you make a snack?" Cora asks Logan.

"You may want to ask your mom first," he tells her.

"I think you should go, and I'll cancel your flight for tomorrow. Just do paperwork in the office until I decide what to do with you."

Logan looks heartbroken, and I feel the same. I liked Dickle15. I knew if we met it would most likely be different. Then he stopped talking, and it proved to be a lose/lose situation.

"I'm so sorry," he says while grabbing his coat and boots.

"Mom, I don't want Beefcake Batman to leave. It's snowing really bad too."

I can't listen to Cora. She doesn't understand, although I don't understand either.

"I put up with crap like this for years, Logan. I just can't."

"Crap?" he responds. "I wanted to meet you so fff—orking bad," he catches himself before cussing in front of Cora.

"Well, now you have, and you can go … spoon yourself tonight."

Cora giggles. "What are you talking about? I can give you guys a fork and a spoon. They're right here."

"You wanted to meet me because I knew nothing about baseball, right?" I retaliate. We had that conversation more than a few times, and now I know why. I hadn't heard of him, and I was safe.

"No. Well, yes, I wanted a clean start. I didn't want to be known as 'that guy' anymore. You can't fault me for that."

"I don't." I press my hand onto the kitchen island, needing it to hold me up as my heavy heart tries to anchor me to the ground. "I blame you for not being honest."

He ties his second boot and stands back up. "Haven't you ever wanted something so badly, you went about getting it in the wrong way?"

I can't think clearly enough to answer his question, so I don't. "Please be careful driving home."

He looks down and away from me as he opens the door. "Wait!" Cora says while running over to him. She wraps her arms around him, looking like a little doll compared to Logan's size. She yanks at his shirt, pulling him down to his knees and whispers something into his ear.

"Cora," I say, wanting her to stop doing whatever she's doing. In response to me calling her, she releases his shirt and runs back over to me. Logan looks up at me once more, then leaves a cold gust of wind in his place as the door closes after him.

"What did you just say to him?" I ask Cora.

"I just ... I told him I'd miss him." She's lying.

"Let's get your homework done so we can pack you up for your dad's. I'm leaving in the morning for Florida, remember?"

"I remember," she says with a sigh. "I wish I could go with you."

"Me too, sweetie."

"I like Beefcake Batman," she says. I wish she would stop calling him that.

"I know, but some people come and go from our lives and we need to be okay with that. What's important is that we always have each other, and we'll never come and go. Do you understand that?"

"No," she says as she climbs up on the bar stool. "He likes you too. So, why would you make him leave?"

Her words are making this harder and the hurt worse, and I'm still trying my best to digest all of it. If this was just about Logan for the past week, a man I just met, my heart wouldn't be hurting, but it's not. This is a year's worth of conversations, topped with everything else that happened over the past seven days, which included me taking care of him when he was sick and vice versa. It's like we had a relationship but didn't. My head is just everywhere. "He made a mistake Cora, that's all."

"You don't like mistakes, do you?" Cora asks.

"Cora, it's not like that."

"What if I make a mistake? Will you not like me anymore either?"

I take the seat next to her and pull her hands into mine. "Cora, you are my little girl. I don't care how many mistakes you make in your lifetime, I will always, always love you. Do you understand?"

"Kind of," she says with a whole lot of disappointment settling into her big, blue eyes.

She's not old enough to understand the big picture, but I don't want her to feel any of the repercussions of my decisions. I feel like I've caused her a whole lot of discontent in the last year. "I'm sorry, sweetie. I am."

"It's okay, mom. I'll try not to make mistakes, okay?"

I'm leaving home with a broken heart tomorrow morning, for so many reasons.

But at least my ass cheeks aren't still glued together.

CHAPTER 27

A WEEK THAT WAS SUPPOSED TO BE FILLED WITH HOTEL SEX ... WAS NOT FILLED WITH HOTEL SEX

Four Days Later

"Folks, the flight might be a little bumpy, so we're asking that you keep your seatbelts fastened throughout the trip. We should be arriving in in approximately three hours and ten minutes, where it is currently snowing and the temperature is thirty-two degrees. We hope you enjoy your flight with us today."

I need wine or something. "I hate flying, even in good weather," Brielle whines in my ear. This week has felt like three while listening to her go on about her threesome troubles, a lack of a ring, and no guaranteed wedding date. I'm looking forward to going home, getting my Cora snuggles and forgetting about everyone and everything else. "Did you shut your phone off?"

"Oh, I almost forgot." I take my phone from the pocket of my bag and find a notification from Words With Friends on my display. Actually, there are twelve notifications with new game requests. I open the app quickly, keeping an eye on the flight attendant who's slowly making her way down the aisle. All the requests are from Dickle15, but why twelve games?

I start with the first one, looking at the game board, finding the word," **hi**."

I click "next" for the second game board and find the word: "***no***."

The next ten have either a "***no, sad, mad, low, foe,***" oh, and there's a *"dumb"* mixed in with his two and three letter words. Then, the twelfth game has the word *"**sorry**."* A thirteenth game request comes in, and it's the word *"**love**."*

Love. You can't love someone after a week.

A message on the side pops up next:

Yes, I love you. It's been a year, and during that time, I fell for your personality. No, I didn't know what you looked like, but that was just the extra good part of everything.

I screwed up bad. I wasn't thinking. I wanted to be with you, and men don't always make the right decisions. We can't always handle life properly, kind of like the flu. I originally got your name from a friend, who explained your situation, which, marital-wise, was like mine. After sucking at vocabulary most of my life, I was willing to take a chance. I never thought this silly game would create a friendship, as well as teaching me some words I'll never use in real life.

Anyway, Hannah, I miss you. I'll play another 365 days of Words With Friends with you if it means you might forgive me someday.

"Ma'am, I need you to turn your phone off now."

"Oh okay, sorry," I tell her.

"Told you," Brielle adds in.

I quickly move my fingers along the keys, typing in a short message, then telling him the plane is taking off.

I shut my phone down and return it to my bag. "I made a mistake," I tell Brielle.

"What are you talking about? People do it all the time. You just shut it off, you're not going to get a detention or anything." She laughs and places her headphones over her ears.

"Not that kind of mistake," I tell her, even though she can't hear me.

It's taken me all week to realize some things are worth fighting for. Some things are worth forgiveness. Some things are worth seeing through to get to the other side. It's taken me a while to figure it out, but maybe this was my lesson to learn all along.

Once the plane steadies in the air, I pay the premium fee to gain access to Wi-Fi for the duration of the flight.

I open my texts and type in Rick's name.

Me: I'll be home in a few hours. We need to talk, okay?

Rick: Sure thing, babe.

Me: Is Cora okay?

Rick: She's perfect.

Me: Thanks.

Rick: Do you need a ride from the airport?

Me: I have a car scheduled, but thank you for the offer.

Rick: Anytime.

I put my phone away and lean my head back into the hard cushion that's a little high for my head, leaving my neck craned in an awkward position. I'm not going to be able to fall asleep like this, and I just want the flight to go by quickly. Instead, I place my elbow down on the armrest nearest to the aisle and rest my head on my hand.

I'm able to fall into a semi-restful place, but it seems like only a few minutes pass when I'm nearly knocked unconscious by a food cart. "Oh my goodness, I'm so, so sorry. Are you okay, ma'am?"

The flight attendant, who oddly looks like Brielle, kneels beside me and places her hand on my knee. "Can I get you some ice?"

I don't know if I'm out of it because I was asleep, or if my head got hit that hard. "Yeah, and maybe some vodka and orange juice too."

"I don't know if that's the best idea," the woman says.

"Please?" I beg.

"Is that your friend?" she asks, pointing to Brielle.

"My colleague," I reply.

The flight attendant leans over and taps Brielle on the shoulder, waking her up too. Brielle peels her headphones off her head and rubs her eyes. "Is everything okay?" she asks.

"Um, I'm afraid we just knocked your colleague's head pretty hard with the food cart. I'm going to get her some ice, but she's asking for vodka too."

"I'm not her mom," Brielle says. "Although, she's old enough to be *my* mom."

"What? No, I'm not!" I scold her. "Women can't have babies at seven, Brielle."

The flight attendant folds her fist over her mouth. "I'll be right back with the vodka," she says.

Finally, someone who understands me.

"Sorry, I guess I had the math wrong on that one," Brielle says.

"Just a little," I tell her, with a look that makes it clear she is never to announce that again.

"Are you okay?" she asks.

"No, not really."

"Where did it hit you?"

"It's fine," I tell her.

"Let me see. I'll check for a bump."

"Really, it's fine."

The flight attendant returns with an ice pack, a cup of orange juice, and a tiny shot bottle filled with vodka. "Thank you."

"It's on the house," she says.

Uh, yeah, I'd say that should be a given. Not worth it.

I down the shot and lean my head back to try and sleep off the rest of the trip. The vodka does its job, and my eyes pop back open as we touch down on the runway. Thank goodness.

"I want to go back to Florida," Brielle whines.

"Maybe you should just move there? You're still free as a bird. Do what you want with your life … whatever is going to make you happy."

"You want me to quit and go away, don't you?" she responds.

"No, Brielle. I'm just being a mother figure to you. After all, I *am* old enough to be your mother, right?" I roll my eyes and lean forward for my bag.

"Well, you're firing Logan, so maybe you should hang onto me for a bit longer before you have no one left to help you."

I look over at her and furrow my brows. "Take it easy. I was just trying to be a friend. If you're not happy, make yourself happy."

"Ditto," she says.

"I'm working on it," I snap back.

"I can tell." Brielle rolls her eyes and nudges me out of my seat so she can grab her hot pink duffle out of the overhead compartment.

Neither of us says much to one another as we make our way off the plane and down to baggage claim. "I'm sorry, Brielle. I was just trying to help, honestly."

"I know I annoy you, but you don't have to be so obvious about it."

Why is she acting like this? "Did something happen?"

"Nope," she says with a clipped tone.

"Okay."

"I'm lying. Something did happen," she says.

"What? What happened?" What could have happened? We haven't left each other's side in days.

"It was me," she says.

"What was you?" We're standing in the waiting area of the gate we just deplaned from, and people are staring at us because I've been a little louder than I should be.

"I told Logan to look you up on Words With Friends last year after Rick left you."

"What?" I shout. My blood runs cold, yet my face feels like it's on fire. "This is a joke, a goddamn joke right now, right? But it's not funny."

Because I'm still yelling, a TSA security officer approaches us. "Ladies, is everything okay?"

"No, she created a stalker and sent him to me!" I continue, now sounding like a nutcase, and officially making a scene.

"A stalker? How do you create a stalker?" the TSA officer asks, seeming more curious than serious, despite my erratic behavior.

"He's not a stalker," Brielle laments. "It's Logan Grier. He's a friend's friend of Adam's. We were all out for a party one night and someone mentioned setting him up with a nice woman who didn't know a whole lot about sports ... and well, I made magic."

"You made magic?" I huff. "You set him up with me through a stupid word game. Then, when things didn't work out that way, you—"

"Told him there was an opening as a temp, and you might prefer that way of meeting someone, versus the online dating thing that hadn't worked out for you." Brielle is biting her thumbnail. Maybe she just realized how asinine this all sounds or how stupid it is to interfere with someone's life the way she has. How could she be so deceitful? "He told me you probably wouldn't be too happy when you found out the truth, and that he'd just keep trying to meet you through your word game conversations, but I was impatient. I wanted him to make a move."

"This was all you. All of it. I tossed aside a great guy because you had to interfere."

"Wrong. I found you the great guy, Hannah. I was trying to help you. You were so miserable, and I just wanted to see you happy again. Forgive me, please." I don't think I've ever seen Brielle angry, not like she is right now. But how can I just be okay with this? I can't be. I've been blindsided, and I feel like a fool.

"I don't know what to say right now."

"Ladies, can I get back to my job now, or should I pull up a few chairs and invite some people over to watch your Jerry Springer episode?"

"We're fine," I hiss.

"Oh, and if Logan Grier wants to date you … come on now, even I wouldn't turn that guy down, and I'd be eternally grateful to the friend who made it happen!" The security guard walks away chuckling, which kind of infuriates me a little more. I'm a joke in everyone else's life, it seems.

"Don't blame Logan," Brielle says. "I saw how happy he made you throughout the year you two were just chatting through your game, and I had to interfere. I just really thought you two needed to meet. I messed everything up."

"He's a grown man. He could have opted not to take your advice," I tell her.

"Yes, but he really liked you, and I insisted it was the best way to make things happen. I know how easily people are persuaded when they have feelings for someone. Plus, you know how relentless I can be when I set my mind to something. He really didn't have the option to say no," she says.

I'm getting the feeling this isn't completely about Logan and me. "You know how easily people are persuaded?"

"I'm not as blonde and dumb as you think I am. I broke up with Adam, for your information."

"I had no idea, Brielle. I'm sorry."

"It's fine. I did it before we left so I'd have the week to be distracted."

I drop my shoulder bag to the ground and wrap my arms around her neck. "I'm sorry," I tell her.

"I promise I didn't mean to hurt you. I just wanted you to be happy, but I shouldn't have pushed so hard."

"It's okay," I tell her. "I may never have met him if you didn't pull your shenanigans."

"It's true," she cries out through a crackled groan.

"And, now I've gone and ruined things, so I guess that's just the way it goes. He was out of my league anyway, and in the short amount of time we were together, look what I put him through. I gave him the flu, and he had to rescue my glued-together ass cheeks. He's better off without me."

"Don't say that," she tells me.

"It's life." I grab my bag, and as we head toward the airport's exit, I feel defeated. Maybe I'm just meant to focus on being a mom and excelling at work right now. I can go along with the notion of that being life's great plan for me.

"I need to get my bag," Brielle says. "Will you wait for me?"

"You didn't check a bag," I remind her.

"Yes, I did. You were standing right there."

"I know. You didn't check anything. We checked in at the kiosk and went right to security."

"Must be that old age getting to you again," Brielle says.

"Or that blonde is seeping into your brain," I reply.

"I have a bag coming. Just wait a minute, okay?"

I lean back against a post in front of the baggage claim area, expecting that we'll be waiting here for however long it takes Brielle to realize she didn't check a freaking bag. She's acting like an excited dog waiting at the conveyor belt as the alarm rings with the warning that the bags are about to roll out.

I close my eyes for a moment, taking in a deep breath, but I'm left with a gasp as a hand clamps around my arm, pulling me away from the post I'm leaning on. "Ma'am, I'm going to need to have a word with you."

When my panic eases, I find a pair of familiar eyes in front of me, but the vision disappears just as quickly when his hands cup my cheeks and his lips crash into mine. I instinctively loop my arms around his neck, squeezing him like I need him, like I want him, and like I never wanted to walk away. His hands glide back into my hair as his fingers comb through my loose waves. His touch takes my breath away, causing our lips to part. When he tilts his head back and gazes into my eyes, a smile curls into the corner of his lips, matching the smile I have for him.

"Take me back," he says.

"I never had you in the first place," I remind him.

"You had me with a shattered heart, Hannah. You fixed mine, and I want to make yours whole again too."

"You already have, Logan. I think I've come to realize that fate doesn't always work the way we hope, and sometimes we need to take matters into our own hands. I see now that's what you were doing, and I love you for that."

"Really?"

"Really. Some might even say I came down with the man flu since I saw you last. It's bad. I'm not sure I'm going to make it without someone to take care of me."

"All you need is some soup, juice through a straw, and liquid Advil—it's like magic." Logan laughs quietly and kisses me again. This time I hear Brielle clapping behind us, and I remember we're in the airport, and we're being *that* couple.

Logan turns to face her. "I told you she'd be pissed," he says to her.

"And I told you she'd get over it," Brielle argues.

For once, it's my turn. I get the romance. I get the guy who wants to fight for me, instead of with me.

EPILOGUE

Six months later

The moving truck pulls up outside, and I take the deepest breath I've taken in a long time. "I know this is hard," Logan says.

"This is where Cora's life began," I tell him.

"You'll always have your memories, but it's time for something new. This is healthy for all of you," Logan says as he places his hand on my slightly swollen belly—the miracle he was told he'd never experience. The miracle I wasn't sure I needed in my life until the moment we found out. That's when everything in my life fell into place. A family—what I never wanted to lose and what Logan has always wanted to have.

When I returned from Florida last fall, I told Rick we needed to be farther away from each other. The arrangement wasn't working, and it was causing unnecessary stress and discontent in my life. I wanted to start something new with Logan, and I didn't need Rick's influence in that. I also didn't want two sets of spying eyes watching it from next door.

It wasn't an easy transition, going through the process of selling the house and packing up ten-years-worth of belongings, but today feels like a fresh start, and I am I'm ready. I deserve it.

"I can't wait to live on top of the mall!" Cora shrieks.

"You know that doesn't mean we're going to be shopping every day, right?" I tell her.

"Uh, yes it does," she replies with a giggle. "I need to buy so many toys and clothes for my baby sister, Mom." Cora's world is bright and full of love, happiness, and excitement.

I was worried she'd miss the house she grew up in, but I'm glad she isn't upset about that or moving twenty minutes away from Rick. Cora was forced to grow up quickly while dealing with this divorce at four and five years old, and I'm grateful for her current understanding. Whether it will always be that way or not, I don't know, but for now, I hope I'm doing what's best for her.

"They've got everything handled from here," Logan says. "Let's get over to the condo so we're there when they arrive with your stuff."

I take one last look around, mentally shutting off the light switch. It's time for the next chapter with Logan, Cora, and baby-girl Dickle.

As we arrive at Logan's condo, we take the few personal belongings we packed in his truck with us up to the penthouse. One thing I never considered about Logan was the lifestyle he was accustomed too. He isn't showy, but he knows where to spend his money, and he does so with sense and style. It's like a dream here in this open space with views on all sides of the condo. Plus, the best part is the incredible man I get to start a new life with.

Cora is already dancing around her new room, and I'm taking in a fresh breath of new air.

"Cora," Logan says with child-like excitement in his voice. "What do you think? Do you like what I did?"

I don't know what he's talking about so I head down the hall to her room and peek inside. "Holy crap." He decorated her room to look like a princess's castle—it's a bedroom any little girl would dream of.

"This is all mine?" Cora asks. "Will I be sharing it with baby Dickle?"

"You told her that name?" I ask Logan.

"No, I did not. She must have heard you. I don't think I've called our daughter by that ridiculous name, Hannah." Logan laughs, pointing his raised brow at me. "Maybe you should just call your sister 'baby girl' until we have a real name for her."

"No, I like Dickle," Cora laments.

Logan lowers his head and laughs a little more. "Anyway, this room is all yours, sweetie," Logan tells her.

Cora runs into Logan's arms, and he lifts her up and swings her around before placing her on top of the castle that has a gated play area with a small table and a tea-party setting. "I love it!"

"Watch this," Logan says. He climbs beneath the platform, and his head pops up through a hole. He rises up a foot and rests his elbows on the little table. "I'm too big to climb up, so I made a different entrance so your mom and I can join you for your tea parties." Cora covers her mouth and giggles so hard her eyes squint shut. "I have one more question too …"

"Whatever it is, the answer is yes," Cora says.

We'll need to work on that as she gets older.

He leans over and whispers in her ear, and Cora says, "My answer is still yes."

"Okay, good." Logan disappears from the hole he climbed through and doesn't pop back out from underneath the castle's platform for a long minute.

I don't know what he's doing, but my phone's buzzing in my back pocket. Probably Alan wondering why I decided to take a personal day when I'm not sick or dying.

I turn on the display and find a Words With Friends notification. What the heck?

I open it up, and it's a blank game.

"Logan, did you just send me a game request?"

"Yeah, sorry," he says climbing out from under the castle. "I was hoping I'd get lucky and have certain letters to choose from but …"

He has a pile of wooden tiles that he places down in front of me, spelling out the words: M-A-R-R-Y M-E

"Oh my gosh," I sigh, feeling my chest tighten like a knot.

"I thought I would never have it all, Hannah. My world seemed to end when my baseball career ended, and I thought that was it for me, but you and Cora have proven that I can have it all, and this is better than I expected life could be. I want this—us, plus a cute kid with a sassy attitude who I can have tea parties with."

"I do like tea parties," Cora adds in. "And I love Beefcake Batman, Mommy."

My hands are pressed against my chest, preventing my heart from exploding.

I glance back down at my phone from the notification he sent and realize there's a little bit of fate playing with us today because *I happen to have the letters I need on the game board to respond to his question.*

I place the letters, Y-E-S, out in a row and click play. When I look up, he's on his knee with a ring in his hand, smiling, with a look I've only seen when I watched the video of him walking up to the plate on the baseball field. I wondered what it would take to bring that smile back.

"Mommy, say yes!" Cora says as she climbs down from the platform.

He asked Cora first, which means he can have my heart.

"I already did, sweetie."

"You did?" Logan asks? "I didn't get a notification." I throw my head back and roll my eyes. "Damn Internet."

"Yes, Logan, I will marry you." I rush to him and wrap my arms around his neck, kissing him with as much force as I can offer, so he knows how much feeling is inside of that three-letter word. "You'll always be my Dickle."

As the moments pass by, and Cora's hug loosens from our necks, she looks at Logan and says, "Tell her."

"Tell me what?" I ask, looking at them.

"Alan just announced his retirement, and Brett was promoted. Oh, and Nick and Taylor were let go on several counts of sexual harassment. Weird, right?"

"So weird," I say with a laugh.

"Oh, and I might have overheard who the new vice president of the company is going to be …"

"What? How would you hear that?"

"Brielle was at the company meeting this morning," he says with a laugh. *I missed the company meeting—it's the first one I've ever missed.* "Your name was announced, and they said you'd be claiming your new title tomorrow."

Holy crap. "Are you serious?"

"Serious as ever," he says.

"What about you?" The six-month temp term was only extended a few weeks, and there hadn't been an approval from Alan on making Logan's position permanent, so I've been worried about how that may turn out.

"Tech needs help, so I'm switching departments. It's more of my thing anyway, and that way, we'll keep our personal life separate from work."

"So, when I need IT support …"

"I'm your man, baby."

"Yes, you are."

Made in the USA
Middletown, DE
23 July 2018